N

Haint (a short story)

Handsy (a short story)

by Jon Goode

Mydas (a novel)

Haint (a short story)

Handsy (a short story)

by Jon Goode

GOODESTUFF ENT LLC

Atlanta, GA

Printed in the United States of America

First Printing, 2020

ISBN-13:

978-0-9965004-1-8

GOODESTUFF ENT LLC

Author: Jon Goode | IG: @jon_goode

Cover Art: Dr. Fahamu Pecou | IG: @fahamupecou | www.fahamupecouart.com

Graphic Design: Verbal Slick | IG: @verbalslick

Editor: Lia T Bascomb Ph.D

Dedicated

To Barbara Goode, the first person I saw

pull gold out of thin air.

TABLE OF CONTENTS:

1. MYDAS (a novel)

2. HAINT (a short story)

Chapter 1 | Blood. Money

I stand by the counter and eye a seat near the rear of the room. This is where someone, possibly you, is supposed to mention Rosa Parks. Pangs of guilt should then immediately compel me to find a table closer to the front. Sorry Mrs. Parks, and possibly you, it's not going to happen. I take note of the exits as I walk toward the back of the room. Grounds For Approval is one of these new, cool, hip, awakened coffee houses according to the reviews written by people promised a free cup of coffee if they'll write a review that says, "Grounds For Approval is one of these new, cool, hip, awakened coffee houses." It's two shotgun rooms, side by side - so maybe a double barrel shotgun room? - separated by a crudely cut entrance and exit between them.

"...*shoot, hunt! Shoot him 'fore dawn come!...*" covered in sweat, Bart Barker of Barker and the Celestials shouts loudly from a wooden bandstand somewhere in my mind. My father plays bass with one hand behind his back.

My parents loved that kind of juke joint, hair down, sleeves high, sweaty, belly rubbing music. Everyone in Alabama does... or at least did. I'm sure no one here, or even there for that matter, would remotely remember that song now. It's all *Plink Blink Bloop* music with the kids today.

1

I look about and take in the room. The tables for two, that can barely accommodate one, all have their round tabletops painted different colors: green, yellow, blue, and red. My mind imagines giants playing a helter-skelter game of Twister while having a low-fat latte. In the center of each colorful table sits a synthetic rose, in a vase of real water. Why? I touch one of the plastic-like thorns on a red table as I pass. It bends to my touch and I think, only the thorns of real roses can hurt you.

The walls of Grounds For Approval that aren't exposed brick are painted a benign color that makes you long for exposed brick. The art work, mounted crooked in an effort to be edgy, is a *Nuevo EurAfrican* rip off of BasILLIka who is himself a rip off of Basquiat. It's a copy of a copy of a copy and its message and meaning are diluted appropriately. The acrylic on the canvas is all sharp angles and crossed out words that didn't mean anything to begin with. It's the kind of art people pretend to understand because it's new, cool, hip, and awakened, although they're just as confused by it as you and I.

"*... do your work baby. do your work now...*" Barker is all white teeth and brown liquor vocals. He sits inside my thoughts looking at the art and whispering lyrics in my left ear. My mother, with one arm behind her back, is playing drums in my right.

I tap my toe as I hum the melody to myself. All of the cattywampus, catty cornered canvases have the effect of making me feel slightly off balance, sea sick, as my head tilts to — to view one — and fro to view another. I give up on the deep art, anchor my mind on

2

solid ground, and continue counting exits. That's what's most important. The emergency exit at the rear of the room and the front door are the only ways out that I can see. Noted. I survey faces without looking anyone in the eye too long, and feel body language as I navigate toward my seat. This is mostly habit, due diligence. No one lifts an eyebrow, or has that ceiling light of recognition that comes on when it dawns on them that they know who you are. I feel fairly sure no one has or will recognize me here. Pictures of me are mainly rumored to be fakes, artistic interpretations, or dramatic renderings. I haven't been recognized by a random stranger in a very, very long time, but it has gotten weird, and sometimes dangerous, the few times it's happened.

In truth, Grounds For Approval is nothing new or hip. The exposed brick, skewed art, double barrel layout is the blueprint for all new, cool, hip, awakened coffee shops. You can walk a block south to *Bump and Grind* where they feature a cocaine infused Colombian drip, and it'll be the same layout with a different artist on the wall; but I must say the patrons there are far more alert. You can stroll two blocks east to *Bean Bag* where dehydrated coffee beans are sold to patrons in tobacco chew sized pouches and just kept in the mouth, against the gum, all day for a constant caffeine fix. The only thing setting Grounds For Approval apart is that you can order your coffee and pay for it through the latest *H-App* in your hand seated *iPalmPhone II*. You receive a *reading* when your order is ready, you go to the counter near the front - sorry Mrs. Parks I'm still not going to do it - and your half caf, double cream, caramel, shot of vanilla, extra whip macchiato, which flies in the face of the definition of a macchiato; or your vegan,

3

gluten-free, sugar-free, soy-free, non-GMO, organic blueberry muffin; or your socially conscious, donate a dollar to prevent interstellar pollution, locally grown and respectfully harvested, halal strawberry scone; or whatever your overly wrought order of choice is, will be waiting.

I've been here once before and still have yet to see a single employee. It's as if Oompa Loompas, The Fellowship of the Ring, or some magical mystical, possibly elfin, coalition of invisible baristas are just below the countertop pumping out complicated, strenuously defined, coffee and confectionary delights all day.

I'm just sitting down near the rear emergency exit when I see him enter. He looks like a reporter. Like he *Mersenned* the word "reporter" in his *iPPII* and cut and pasted the first and most obvious image overtop of himself. The trench coat, the felt stingy brimmed hat, the trousers just a touch too high so that you can't miss his patterned socks. It goes beyond cliché into costume. Even his name at the bottom of his ridiculous post on the *blanket cork* inquiring, "Does anyone know, or have information regarding, the whereabouts of Midas or anyone claiming to be Midas. Yes, that Midas. *Amazon World Solar Times*, the most prestigious *mind reading* on the planet, is interested in having him, her, or them come forward and share the Midas story in a series we're producing entitled: Myths Demystified. Only serious inquiries need respond, via this *cork,* to Kent," is a costume.

Kent spots my light grey plaid cap immediately, and moves through a throng of people having a silent VR birthday party near the front amongst the Twister tables. A woman takes a deep breath, her hand glowing as it covers her open eyes, providing her with whatever VR experience the group has agreed to enter into. She blows hard into Kent's face, the lights on her noise canceling headphones blinking green, then red, then blue in sync with all of the other party attendees, and some of the tables. Kent is clearly taken aback and begins blinking rapidly and moving away from her as quickly as he can without crashing into someone else. She's smiling broadly, totally oblivious of his presence and her breath crashing on the shore of his stubble covered chin. She must be the birthday girl, blowing out her imaginary candles. All of her friends are also staring into the glowing VR players in their hand. Their heads are all faced in arbitrary directions and hanging at disjointed angles, much like the paintings on the wall. You would think that everyone is not looking at, and seeing, the same thing. Which of course they are. The birthday girl cups her other hand to her chest and raises her shoulders just as everyone begins lip syncing what appears to be happy birthday, not the Stevie Wonder version either.

The blinking red from the noise canceling headphones registers and puts me at ease. When I first entered I saw a flash of reddish maroon out of the corner of my eye, just to my right and slightly behind me. I turned but there was nothing there. Few things can move so fast as to evade my sight. I'm faster than I look.

"... *put on your red headdress and then you go down under*..."
Bes is dancing frantically, throwing her sweat over the entire band as Barker laughs his, just north of tuberculosis, laugh loudly into my frontal lobe.

5

Kent navigates through the crowd, careful not to ruin anyone's birthday experience. He looks like a master thief negotiating a security laser maze. Some people call Virtual Reality fake. They dub it fantasy, title it *FauxFillment* or *FauxReal,* but what is life but what you see and hear and share with your friends and family? Are the times I share with others, that we all revel in, talk about and remember for years to come, no matter if they are VR or Real Reality, not real? If I had an RR experience that I was too inebriated or mind altered to remember, in the ways that matter, did it happen? Is it real? There are those that say VR is the only ethical and safe reality to be had. It's a reality of your choosing. It leaves no carbon, or criminally indictable, footprint. Many of those people feel like RR should stand for Reality Rape. They argue that it's a reality that's forced on you whether you want it or not. I've been seeing more and more people wearing the "RR is Violence," buttons, clashing with people sporting the "VR is *FauxFillment"* t-shirts. People are pretty entrenched in their stances. The last time I remember people being this dug in on their opposing views was during the early 2000s iPhone versus Android, or Yanny versus Laurel debates. For the record... it was Yanny.

Kent walks up and extends his left hand. He must have had his phone seated in the right. We shake hands. It feels awkward to me. Mine is seated in my left so I take his left with my right. The move, to someone watching at a distance, might appear as if I am about to kiss the back of his hand. He chuckles, aware of the optics. He's clearly used to, and gets a kick from, the appearance these types of handshakes give.

"Thanks again for agreeing to meet with me, Mi..." Kent catches himself before saying my name. I feel the muscles in my legs twitching, adrenaline flooding my system, ready to move swiftly toward the exit.

"...*Shoot him 'fore dawn come!...*" Khadijah, her hands slick from Bes' sweat, pulls me to my feet and points toward the exit as Barker flips a table deep in my imagination.

Kent notes my reaction and looks at me, his eyes squint slightly, as if to say, he really believes he is who he says he is. He then looks about the room where there are only the VR birthday partygoers playing what looks to be an adult virtual version of pin the tail on the donkey. Everyone else in the coffeeshop is lost in their hands. He turns back to me, smiles a condescending smile, and begins again, "... thanks for agreeing to meet me," he says as he settles into his seat and checks a new message that has illuminated his phone, simultaneously. I smile and nod. He doesn't notice.

"We're honored to be able to share 'your' story with the *Amazon World Solar Times* subscribers," Kent says, his eyes still glued to his palm. This is the norm for here and now. People here, but there. People with you, but far away. People who demand your time, and then take it for granted. It's not even considered rude, it's just... the norm. I can see the content of the phone message reflected off of his glasses. The nonprescription lens, horn-rimmed glasses are also, clearly, a part of his reporter's costume. He's finished with the message and is now perusing the cafe's menu.

"We're going to run it on Monday as a *Waking Lobe-ular*. As soon as our readers wake and their consciousness registers with our servers it will be downloaded into their frontal lobe and available for *mind reading*." He says all of this as he places his order. His order is going to be something really ostentatious and difficult, I can feel it.

He smiles as if pleased with his beverage and pastry choices and looks up, truly noticing me for the first time. He tilts his head to the side a bit, like confused *Game-Neins* do when presented with something non-binary; like I did trying to view the art as I approached my seat. His brow furrows a bit.

"Not what or who you expected?" I ask. I maintain my smile. It's one of my greatest weapons.

"In truth I didn't know what... who to expect. You said you'd be seated near the rear in a light grey plaid newsboy cap. That's all I had to go on. No race, gender, genus, continental, or planetary designation. Nothing. No one seems to know anything about the legendary and elusive Mr. M. I've seen drawings of you or course. When I'm in Asia you're Asian. When I'm in Africa you're African. When I'm in America you're white."

"Interesting Mr. Kent. Everywhere else you denoted the designation of the people of the continent, and not their color. But in America..."

"In America, American means white even though they've been in the minority, except in seats of power, for a while now. Is that really interesting Mr. M? You can't be who you say you are and not know that."

"I thought it interesting that you said what I know, you know, and everyone knows, although few seem to voice that truth."

"I am a journalist."

I chuckle. His tilted head is now straight as an arrow and his eyes previously on his phone, on the menu and about the room, are now fixed intently on me. Just what I want.

"I'm just saying Mr. Kent, in my experience all journalists aren't given to telling, or even caring about, what's true. They just know what's news, what'll up-sale downloads. You're not here because you think my story is true. I know that. You're here because you think possibly it's interesting. It's quirky. I'm mad. You're here because it's, maybe, news you can sell." His eyes stay intently and intensely on me as his lips, a straight line after my comment about journalists, curl into a bit of a sneer.

"All I was attempting to say Midassss," he looks me square in the eye as he says my name in a conversational, and adversarial tone, dragging out the S, "about Asians, Africans and ... white people is that geographic regions and races tend to cast you in their own image. You're like a folk tale, make believe. You're *FauxFillment*."

I don't allow myself to react. I don't even look around to see who might have heard. I feel confident everyone in this room is properly distracted. I note that Kent is a person that when he feels

9

attacked will strike back, even if it's a clumsy attack. I maintain eye contact and reply,

"Ah. But not so much of a folk tale or fantasy that I could pull you from your phone?"

I look over at his glowing hand, catching him off guard. He turns his palm down toward the table. Before he can speak I sit back, lighten my tone and continue,

"So you were anticipating someone more exotic perhaps? A Plutonian or a Sociaphite or a Troll come down from the hills and here I sit, a mere black man."

"What's your age may I ask?"

This is his attempt to either get under my skin by insinuating I'm childish, or him trying to catch me off guard. Either way it doesn't work.

"Why do you ask?"

"Well for one, stories about you," he places air quotes around the *you* with his fingers, "have circulated since, forever it seems. You may be insulted but in truth you are more bedtime story than man walking amongst us. The first recorded mention of Midas in modern times has been traced to a *blanket cover* from 2030 I believe. There are rumors of you being featured in news articles before that but The Great Hack of 2027 erased all news media prior. Then of course there is the lore about the Midas of antiquity and questions about if you are he, and if so, if you are eternal; or is this all sugar-plum-fairies and now-I-lay-me-down-to-sleep. So you're rather like Bigfoot or Spring-heeled Jack or Arthur Edwin in the imaginations of the people who still care to imagine. To tell you the truth, I'm not even remotely convinced you are who you say you are, but that's what I'm here to find out isn't it. Also, just so that you know... No one uses the term 'black' to refer to people anymore. It's ... well, it's unused. The *Noir Nationals* frown on it."

A constant and genuine smile is my only response. He returns a disingenuous grin before continuing with,

"But you, of course, already knew that."

"I did, but I choose what words I use, no one else."

I give Mr. Kent a knowing wink at the end of the statement. My time in the south has taught me, you can say all kinds of rude things so long as you put a wink or a smile or a bless your heart at the end.

"Mr. Kent I reached out and agreed to this interview for a couple of reasons, the foremost being I think it's time to share my story." I place air quotes around the *my* with my fingers, "I haven't told it in so long perhaps it's time that I heard it again, too. If you don't believe I am who I say I am by the end then all we've done is share a delightful afternoon together watching adults, lost in birthday fantasy, play pin the tail on the... something. I only ask three things, one that you from this point forward refrain from using my name, two that you keep an open mind, and three, the coin. If you agree to the prior, will

11

work on the medial, and have possession of the latter we can begin to see if I'm me."

I can see that he's fifty-fifty on whether to call it a day or move forward. He's going through all manner of, I don't need this shit, conversations in his head and calling me things the *Noir Nationals* would frown on. I can also see that he's curious though and curiosity has certainly transfixed some fickle felines.

The coin I mentioned is a two-fold request. Number one, I sent the message asking him to bring it, encrypted to his back channel personal *reading* and not to his all too easily hacked office address. If someone read his office correspondence and showed up without knowledge of the coin then I'd know it's not Mr. Kent. I agreed to and need this interview to be with Mr. Kent. Number two, well, hopefully we'll get to that later.

Kent regards me for a moment, his eyes hard, before standing, taking his hat and coat off, draping the coat over the back of his chair and placing the hat on the table,

"An AODO original," I say as I eye the trench coat, "Those don't come cheap."

"Not at all but you'd be amazed at what you can afford if you save a little. Of course you supposedly being who you are, would know nothing about having to save would you?"

"... *I heard you gone run down fast, laugh, and listen to 'em play them tunes...*" Rose rubs my back, her nails jagged, her hands hard,

as Barker puts his arms around my shoulders to let me know he hasn't
left my thoughts just yet.

Kent reaches into his pocket and fishes out an *Aquarian quarter*.
That's what we call them. To Aquarians they are worth little to nothing
but tourists love to get their hands on them as proof positive of an other
world visit. He hands over the coin with its smooth sides. The value is
denoted by the serrated edges. Analog, non-digitized, money fell out
use in all of the worlds some time ago, but when these coins were in use
they were all the same size, color and shape. Their worth was indicated
by the number of little sharp ridges on the edges. Although this is called
an Aquarian quarter it really would have been worth, in its time, twenty
dollars by U.S. standards. Kent extends the coin to me. I smile and take
it with my right hand.

Kent doesn't care why I want the coin. If the coin gets him the
interview then so be it. He takes a deep breath before asking, "Do you
mind if I record this? I want to be sure not to misquote you or skip any
of the important details."

I took note of the fact that his *Occ Recorders* were already on
when I caught the reflection of his eyes in the lenses of his costume
glasses. No worries though, in a time where everyone is constantly
surveilled by everyone else, I'd turned my *Occ* and *Aud Scramblers* on
the second my *SUberAutPrime* service driver picked me up in his,
almost glowing it was so bright mint green, vehicle from my
comfortable little split level *DomiCas*. In Orwell's dystopian and sadly
accurate novel *1984* he said that Big Brother is watching, but he could

scantly have guessed that in 2271 everyone with a phone would play Big Brother's role; and here in 2271, everyone has a phone.

I look Mr. Kent in his eyes and stare at the blinking red dot he's cleverly positioned to where it'd be mostly obscured by his eyelids, just to be sure he knows that I know that he's already recording, and I say, "*Aud*, no *Occ*."

His cheeks, hued darkly enough to signal his African linage but imbued with a pastiness that testifies to the pale ape that tore through the delicate limbs of his family's tree somewhere in the past, blushes red.

"I ... I... I apologize. I didn't even realize it was on." His mouth speaks this lie but his red cheeks tell the truth of it. "I did an interview earlier and must have forgotten to turn it off." He blinks twice, holds his eyes closed for an extra second and touches his chin. When he opens his eyes, he opens them wide enough for me to see he is no longer *Occ* recording. He rubs just past his right temple, near his ear and shakes his head as he registers the feedback I knew he would be soon experiencing and says, "You've got an *Aud Scrambler* on?"

"And an *Occ Scrambler*," I say maintaining my ever-present smile.

He leans in and whispers, "But, they're illegal."

I lean in even more closely, "Indeed they are. As is a reporter *Aud* and *Occ* recording a person without their permission but let's neither of us hold the other in contempt for their sins. I'll turn the *Aud*

14

Scrambler off." I take a deep breath and continue, "You should be able to hear me clearly through your recorder now."

He looks at me quizzically "How did you? I mean you didn't touch any..." I sit back in my seat.

"I'm sure you have better questions than that for your readers Mr. Kent."

He nods, the corners of his mouth turning down a bit. I have no wink to serve as remedy this time. He says, "Friday, 2 p.m. 2271, interview with, the golden child, session one."

After describing me as the golden child, it's bold of him to think there will be more than one session.

"... *break it down baby now*..." Barker laughs and agrees.

"So. Is... you know... your birth name?"

"No."

"What's the name your mother gave you on that fateful day she looked down into her new born baby boy's," he looks over the top of his fake prescription glasses, into my all too real pupils, and continues, "black eyes with a gold halo?"

"I can't tell you."

"You don't know?"

"Oh, yes, I know. I guess I misspoke. It's not that I can't tell you. It's that I won't tell you. People keep very few things to themselves these days. Everything is covered by *The Blanket*. Your name, age, solar identification registration, retinal scan, initial embryonic DNA sample... everything. What my mother chose to whisper into my ear on cold mornings when she woke me up to go to school, I choose to keep to myself. I hold it close. I treasure it."

"I see ... so, when did people start calling you... you know what?"

His dancing around my name, as I asked, has an interesting result I hadn't anticipated. It has the affect of making me feel like Voldemort in those now ancient tales of magic and mystery. Like I'm the villain in this story and I'm pretty sure I'm not. Then again it's rare that the villain thinks of himself as one isn't it?

When did people start calling me... you know what? I don't have to think long or hard. It was the moment that changed everything. The moment revisits me like the ghosts of dead ancestors in the midnights of our struggles. I don't speak. I just remember. I rub my nose with my left hand as the memory starts to live again in my skin. I'm careful. I want to measure my words and roll them out like homemade buttermilk biscuits so that they may rise properly; because words, like biscuits, can't be unmade. Can't be undigested. Once they're pulled from the mind's oven and presented to the world they can only be consumed greedily or ignored completely, but never undone. I will however tell you in whole, what I told Kent in part.

"...*shoot, hunt! Shoot him 'fore dawn come!...Sangin' bangin' out them tunes...*" Barker stands, gives me a knowing nod, walks through the crowd and out of the front door. His voice in my mind disappears as my own grows louder.

Chapter 2 | Blood. Relative

I was thirteen the first time someone called me Midas. I wasn't sure what they meant by it and the condition under which the moniker was attached to me, was less than ideal. All I could think of was the corny car commercials that would air as my dad yelled at the football players on TV as if they could actually hear him, "Bruh! Why yew throwed dat!?" "Really doh, really! Yew gon ruhn on ferst don!"

He would spend his entire Sunday, arm chair coaching the games; the same games my mom was boycotting and saying that we all should. She would come into the living room with her arms crossed against her breasts, shaking her head slowly from side to side like an oscillating fan on the first setting. Her face was a portrait of disappointment.

"Not even for your son?"

"Wha? Wha yew talm 'bout nah Quita!?"

My mom was Michigan born and private school educated. She came from money, culture, and breeding. She was a Duvernay. Her father descended from the New Orleans Duvernays and that still meant something in certain parts of the country. She was pretty by the standards of most men, and quite a few women. She was tall, with

Statue of Liberty perfect posture that made her seem taller. She had the complexion of hot coffee with two creams and one sugar just before you stirred it, while it was all still swirling and fighting for an identity in the cup. She spoke "good," "proper" English. So much so that when she answered the phone's at the Michigan Department of Labor, a job she took because she had to but always felt was beneath her, people often assumed she was white.

One white woman even commented, "I'm so glad they're hiring more of us down there. Last time I came in," she paused and began to whisper like school girls in the back of the classroom clandestinely discussing the boys they like, "...well, the last time I came in they had nothing but niggers working."

She'd meant it as a compliment.

Dad was Alabama born and juke joint raised. He was born poor even by poor people's standards. He was the color of the cheap pawn shop .38's, the ones they didn't even bother to keep behind the glass: rusty, reddish, blackish, brown. The throw away guns that already had the trigger and grip wrapped in electrical tape. That's how he'd felt for most of his life: thrown away, bound, easily triggered. Dad wasn't good at math, or English, or most of the things taught in school. He couldn't get the words or numbers to make sense on the page. In poor, inner city, Alabama public schools they didn't give confusion between the eye and mind a proper name or diagnosis like dyslexia. They didn't put you in a program to help you tread water in the sea of words swimming on the blackboard. No. Instead they called you developmentally delayed on good days, fucking retarded on bad days, and nothing at all most days. The school teachers and staff held you back and ignored you. The student body teased and made fun of you. Ashamed and angry, undiagnosed or misdiagnosed and maligned, tired of fighting and confused, anyone in their right, or wrong mind would eventually drop out. Which is what dad did at the age of fourteen in the sixth grade. He did find one thing he was good at though. Reading and writing weren't his thing but he certainly could talk. Especially to women. Early in his youth he'd discovered he was adept at pouring the honey elixir of long dead and forgotten Greek gods and poets into the ears of young girls and older women alike. Slick as owl shit, is how his rap to the ladies was described in the south. I, being unfamiliar with owls and their excrement, would have to take their word for it. Later in his teenage years, pop would wrap that silver tongued southern rap—which was equal parts break beat and broken English—up in the clothes and cars of a semi-successful street hustler. No matter the cars or clothes or how smoothly the words swam to the surface of his rich, fluid baritone, he still had Alabama all over him, and it was especially thick around his tongue.

When mom was mad or irritated with dad her speech would become even more keen, proper, and pronounced; and her words would leak slowly from between clenched teeth like air from a tire with a nail in it. When dad was upset he offered up a word soup that no one could easily digest or decipher. Dad's nickname was Ray Ray or Trump. Everyone called him that, even mom, except when she was mad.

"You know EXACTLY what I'm talking about... Raekwon. You're going to sit here while those owners disrespect the players, and support this madness?"

"'Quita... I'm nah sah-portin it. Uhm jus wachin' it! Lissen, I bus my az at dat gay-rog all week. Jus leht me wach dah game 'n peace. Dayum!"

Dad did oil changes and brake jobs at a garage down the street and was paid under the table. His quick-talking, house-breaking-in, drug-selling, semi-successful street hustler life got him into real trouble in his late teens. He was locked up for a couple of years on a B&E and aggravated assault charge. He said he wasn't there that time. He swore that the previous caper had scared him straight. His "friends," however, said he was there, and their swearing knocked time off of their sentences. Pop had to walk through life with the word felon scarlet lettering every job application he put in thereafter. Not that he put in many. He wasn't a fan of working anything but the corners. My mom, just eighteen, found herself down south visiting relatives when she bumped into the twenty-one-year-old charismatic, freshly paroled, man that would be my father.

"Fine, Raekwon, watch the game then! Raymond! Come in here with me! You don't have to watch these mennnn," her eyes fixed on dad as she elongated the word men—it was a clear indictment of some sort — "degrade themselves."

When I clearly hadn't moved at the speed she felt I should have, she added, "Raymond! I am not going to tell you twice! Come on!"

21

Which was technically her telling me twice but who had time for technicalities when an ass whipping was imminent.

Mom only called me Raymond when she was mad at me or dad. Most days I was Little Ray or RJ, short for Ray Junior. This was just a few years before everyone started calling me Midas, even my parents. I'd never be Little Ray again after that.

Mom and dad met early in the summer of 2005 at a roller rink in Birmingham, Alabama. Dad was all big laughter, warm southern drawl, compliments wrapped in clever metaphors, "Gurl if Gahd made anythin' fihner he kehpt it fo hissef," and what felt like boundless energy and potential, even after his incarceration. Mom was all buttoned up, sit with your legs crossed so tight you can hold a piece of paper between your knees, don't listen to these hard-headed boys, don't drink that fire water, don't dance too close, remember yourself, leave room for Jesus, and don't, don't, don't, get pregnant. By the end of the summer she'd had corn liquor made by my father's half brother's girlfriend's uncle, she'd danced so closely with dad at a sweaty juke joint just outside of Birmingham you'd have thought they were in the same skin, she'd gotten lost in his syrupy smooth southern speech, she'd forgotten herself, and indeed, by summer's end, she'd discovered she was pregnant. When my eighteen-year-old mother called her parents with the news that she was having the baby of a twenty-one-year-old high school dropout, Alabama parolee, they were less than pleased, and less than supportive. Her father told her he'd schedule an abortion for her the next day. Her mother said that he was being silly and ridiculous, that the abortion would be scheduled for later that same day. My mother refused. All eighteen years of her stood tall and announced that she would indeed be having her child, their grandchild, me. All that education, the ballet lessons, the trips to Martha's Vineyard, the etiquette lessons, the pony, all that breeding, all that potential... wasted, they thought. It was a scandal her mother couldn't endure and an embarrassment her father wouldn't. Her parents wrote her a check, and wrote her off. They abandoned her in Alabama with cousins she barely knew and an uncertain future. My mom's parents, the grandparents I'd never meet, counted their lucky stars that they had another daughter, Quinchelle Duvernay. Another chance to get it right.

Mom was crushed by how quickly and completely her parents could cut her out of their lives. She was inconsolable but determined to return to Michigan. Her parents could deny her their love and attention but they couldn't deny her existence. Dad, in love on the one hand, and thinking mom's parents and their money, would eventually come around on the other, broke his parole and returned to Michigan with her. He started taking, temporary, under the table work and odd jobs to support his soon to be family. He figured it would be just until Mom's parents saw the light. They never did. They chose the darkness instead.

I look up and notice I've said little to nothing of substance to Kent. He is staring at the brick wall behind me and if I had to guess I would imagine he's preparing a grocery list. Just then his hand lights up and so do his eyes. His order is ready.

"I'll be right back," he says as he stands, navigates the laser maze of birthday attendees, and returns with his Oompa Loompa

23

produced beverage and pastry. I smell cinnamon and vanilla and nutmeg and pumpkin and ostentatiousness.

Before he can return to his seat I extend my lighted hand, palm up and say, "I apologize Mr. Kent it appears my order is ready as well. Would you mind terribly grabbing it for me before you sit?"

Kent's body language suggests that he does mind terribly. I smile, wide. He nods, sets his drink and pastry down on the table, double dutches through the crowd and returns with my coffee. To ask him to mother my coffee by adding two creams and one sugar seems a bridge too far, so I drink it black. It's a strong cup but clearly not as strong as Kent's.

Kent's cinnamon, vanilla, nutmeg, beverage sends him into a small coughing fit. Anyone not lost in VR birthday fun turns and eyes him with concern.

"Are you okay Mr. Kent? Wrong pipe or am I going to have to act like I know the Heimlich Maneuver or the Lyacinth Procedure?"

I wave and nod at the onlookers in an effort to let them know everything is okay. I sincerely hope everything is okay. I keep my head tilted forward so that anyone looking at us can only see, at best, the lower half of my face.

Mr. Kent gathers himself,

"I do apologize. I think they must have put a little cayenne on top. In truth I don't mind it really but I just have to be ready for it."

I think to myself, as complicated as his order was he'd be lucky to just get a sprinkling of cayenne and not *Martian powdered smear*. Talk about spicy. That stuff would have Satan butt naked in Alaska, standing inside a freezer, asking for a glass of ice water.

The initial cough inducing surprise of the drink was short-lived because now Kent is gulping it down greedily. I begin speaking again just as Kent is taking the first bite of his pumpkin spice something or another.

"As a young man I attended Kaneeka Chisholm Junior High."

"... on the east side of Flint?" He says, a few crumbs spilling from his mouth onto the table.

"Yes. You know it?" I reply with my eyebrows and the corners of my mouth raised.

"Of course. I was raised in Flint. We were taught about it in elementary school. It made national news in its day. The first public school named after the second African American, and first female, President of the United States. It's been closed for... I don't know... a hundred years? You, went there?"

Through the passage of time I had become not only handed down folklore, but had found myself caught in the torrent of publicly taught history. I decided to add to the lesson.

"Did you know that one of President Chisholm's ancestors ran for president back in the 1980s?"

"I can't say that I knew that. I don't imagine many people would know that today. Clearly he did not win."

"She... clearly she did not win."

"What? Interesting. So President Kaneeka was fulfilling her family's destiny by becoming the first woman to ever hold the office of president."

"Indeed, and to answer your question," I decided to answer the question he'd asked at the top of the conversation and not the most recent.

"It was after a fight I got into at KCJH that Midas was born."

"A fight over?"

"What else? A girl."

"Interesting." Kent says interesting like a character named Spock from an ancient science fiction broadcast. Today's science facts, however, have far surpassed what was centuries ago thought to be flights of fancy and fiction. Kent continues, "I don't think that people think of you as, human in that way, or human at all."

I laugh, perhaps too loudly,

"Mr. Kent I assure you, I'm hyper human in some ways."

If only he could have asked Felicia Alford, she would have testified to it. We were all 12 and 13 back then at KCJH. We were children, little boys and girls, but due to either genetics or hormones

Felicia already looked like a woman. Male teachers fought to not give her a second, or third look as she passed them in the hall. Her hips would rise and fall like bad credit scores, and were as round and sweet as corner store-stolen cherry blow pops. Female teachers hated her for reasons they couldn't readily explain, or admit. She looked like what their earnest New Year's Eve resolutions said they'd look like as Old Lang Syne ushered them into 365 new days of broken promises. Felicia never dressed provocatively but she couldn't hide curves that girls her age—and women three times her senior—envied; and that grown men were ashamed to admit, and young boys all to eager to confess, they desired. She seemed unaware of all this attention and, at times, derision aimed at her. Also, unbeknownst to Felicia, we were a couple. I'd never said more than hi to her in the halls as we passed each other. I'd never called her at home or inboxed her on *Shush* or *PassedNote* but I just knew that once I let her in on the surprise, about our relationship, she'd be with it.

You can't imagine the shock and awe I felt as I walked up on Felicia, between classes, sharing *3-D vmojis,* in the hall, by the lockers with Preston Scott. *3-D vmojis* where everyone, including me, could see! Hearts and smooches and cuddles just floating in the air above their heads as they stood next to her locker. Preston stood rocking back and forth sheepishly with his hands in his pockets. His smile was as wide as the hallway, and his teeth were game show host white and perfect. Felicia's back was against her locker and her hips jutted slightly forward as if pointing to him. She had her arms crossed against her chest, creating an artificial barrier between them. Her eyes though, her

27

eyes told the truth of it. They were drinking him in like a lunchtime juice box. And not just any juice box, a box of red juice.

Didn't Preston know that she was MY girl! I figured it was just a misunderstanding, a clear mistake, and once I explained it to Preston... and Felicia, they'd both understand she was indeed MINE. So I walked over to Preston and punched him in the face. This was not only an awful attempt at explanation but also a terrible idea.

Preston was an anomaly. He was probably the smartest kid in the school, perhaps in any school, but he had already, at the tender age of thirteen, been kicked out of two schools for fighting. One of the fights was with a teacher—a fully grown, teaching, adult, man—and he'd won. My punch had clearly caught him off guard, much the way an insect catches a windshield off guard. Felicia covered her mouth, with her beautiful hands, and Preston, his head still turned slightly east from the force of the blow began to laugh, a strange, guttural, low, dangerous laugh. I could feel the kids in the hall starting to recede into the walls and push themselves into their own lockers in an effort to get as far away from me and whatever came next as they could. Preston turned his head slowly toward me, like creepy ventriloquist dummies in old archived *Kudzu* films, his laughter growing louder. I began to laugh too because, why not. I wanted to hit him again with my aching hand, but what I had done so easily as I approached now seemed impossible. I wanted to run, but my legs had divorced themselves from my mind's commands. Once Preston's head had completely turned or maybe just before, I can't be sure, it happened so quickly, he punched me hard, twice, in the nose. His fists were clearly traveling faster than my nerve endings could register because the pain didn't immediately find me. After the third punch though the pain kicked in, just as my knees gave out. When you're standing the floor doesn't seem that far away. When you're falling however it seems to take forever to get to it, but get to it I did. I was laying on my back staring into the fluorescent ceiling lights. The *3-D vmojis* were still floating in the air, like tweety birds around the heads of characters knocked unconscious in *Kudzu* cartoons. I could feel the blood, hot and thick, running out of my nose and down my cheeks like molten lava. Suddenly all that was ceiling and fluorescent and *vmoji* was blotted out by Preston's face as he stood over me, his fists clenched and trembling. He shouted, "You should use your words!"

Which seemed like sound advice, that I wouldn't get to use because of my pending death. I accepted that I was going to be killed right there and then by a guy who was stealing my girlfriend, unbeknownst to her. Preston looked at my face and his expression went from anger to confusion. He looked at his own fist, the one he'd punched me thrice with so far, and seemed even more perplexed. He held his hand up beneath the florescent lights and turned it from side to side, examining it, then looked at me and said, "King Midas?"

"A king huh? Your ascent to the throne was sudden and unprecedented. Did you know who Mi... who that was?"

Kent's voice comes to me almost as if echoing through those long KCJH hallways. It pulls me out of the memory and back into the cafe.

29

"Excuse me?" I say as I gather myself. I find my hand unconsciously rubbing the bridge of my nose. The skin remembers.

"When," Kent takes a moment to recall or quickly replay the name in his *AudRecorder*, "Prest. Preston, called you a king. Did you know who that particular king was?"

I chuckle, remembering my confusion at Preston's proclamation.

"No, actually I didn't. I thought to myself, mufflers? but by the look on his face I knew something different was going on. To be honest I really didn't care what he was calling me so long as he was no longer hitting me. I mean up to that point his right hand was working overtime. His left hadn't even punched in yet."

Kent chuckles at the pun. It's the first, more warm than confrontational, moment we've shared. I continue, "I discovered in that moment, in the halls of KCJH along with everyone else, that somehow my blood had become liquified pure gold, and that when it cooled it became solid gold."

"You say, had become? It hadn't always been that way?"

"No. Certainly not. I'd had scraped knees, cuts, all the injuries that kids self inflict in pursuit of fun. A fun that to our parents looks more like repeated, laughter filled, attempts at suicide. My cuts and abrasions had led to burning rubbing alcohol, band-aids that don't come off easily, and itchy scabs, but never gold. It had been just good old-fashioned red blood up until that moment."

"Hunh. Interesting."

"Indeed. Anyway, I got up and ran home. I felt lucky to have not been capital murdered. I didn't mention any of it to my parents. I just went to my room and began tidying up. I organized books and put away action figures, Legos, and my little chemistry set. I didn't know what to do so I just cleaned my room in silence. It was something I could control and I needed some semblance of control in that moment, I think."

"Why didn't you go to your parents? Were you embarrassed about the fight? Do you think you were in shock, or had a concussion? Maybe that's why you were just mindlessly cleaning. The trauma to your head could have impaired your vision or caused you to hallucinate and see the blood as gold."

Kent is doing what any rational mind would do, and several have done. He's looking for a pedestrian explanation for a, reportedly, extraordinary occurrence. When something gets beyond the lines of what a sane mind considers reasonable, then that mind does everything it can to push that thing back inside the lines, back inside the known parameters, back inside of the comfortable boxes. Unfortunately, my story comes with little comfort.

"It wasn't mindless cleaning, it was definitely mindful. If I was hallucinating that would mean that Preston and everyone in the hallway was sharing my hallucination. The lunches at KCJH could be a trip, but I don't think they ever sent us on an actual trip. And I didn't tell my parents because at the time I don't think I knew what to say, or how to explain it, or if it was even really real. I mean, it had clearly happened, but was it something that would continue happening? In the following days and weeks at school, however, it became all too real."

"How so?"

"Kids initially were giving me a wide berth in the hallways and teachers would just stare at me as I sat at my desk. It was like I was patient zero for some new dangerous contagion. Then, faster than you can say Leprechaun, word spread around the school that Preston's parents were able to use what was left on his hand to pay off their car. The next thing I knew I went from kids not wanting to touch me at all, to every kid in school wanting to fight me all the time. It got out of hand. The teachers wouldn't stop it or intervene either. They'd come running and stand by waiting. The janitor would be off to the side with a mop. Getting from math to English had become Thunderdome, so I stopped going to school. The school administrators called my mom, told her about my lack of attendance, and insisted I return. When I got home after a day of pretending I was at school mom and dad were both sitting on the couch, waiting for me. I knew this was coming. I knew they had questions about why I wasn't going to school."

"You were finally at a point where you were ready, or at least willing to speak with them about it?"

"I wasn't, not really. Before they could say anything I pulled out a small knife, cut the palm of my hand and dripped gold onto the dining room table. My dad stared in disbelief and said, 'gold?' My mom who at the moment could not care less about what it was shouted, 'Boy! Stop making a mess!'"

I can still see their faces. The surprise in his. The frustration in hers. I've seen both of those expressions in Kent's face in the short time we'd spent together thus far. I continue, "I explained almost everything to them that afternoon."

"Almost? Why almost everything?"

"Your girlfriend must love that you're an active listener Mr. Kent."

"Please don't try to deflect. You invited me here to tell me the whole story. So tell me the whole story, please. Our readers deserve your complete and unvarnished version of the truth."

Mr. Kent is not wrong, but we don't always get what we deserve in this life, and more often than not, that's a blessing. I debate, for a moment, asking him if the truth has versions, or if the truth is just the single and solitary truth; but feel like that will take us somewhere he nor I have time to go. Instead I decide to go another route,

"Have you ever had gumbo Mr. Kent?"

"Gumbo, girlfriends, and bears, oh my. Where are you going with this Dorothy?"

Of all the things lost to time can you believe *The Wizard of Oz* has survived? I see the ruby red slippers in my mind and look over my shoulder unconsciously. I turn back to face Kent.

33

"Gumbo. You ever had it?" I resist the urge to call him Scarecrow or Cowardly Lion.

Mr. Kent sits back in his chair and exhales as if exhausted by this conversation already, "... Yes. Yes I've had gumbo."

"Well then you know."

"I know what!?" He bolts upright in his seat, bumping and jostling the table slightly. His frustration getting the better of him. He takes a deep breath and sits back again.

"You know that a good story is like gumbo. It takes time. It's got to stew a bit. It has key ingredients that make it delicious, that make it worth the wait. But each ingredient has to be added at the right time to make it gumbo. Rush it, add the wrong thing, or add the right thing at the wrong time and you ain't got gumbo. You've got soup. Perhaps a delicious soup, but it ain't no gumbo."

"I'm not writing a cookbook. I'm writing an article about you and your supposed life. I don't want any gumbo. I don't want any soup. I just want the truth."

"Then you're in luck because gumbo is the truth. So as I was saying, I told them about what school had become for me. I told them, I feared for my life. My mom withdrew me from KCJH the very next day and began homeschooling me after she got home from work. The story of the fight, however, had a life of its own. It had transformed from Preston punching me and getting my blood-turned-gold onto his fist, to me touching him and gilding his entire body, to me looking at him and

34

turning him and anyone within my sight into golden statues. Reporters caught wind of this sensational tale of the kid that could turn people into gold and started camping out on our lawn so that they could get an interview, or just a photo of the real life Midas. My dad threatened to shoot them, and my mom threatened to sue them for harassing a minor. They backed off and things seemed to cool out. Then one day while mom and I were walking to the store a car jumped the curb and tried to run us down. The driver kept screaming that my blood could save. He kept yelling something about Midas and then Jesus. Other maniacs tried to break into the house, or run up and force their way into our car. So we moved to a place where we hoped we wouldn't be recognized. Waukegan."

"Waukegan? I'm not familiar," Kent says. I notice that unlike before I'm no longer fighting his phone for his attention. He's a bit frustrated but I have his full attention.

"Waukegan is a suburb of Chicago. It's much smaller than Chicago but still large enough that one can be an anonymous face in the crowd. A place where if you stick to yourself, you can disappear in plain sight."

"And were you able to?" Kent sits up again, and moves to the edge of his seat. He's back from his small tantrum. Mr. Kent may be easily upset but he also doesn't live in that space long. Noted.

"We were," I let out a sigh as memories of Waukegan, and the briefly peaceful respite we found there, lightly flutter like a butterfly through my memory. "Yeah, for a little while, we were."

"And that's good. Right?"

Now it is my turn to sit up straight, lean forward, and move to the edge of Kent's personal space. I look into his grey eyes and make sure he's looking into mine before I begin again.

"Mr Kent. Money is an interesting thing. With money comes a power of sorts. With enough money you can influence trials, influence elections, topple nations, prop up dictators and so on and so on. Money is, in and of itself, indiscriminate. It neither loves nor hates, wants nor needs. It is a blank canvas awaiting your influence and direction. It is the will of men and women that brings nobility or malignancy to money, that bends it to righteous causes or wicked deeds. First Timothy six and ten is often misquoted as reading, money is the root of all evil. In truth that verse reads, the *love* of money is the root of all evil. Some even read it as saying the desire for money is the root of all evil. In the end, money doesn't make anyone anything they are not. It just makes them more of who they are.

"First Timothy six and ten?" I can tell by the way he asks the question that I have stepped into a place Kent doesn't visit or even care for. He continues, "From, the bible? I mean the Christian bible?'"

By the way he says the word Christian it's apparent that to him, Christianity is like the cheese in the old mousetraps. Many have gotten their necks broken trying to grasp it.

"Yes, the Christian bible. I know celebrity and cyber-based designer religions are all the rage these days. Piecemeal prophecy and patch-working passages from books eons old alongside memes created yesterday, is the way of the world; but there was a time when doctrine was digested whole and faith not consumed so a la carte."

Kent's grey eyes seem to darken a bit before he speaks,

"And look where that got us. Wars. People using scriptures to enslave and embolden. Fights over parcels of land people laid claim to because of loose interpretations from this book or the other. The deconstruction of the organized religions and rise of these smaller, shaken not stirred, hybrid, peace meals put an end to all of that. It was for the best. Also, I thought you said you liked gumbo. Things all mixed together like Buddha, Jesus, Muhammad, Lao Tzu and @777Spiritual_Faith_PoleDancer swirling together in a delicious stew. No?"

I don't immediately respond but think, touché Mr. Kent. Kent takes my lack of response as a response it appears. He doesn't sit back. I think he would consider sitting back now as retreating in some way, and he's currently not in a mood to give up ground. Not on this particular topic and not when he's gained so much. With his eyes still locked on mine he asks, "Would you consider yourself a religious man?"

This is a question I've certainly asked myself through the decades. My mouth offers an answer that I'm not sure my mind has fully endorsed.

"I've seen a lot Mr. Kent. More than I'd expected to in one lifetime and perhaps more than any one person should. In all I've seen

37

I've also grown to know that there's something bigger at play. Some call it God, some call it the universe, different religions and different cultures have called it different things, but they all agree it exists. Even the designer, hodgepodge religions don't refute this point. Even @777Spiritual_Faith_PoleDancer would agree."

"So you are a religious man then?" Kent moves closer, just inside of my comfort zone now. He seems anxious for an answer. My brain and mouth get on one accord and I give him one.

"Where belief in something bigger than ourselves unites, religion divides. I can't refute what you say religion has done though that's more about man than the religion itself; but it has seemed impossible to divide the two. So am I religious? No. I hope we are all bigger than religion by now. I hope we've dropped religion and picked up God. Just like I hope we can differentiate the difference between gumbo and a swirling, delicious, stew."

"I see," Kent says, the wheels in his mind seem to be spinning in an effort to find a response. Ultimately, he finds his way back out of my personal space and settles on, "I'm sorry I interrupted you. This interview is not about religiosity. It is, as I said, about you. A moment ago you were speaking about money and character. Let's return to that."

I don't mention that religion or my lack thereof is a part of me. I don't want to throw rocks at that hornets nest again. So I return to where we left.

"Yes. I was saying money can only expose character. It can't build it. Money will only make you more of who you are at your core, deep down inside. My father was at his core a man that had chased money and its trappings his whole life. Cars, clothes, drugs, excess. It was what he wanted, what he felt he'd deserved from his earliest memories I would suppose. He also felt like either society, the government, schools, people, bad luck, God, Satan, or all of them, had in some way denied him access to these things. In truth he'd only come to Michigan with mom betting on a pay day down the road. A road that had gone from long, to longer, to never-ending.

"Mom was a spoiled rich girl that had been, through choices repugnant to her parents, separated from their money. Money she considered her birthright. Cut off. Discarded like Thanksgiving's leftovers on the Monday after. She, like dad, loved the trappings that money could afford. While dad had only viewed those trappings from the periphery, mom had lived in the center of it for all of her formative years. Working at the Department of Labor was for her like toiling in level one of Dante's nine circles of hell.

"Now imagine, those two, having a child that basically has unlimited *ByteBill Blings* running through his veins. Every-time he scrapes his knee it's a mortgage payment. Every time his nose bleeds it's the full purchase price of a new car. Imagine having my father with his desires. Expensive cars, the latest clothes, designer drugs, and women, lots of women. Imagine having my mother's wants. Decadence, opulence, a need to show her parents that she can not only survive but thrive without them. Can you see them both, young, in Alabama, unexpectedly creating a child and having to make a way. Then imagine them, not as young, broke, weary of life, tired of struggling, tired of each other, and hiding out in Waukegan with access to limitless wealth. All they have to do is strike gold."

The turn of phrase, strike gold, is not lost on Kent whose back straightens a bit when I say it. I can see the wheels of his mind turning, already trying to figure out where to place that line in the *mind reading*.

"We were living in Waukegan. Neither mom nor dad were working. They were afraid that someone would discover that they were the parents of 'Midas.' I thought they were afraid that someone would do something to me but over time I realized that they were afraid that someone, or some agency, would take me away from them. Take away the golden goose, this one chance they had to get, and be, everything they'd ever wanted.

"One night, after we'd been in Waukegan for about two months, mom and dad both came into my bedroom. The hour was very late. They were both fully dressed, wearing coats and shoes."

My eyes go to the front of the cafe but all I can see is our old apartment. My hands feel hot as they grip the chair's arm rest. The soles of my feet burn as I begin to grind the heels of my shoes into the cafe's stone floor. The skin remembers, as I begin to also.

"One of them turned on the overhead lamp, waking me from my sleep. I shielded my eyes from the sudden and unexpected flood of light with my hands."

The dancing, lip syncing, smiling, silent VR birthday partygoers, their hands covering their faces, all seem to be mimicking me that night.

"In the spaces between my fingers I watched through squinting eyes as they approached. Mom's smile seemed, painted on, fake, something about the corners of her mouth seemed sad or afraid. Hers was the smile of a circus clown, of someone offering delightful distractions and feigning joy so that you might not smell so clearly the elephant shit in the room.

"Mom sat down gently on the bed, her right hand behind her back, while dad stood. Dad didn't bother to smile. His eyes were determined, the pupils black focused pinpoints. His mouth twitched from, what I understand now to be, him grinding his teeth. His right hand was behind his back but his left couldn't seem to find a place to be. It rubbed the front of his pants, went into his pocket, came out, tucked into his arm pit, scratched his head. His left hand was confused but his eyes knew exactly where to be, and that was on me. With his left foot he kicked mom's right. Her practiced smile gave way to genuine anger for a brief moment as her head turned ever so slightly toward him. Then she remembered herself, remade her smile like bed linens after a rough night of sleep, turned full toward me and said, 'Since the incident at the school things have been... hard for us... for us all. We had to leave Flint with little to nothing and come here. For you. For your safety. And and AND, we were happy to do it Mida ... R.J.'

41

"Dad began to shift anxiously from foot to foot. It was clear this was taking longer than he'd hoped, or wanted. As mom spoke I looked into his face. His color was off. Ashen. As were his lips. I'd earlier noticed the focus in his eyes but not the glaze. I don't know how I'd missed it. He wasn't well, which didn't bode well for me.

"I'd heard certain key words in all that mom said after calling me 'Mida...': poor, tough times, sacrifice, blood, money. When she finally took her hand from behind her back—a hand that had held me when I was sick, a hand that had picked me up when I fell, a hand that had rock-a-bye-baby'd me—when she took that hand from behind her back, she was holding a syringe. Dad, his reaction Pavlovian, licked his lips. I hardly felt the pinch as the needle entered my arm. I kept my eyes on dad the whole time. His right hand came from behind his back. He was holding more syringes. No one spoke. The room was as silent as a patient after hearing their doctor say, malignant. We just quietly took inventory of each other. In them I saw pitfalls and snares to be avoided. I saw where the wrong people, role models, and ideologies can lead you. It was as if I was reading one of those ancient *Choose Your Own Adventure* books and here on page 13, was the unfortunate conclusion to a story that began with so much promise. I don't know what they were seeing in me but I'm sure it wasn't their son.

'Now that wasn't so bad was it?'

"Mom said as she removed the last needle from my arm."

Kent's eyes, that had been on mine, watch as my hand rubs my arm where the needles had pricked me all those years ago. I didn't realize that my hands weren't on the armrests of the chair anymore. I stop rubbing my arm, return my hands to where I thought they were, and continue.

"She dabbed at the little gold droplets that formed on my skin after the needle's exit with a piece of cotton. There was no guilt in her face, just the gilt against the cotton. She almost threw the cotton ball in the trash, before thinking better of it and instead tucking it into her coat pocket. Dad took the syringes from her hand, so frantically that he almost dropped one, and left the room. Mom stayed and tucked me in, her smile genuine now, the look on her face one of relief.

'... I ... I'm sorry R.J,' she said, before laying her head across my narrow chest and sobbing.

'Wha dah fuhck dis is!'

"Dad shouted as he re-entered the room, a glass in his left hand, a syringe in his right. Mom sat upright, her posture still perfect. She could hear the urgency in his voice. She looked at the ashen man that used to be her shiny husband,'What Ray Ray!?'

"He walked over and showed her the small glass with what appeared to be blood covering the bottom of it. Plain, old, red, blood.

'Where'd you get that?'

'Fruhm dah say-wrenge!'

"He said waving his right hand and its contents.

"Mom looked at me, looked at my arm, took the piece of cotton from her pocket and looked at the gold that lived where she'd dabbed my arm with it. She took the cup and syringe from dad, like a mother snatching scissors from a child. She threw the blood in the cup onto the hardwood floor, and squirted some fresh blood from the syringe into the glass. They both peered down into the glass, like lottery ticket holders one number away from being millionaires, holding their breath and hoping. Blood. Plain, old, red, blood. No gold. How?

"Dad's pinprick pupils now settled angrily on me,

'Where's dah goald at bwoy?'

"He asked like a burglar questioning a bank teller during a robbery gone wrong. I just stared at him. At those beady eyes. Eyes I didn't know anymore, maybe never knew. It's amazing how you can look but not see. As long as I'd been looking into my dad's eyes, had I ever really seen them? Had I ever paid attention? His eyes were black like mine, but without the gold halo circumnavigating them. I said nothing in response to his query. There was nothing I could say. I didn't have an answer. He took the cup from mom's hand and smashed it angrily against the floor.

'Where. It. At nah!?'

"The burglar was growing more and more irate with the teller's silence.

'He doesn't know Ray!'

"Mom shouted, clearly sensing dad's growing frustration, his anger, and the danger inherent.

'Yay he dew! We moov'd here'n fah 'im! An' nah he on't wan share 'is goald wit us!?'

"He started to move closer, and to ball his fists. Preston? I suddenly felt like I was back in the KCJH hallway staring up at the florescent lights. Mom extended her hands toward him, her palms out, a plea for him to stop. He ignored her plea and pressed on. She stood and pressed her hands and full weight against his chest.

'Raekwon! Stop it!'

"She had the affect of a six foot wall trying to stop a twelve foot wave. He rolled right over her. He grabbed her hand and threw her halfway across the room. There was nothing between he and I now. Not time. Not distance. Not even love.

'R.J.! Run!'

"Until she spoke the words it was as if that idea had never occurred to me. I'd never run from my parents. I'd always run to them. I'd been told during spankings, 'don't you run from me.' I'd been told in grocery stores, 'don't run where I can't see you.' I'd been told in church, 'don't you run up in here.' Running from them seemed unnatural, but clearly we were all doing things that night we'd never done before. I feigned right and bolted left. His hands grabbed for me like that giant silver metal claw in those blinking, flashing, pulsing machine's that used to sit just outside of grocery stores. And just like those claws he failed to seize the prize. I was past him in a flash.

'Hay nah! HAY!'

"I heard his voice shouting as I ran up the hall. I heard the heavy fall of his shoes as he turned and began to give chase. I had no idea where to run. None of the doors in the house locked. The door to the closet in their bedroom opened inward. If I could get in that closet and wedge something or even myself against the door, maybe I could hold him off, maybe mom could calm him down, maybe mom would call the police. There were a lot of maybes, but maybe was all I had at that moment. As fast as my feet would take me I ran for the closet. I could hear him, the thud of his shoes against the wooden floor. I ran into the bedroom and dove into the open closet. I had no sooner shut the door and pressed myself against it, when he slammed the full weight of his frame into the door. I was knocked against the back of the closet. He had readied himself for the blow but was still thrown backward a bit himself. I rushed, slammed the door shut, and pinned myself against it. He kicked the door, and my feet came from under me. I pushed my back against the door, harder, but knew that his next couple of kicks would big-bad-wolf my refuge. I braced myself for the next blow. I dug my heels in against the floor as best I could but my feet kept slipping. I tensed my shoulders. I closed my eyes tight and waited. And waited. The blow didn't come. I didn't realize how fast and heavy my breaths were coming until they finally slowed a bit. My shoulders relaxed. My feet that had been trying to find purchase against the floor stopped and only then did I feel the slick viscous fluid beneath them. I started to feel

46

the pain in my feet. I opened the door and saw the trail of gold leading to the closet, and the pool of liquid and quickly solidifying gold growing beneath me.

"When I'd run from the bed I'd run through the shards from the broken glass. I'd cut my feet and tracked gold through the house as a result. Fear had muted the pain. I limped over near where my mother and father had busied themselves collecting the gold from the floor as it cooled and solidified. Neither of them looked up or registered my presence. It was almost as if I wasn't there. As if the ghost of their son now walked amongst them. I hobbled my way into the bathroom, found a pair of tweezers and began slowly and painfully removing the pieces of glass lodged in my foot. The gold acted as a coagulant and almost as soon as I removed a piece of glass the bleeding would slow. If I pushed the skin together after the glass had been removed the bleeding would stop completely and the gold somehow work to seal the cut. I removed the last piece of glass, wiped my feet with a towel and sat on the bathroom floor with tear stained cheeks as the gold closed and mended the last of my wounds.

"Eventually, once they'd collected all that they could, my parents became aware of my absence. They tracked my gilded footprints to the bathroom. There was a light knock on the bathroom door and then the turning of the door handle. My mother came in, her eyes on the floor. I don't know if she was ashamed, or simply looking at the precious metal leading to where I sat with my back against the chipped paint of the bathroom's far wall. She finally let her eyes land on me. There was genuine concern there. This is the look that had greeted

47

me when I was fevered and would rouse from a sweaty delirium. This is the face that dropped me off for my first day of kindergarten and didn't think I saw her circle the block and park at the far corner to make sure I was alright. This was my mother, returned to me. I wanted to say something, anything, to let her know I still loved her. To let her know we would get through this madness, but before I could speak she looked at my injured feet and said, 'Where are the towels? The towels you used to wipe your feet, where are they?'"

Chapter 3 | Love. Bytes

I don't realize that I am looking down at my feet until I look up into Kent's face. How long have my eyes been on my shoes? Brown brogues with worn heels in desperate need of a shine. They're really not anything to look at, but they are a fair description of how I feel in this moment. Brown. Worn. Dull.

I look into Kent's eyes and can't help but notice that there is an excitement there. The clear love of a good story, true or not, is actively working overtime and extra shifts in his pupils. In the deep creases of his furrowed brow, however, lives the fact that he's distressed and pained to hear such a sad tale of mistreatment. His brow suggests that he's so affected in fact that it makes me wonder about his youth, his childhood, his story. His brow speaks to his empathy and humanity, but his dancing eyes remind me that he's a journalist. That there's a part of him that's elated to be the one that's going to bring this tale of adolescent woe and discovery to the *mind reading* world. I can feel the conflict in being pained and elated radiating off of him like heat from a hot iron on the floor that your foot is inching dangerously close to. People having dueling emotions is nothing new. In those early Midas years I both loved and loathed my parents, every day, all the time.

To say those were complicated times would be an understatement. With the demise of paper money, that you could move hand to hand, came the rise of bitcoin, that you could move continent to continent. Bitcoin in time evolved into *ByteBills*, that you could move planet to planet. From anywhere in the solar system you could have *ByteBills* instantly *blinged* into your *iPP finger tip* account. So although it wasn't paper money it was still, literally, money in the palm of your hand or at your finger tips. The bitcoin and *ByteBill* innovations in many ways led to the ubiquity of *Goldilocks Machines*.

Goldilocks evolved from a thing called Redbox. Redboxes were places where you could rent and return movies and video games, vending machine style. This was in the early 2000's way before *EyeSeeViews* or *iPPTube*. *Goldilocks* took the Redbox model and applied it to precious metals. Any time, day or night, you could go up to a sparkling white *Goldilocks*, insert precious metals or gems into its gold pull-out drawers and the machine would scan, digitize, evaluate and register the current market value of your offering. It would then take ten percent and *bling* the balance to your bank account back then, or *iPP finger tip* it now. Currency exchanges around the world were put out of business almost overnight by *Goldilocks* and the owners of the machines found themselves in possession of the one thing that has always counted, always held value in the world, gold. For my parents— people who wanted the finer things, weren't fans of working, and not averse to doing whatever they had to do to get whatever they wanted— having me for a son was a Godsend.

There used to be stories of parents telling kids, "This is going to hurt me more than it's going to hurt you," before spanking them. My parents gave no speeches and held no illusions. They'd always slither in as a pair, leeches, their hands behind their backs so I wouldn't know the agent of my blood letting. Sometimes it was a razor. Other times scissors. A few times, just my father's fists. They always came as a pair so I never thought it was his idea and not hers, or her idea and he was just going along. They always came as a pair and it was the only thing that they did together anymore. They rarely spoke to each other in those days. They'd get their *Goldilocks* deposit, divide the porridge and not speak until it was time to once again strike gold; and then they'd come joined at the hip, joined in their purpose. They almost looked in love when they'd enter my room. They almost looked like who I remembered them to be before KCJH, before Preston Scott. When they'd come in the room I'd always smile in spite of myself and then I'd see their hands behind their backs, and feel my back against the wall. Dueling emotions are nothing new to me.

I'm completely turned and staring at the cafe wall behind me. Even though I'm facing the wall I can feel it against by back. My shoulders come forward and my back rounds like an angry, scared cat. I sigh, square my shoulders and turn around to face Kent. He says nothing but his curiosity about my odd antics is clear. He probably thinks I'm mad. We silently take new inventory of each other. The madman and the journalist. As we quietly stare at each other I notice something I hadn't noticed earlier, Kent doesn't look well. Ashen. Dull. Since we've been sitting his skin has gone pasty and he's beginning to

51

sweat profusely. I'm about to ask if he'd like to step outside when he says, "So, what DID you do with those towels?"

The bathroom. The glass. The blood. The gold. The towels. My eyes go back to my feet. I wiggle my toes in my brogues and grind the heels of my feet against the soft cloud inserts.

Your skin is the largest organ of the body and though not thought of like the brain, it remembers. I have elephant skin, not in texture but in memory. It remembers everything. The glass. The fists. The razors. The bullets. The knives. The concrete. The fingernails. The walls. Any and everything ever used to bruise, scrape, burn, or break it, my skin recalls in painstaking detail. My feet burrow against the shoe inserts as my skin remembers the glass shards freed one at a time from the heel, the ball of my foot, and between my toes. My jaw clenches as my mind sees what my skin can't forget. The tweezers. The tears. The towels.

"I gave them the towels." It comes out sounding angrier than I'd wanted. I'd thought all these years would have dulled the anger. I supposed that the pain would be more emotional than physical now. Alas, no, there it is, right at the surface, a volcano with a calm façade but seething beneath, searing hot, churning, ready to erupt when least expected.

"I guess you had no choice," he says as he wipes his forehead with his hand and stares at the sweat. He looks at my forehead and around the room to see if anyone else is sweating. No one is.

"We all, always have a choice Mr. Kent," I say forcing myself to still my feet, and drawing his attention back to our conversation.

He clears his throat, "Did you have a choice in becoming," Kent lowers his voice again, "Midas?" I already feel like we're both leaning in so close we appear to be nearing a kiss, and whispering so softly only the angels can overhear what's being said. I think about his question for a second before answering. I want to be honest with Mr. Kent but I know there is a line. So here I am again with my biscuit words.

"Yes, Midas was something I ... could have avoided... but I didn't." Now I have his full attention.

"How, and why not?" he asks as I watch a bead of sweat run unacknowledged and un-wiped down his cheek.

Once again I choose which part of the question to answer. I seize on the latter.

"Midas was a necessity. I didn't know that at the time but I'm certain now, Midas was needed."

Kent doesn't press me on the former question, the one I've conveniently skipped. I think if he was feeling one hundred percent and not clearly fevered he would have. Instead he takes a few rapid blinks, swallows hard, and follows me down the rabbit hole that I've led him to.

"By whom?" He coughs and holds up his hand as a sign that he's alright and continues, "Needed by whom?"

"The world in time, but initially my parents."

"Ah I see. Your parents seemed like quite the pair."

They always came in pairs, runs through my mind. An image of them approaching, their hands behind their backs plays through my memory. Kent continues, "Was there any comfort during that time? Someone, something you could turn to?"

"Oddly, there was a chair."

A confusion as yet unseen blankets Kent's face.

"A cheer? There was a cheer?"

Now it's my turn to be confused.

"... A cheer? What kind of cheer would one invent for a time such as that Mr. Kent?"

"I don't know. Sis Boom Rah, I'm being abused by ma and pa? I don't know."

There is a part of me that wants to laugh. I don't.

"No Mr. Kent, there was a chair," I'm sure to enunciate fully this time.

"A chair," Kent scoots side to side in his seat as if to make sure I know what a chair is, "like these?"

"Yes, a chair but not like these. The cheap apartment we had in Waukegan was furnished. By furnished I mean it had in it what previous tenants had left behind before moving on to greener pastures, or deeper graves. The beds, the couch, the tables and chairs were all abandoned. There was this one chair, however, a wooden chair with a high back and an orange velvet cushioned seat. It was a bit wobbly but it felt regal to me for some reason. I adopted it as my own. I even moved it to my room.

I couldn't stop my parents from doing what they felt they had to, and so eventually I took control of the narrative in my mind. When they'd come, I'd sit in the chair like a king taking his throne and extend my arm. That way I wasn't so much a kid being forced into giving by his parents, but a monarch offering freely."

"King Midas?"

"I ... I guess so."

"So after the closet, that was how it was done going forward? With your quiet compliance?"

Goosebumps wallpaper my remembering flesh as I watch my mother's tears as she approaches time and time again, knowing what's about to be done by the pair of them. The corners of her mouth turned up into a mannequin's smile. Wetness streaking her cheeks. The tears of a clown. My father's anger palpable at having to come to me like a child asking for his allowance, but instead of with his hand out, he has his fists balled. My back pressed against the back of the chair, my arms out, palms up, like Jesus asking for your heart.

Later would come my mother's excitement about the clothes and jewelry she was able to afford. My father barely spoke to either of us, or at all. When he did speak to me he'd whisper through trembling ashen lips, I love you. I was still his only begotten son after all. Father why hast though forsaken me? His anger would always give way to embarrassment once whatever want or need that led to the fists, razors, and knives was met. Dueling emotions were nothing new to me, or them. I had become, in their lives, the golden goose that couldn't be slaughtered only routinely butchered. I think all of this but say nothing.

Kent takes my lack of answer as an opportunity to ask a different question, "Actually do you know why the syringe didn't work? You supposedly have gold blood, yes?"

Without knowing it he rescues me from those memories. I tuck them back inside the cigar box I keep beneath the bed in my mind. Where I keep all of my deepest darkest moments.

Now I can talk science and anatomy, things that don't cut so deep.

"Ah! Good question."

"I hope it wasn't my first good question," he laughs and initially I take his statement as a passive aggressive quip but somewhere just under the laughter I hear what sounds like genuine concern that he's doing well. Even if he believes I'm lying the professional in him still strives for excellence. Noted.

"No, not at all. I was just... never-mind. So, I discovered the truth of why the syringe didn't work many years later. I'll describe it this way, in my blood lay the potential for gold but not the necessity of it."

"What? Mr. M you're on some Sufi shit now."

This is the first time Kent, so far a mirror a professionalism, has cursed. He's either feeling increasingly not well or perhaps the distance between us is shortening. I laugh.

"Okay, what I mean is, when my skin is broken, the air, the hemoglobin, the blood's contact with my skin, the thrombocytes and a unique merging of rare and distinct qualities in my genetics and physical makeup merge in a way that turns the blood into gold. If any of those factors are absent then the blood will be, blood."

"Rare and distinct qualities? That's as clear as cumulus clouds."

"Unfortunately that is as clear as I can be."

"As clear as you can be or as clear as you will be?"

"Both mean that what I've told you is as much as I will. So whichever one keeps our conversation going, that's the one I mean."

Kent smirks and pushes on, "How do you know this about your blood? On top of your other claims are you saying you're also a hematologist of some kind?"

"I just bleed gold I've made no claims of being something as rare as a he-man, hemer...

"Hematologist."

"What you said. I've just been alive for a couple of centuries Mr. Kent."

"Centuries to people, but to a mountain only a moment."

"What?"

"I can get all Sufi-ish too." We both laugh this time. Time, conversation, and laughter can create friends where once two strangers stood. I wouldn't say Kent and I are friends but we're something other than we were ten minutes ago.

"Well, in those centuries, or seconds depending on whose clock we're using," I say as Kent nods as if to retort, well played. I wink to acknowledge his nod and continue, "I've had the time and the means to have myself examined thoroughly. Trust me it's the skin, the air, the hemoglobin and the platelets..."

"Don't forget the rare and distinct qualities."

"Yes, God forbid they be forgotten. They all combine to create the gold. Oddly in my research I've found that my biology is now more like the blue blooded horseshoe crab than a red blooded American. It's also why I heal so quickly. My thrombocytes act more like amebocytes in many ways, and they clump like nothing you've ever seen, like nothing that's ever existed. When my adrenaline is pumping it's even more so."

"Meaning?"

"Meaning a knife can slice my skin and cause me to bleed, but if you tried to stab me the blade would only go so far before basically feeling like it hit a wall and if my adrenaline is going then the knife

58

may not get past the very tip. My body's response to adrenaline has increased over the years. The way the glass cut into my feet so deeply when I was a child wouldn't happen exactly the same way today."

"And you know this from experience?"

I hesitate but answer, "... Yes.... and bullets are no different." Kent slides his chair forward.

"Wait, you're telling me you're bullet proof?"

"No, not really. I'm not like Superman in the *EyeSeeViews*. I can be shot and the bullet will enter my body but it'll never reach a major organ. It could break a bone depending on where I'm shot and the level of adrenaline in my system but the bone would mend rapidly, and mend stronger actually."

"And I take it you know this from experience too?"

"Mr. Kent, I'm a black man..."

"A Noir National."

"A. Black. Man. That has lived through some of the toughest times the world has seen since the early 21st century. I don't know how well you know your post-President Trump history and the Blue Lives Matter, pro-police movement that rose as he did; but some members of law enforcement, back then, tired of being caught on body and dash cams doing illegal and immoral things, formed the PVC."

"The PVC? The People's Vigilant Command? Absolutely. Heard all about them."

"I doubt it. The People's Vigilant Command. Yeah, that's what they called themselves but they were better known by the people as The Police Vigilante Command."

"You're saying the PVC were police?"

"They were cops that decided to be proactive and take the fight to the streets. Stop and Frisk turned into Halt and Assault, and then into Search and Shoot. The Broken Windows policing policy turned into broken jaws, broken bodies, broken homes. There was open war on the main streets and in the back alleys of many major cities for years. PVCs wore masks so people wouldn't know who they were. We didn't even know they were cops until one forgot to remove his badge from his belt and it was filmed. He was cast to the wolves as an outlier and found executed in his home soon after, but it was clear to everyone why these attacks were happening so frequently and why no one was ever caught. It's hard to catch a criminal when you assign the criminal to catch himself. The masked assailants initially would scare and beat the people they detained with pipes. So people started calling them PVC, even though the pipes they were using were lead. The name stuck and in time even they began referring to themselves as PVC. They branded themselves The People's Vigilant Command in their recorded and posted proclamations, that looked eerily like ISIS videos. Those who they were attacking had come to know who and what they really were though and so the name The Police Vigilante Command was born. This led to the creation of the Garner Gang, the Brown Boys, and the Rice Regime in reaction. Black and Latino defense leagues aimed at protecting people of color in the streets and named after unarmed victims of PVC mentality. To be clear Mr. Kent this was a time when just being a person of color could get you shot and killed by masked police officers wrapping themselves in a code of silence, the illusion of serving and protecting, and the American flag. I've been shot more times by people paid by our tax dollars than I'd care to recall. But my skin remembers."

"What happens to the bullets?"

"... what do you mean?"

Now it's my turn to be confused by a question.

"When you're shot, you said the bullets eventually are stopped by..."

"The coagulants in my blood."

"Right. So what happens to the bullets? Are you just walking around with bullets frozen in time living inside your body?"

"If I were I'd weigh a ton."

Kent's smile turns into a laugh. His laughter turns into a grimace. What's ailing him has its talons full into him now. He bends at the waist, takes a few deep breaths, composes himself and sits up straight. I don't ask. I just answer.

"The bullet breaks my skin bringing with it some air and some flesh. The hemoglobin and platelets surround the bullet, quickly stop its motion and in the process coat it with gold. The stopped bullet is then either absorbed into my urinary tract, or by my intestines. I have yet to determine what decides which. I pass them either via my intestines with my waste or they're processed through my urinary tract like kidney stones. I always hope they get caught in my intestines because to pass them like kidney stones is .... a pain you wouldn't believe. I don't want to compare it to childbirth because it seems infinitely more painful and difficult to have an entire human being come out of your body, but for a man I bet it's as close as it gets."

"I don't even want to imagine," Kent says, his face is balled up, but I don't know if it's from the pain he's experiencing or the pain he's imagining.

"I don't have to. I know all too well."

"But wait, I've heard people say they wake up in the morning and piss excellence. Are you telling me you shit golden bullets?"

I can't help but chuckle, "I guess I am, but I won't tell you my shit don't stink."

Now we're both just speaking freely, chatting and chuckling like old friends and not recent strangers.

"Does it hurt?"

"Does it hurt? Haven't you been listening Mr. Kent? It's excruciating and..."

"No, no, no I mean when you're shot, is there pain?"

"Hell yeah it hurts. I still have nerve endings," I don't chuckle but laugh fully this time "When I get hit, cut, or shot it hurts. The other day I hit my pinky toe against the corner of the bed and almost passed out."

This time I only get a weak laugh out of Kent. He uses a napkin to wipe his face.

"As I said before Mr. Kent I'm still human. Hyper human in some wa..." before I finish the sentence I notice a woman approaching us with a smile that deserves its own *iPPTube* viewing page and clear recognition in her eyes. This is a look over the years I've learned to dread and avoid. The ease of conversation and growing familiarity between Kent and I has caused me to let my guard down. I haven't been as observant and diligent about my surroundings as usual, as I should be. Fuck. I watch her, smiling, approaching. I notice that her hand is behind her back. They always came with their hands behind their backs. I eye the exit and stand abruptly. Instinctively Kent stands too. I'm sure he doesn't knows why.

"Clay? Clay Kent?" Her voice is warm syrup over hot pancakes on a cold day. My lungs fill with air and my shoulders relax.

I notice now that her eyes are and have been on Kent, and not me, the entire time. Kent looks from me to the approaching woman, noticing her for the first time. His words come out like Porky Pig at the end of a Looney Tune.

"KKKKKim! How, uhm, how, how are. You!?"

"You'd know if you ever returned my *readings* or *grips* Clay," she says playfully although it's clear she isn't joking. She pulls her hand from behind her back, pushes her palm close to Kent's face and shows him the *iPP readings* she's been sending him; and that he hasn't been responding to.

Kent finds some composure and a style of speech not fostered by Mel Blanc. "I know Kim, I know. I'm, I'm sorry. Things have been a bit..."

"Are you okay Clay?"

She cuts him off, and slowly lowers her hand. There is genuine concern in her eyes. The light from the *reading* has illuminated Kent's face. She's noticed now what I'd noticed before and gives voice to it, "You look a little..."

"I'm okay, just a little hot is all."

"Yeah, Clay we all know you're hot!"

She says this while playfully rolling her eyes, and then letting them fall clear and wide back on Kent. Her eyes still hold concern but there something else still beyond her care. Desire.

Kim is a dark complected woman. Her high cheek bones and the curvature of her face suggest Ethiopian perhaps. She is roughly 5'3" but her black, leather, thigh high boots have her standing bow legged and confident at 5'8". Her almond shaped eyes are hazel in a way that she was either born with or her OptiChrome *Swap was done perfectly.* I've seen some swaps where the original color bleeds through at the edges, but not hers. So either Kim's are natural or she's a walking billboard for her surgeon. She's curvy in a real way. Like the natural meander of a mountain stream and not the forced curvature of a mountain highway. In a time where people are always augmenting, improving or doing what some describe as *base dealing* their bodies she looks like she's playing the hand she was dealt; and it's a winning hand. Her form fitting blue jeans and red top allow for her physical perfections, and flaws, all to be known. Which in my mind is, perfection itself. She reminds me of...

"I didn't mean it like that Kim." Kent blushes at her allusion to his hotness. "Listen, I've been meaning to *slap* you back, especially after that night and yeah, we both had a bit too much to drink and then we ..."

Kim turns to me, "Does he ever *reach out* when you extend a *grip* to his *iPP*? Or is it just me that he's ignoring?"

I see now that somewhere in the not too distant past there was a night turned one night stand between them. She thought they had something and he must have poltergeisted. I feel her eyes on me. I thought her question was rhetorical but I can tell by the length of the pause, and the strength of her glare that she expects, no demands, an answer.

"Uhhm... I don't really extend *grips* to Ke... Clay. We mainly communicate via *blanket cork.*"

"*Blanket cork*? I thought people used that for... oh... are you two?... oh. Not that there's anything wrong if you are. I just didn't... oh."

"No, no, no Kim! Nothing like that," Kent says waving his hands as if he's trying to land an interplanetary space falcon.

"Now I see why my *grips* go *unhandled*. Is, is that why it didn't work with you and..."

"No! Nothing like. Tell her..." Kent looks at me, nods and gestures towards Kim.

I pause, turn to Kim, smack my lips and say, "I don't know about your *grips* Kim but trust me he can handle a lot."

I put my hand on my left hip, let my weight rest on that same leg and look at her like, *understand.*

"What!?" Kim and Kent say simultaneously in different octaves as if harmonizing.

Kim waves her brown jewelry laden hand in the air and rolls her neck. Some gestures seem to know no time or space. They're eternal.

"I hear you... whoever you are... and Clay... don't worry," she grabs air, "I won't extend not nar' 'nother *grip* to you chile."

"Kim!" Kent says without knowing what to say next.

"Good night Kim girl!" I say my voice full of conjured sass. She's halfway to the door before I can even finish, "Get home safe boo boo!" The door closes behind her and Kent spins around clearly not pleased.

"What the fuck man! Why would you do that!"

Kent almost topples over and has to use the back of the chair to hold himself up.

"Mr. Kent are you okay?"

"No I'm not okay! What. The. Fuck!"

"Mr. Kent you obviously want nothing to do with Kim."

"Yeah and so!?"

"And now she'll stop bothering you. You're welcome."

"But now she thinks I'm..."

"Forever unavailable. Which is what you wanted right? You're welcome."

Kent's knees tremble a bit and he puts both hands flat on the table to balance himself.

"Kent!?"

"I'm okay. I just got dizzy for a sec. It really is hot in here isn't it?"

"Let's step outside. The cool air will do you good."

"Actually Midas," he doesn't lower his voice this time. I can hear the anger and annoyance. "You know what? I have no reason to believe this isn't all some bullshit. You've been talking and I've been recording but you have offered no proof that you are who you say you are. And actually after seeing your award winning performance for Kim I see now that maybe you're just a good actor with a somewhat compelling story. So what's going to happen now is either you give me something I can corroborate or I'm going to sit down, rest a sec and as you said, consider this a nice afternoon of storytelling."

Kent takes his seat, removes his glasses, and lays his head on the table. He seems winded as if the effort of saying all of that took everything out of him. I don't say anything. I take the Aquarian quarter I've been holding, lay it on the table and head for the door.

The VR Party has evolved into karaoke it appears. I maneuver through the crowd their headphones now glowing green, blue, green, which denotes the silent sing-a-long. I make it through the doors of the double barrel shotgun room, stand just outside, and wait. It doesn't take long.

Mr. Kent comes racing out of the cafe. He doesn't look well enough for racing and running but he manages. I hear grumblings from the other side of the door. In his haste he wasn't as careful with the partygoers as I was and seems to have ruined the *FauxFillment* for some. He doesn't care. He finds me standing there, waiting for him, and stares at me. His glasses fog over due to the change in temperature. He takes them off. He doesn't need them anyway.

Kent reaches into his pants pocket and produces the Aquarian quarter. I smile at the sight of the gold coin. I gripped the quarter so tightly that the serrated edges cut my hand. For the entirety of our conversation my blood was coating and transforming the coin. It's the other reason I asked him to bring it. So that I could prove that I am who I've said I am. Kent looks from me to the coin, then back to me and says,

"Midas?"

I smile and say the thing I wished I'd said to Preston that day in the hall, "Absolutely."

Kent looks both terrified and excited. Dueling emotions are nothing new to me.

Chapter 4 | Midas. Well

We don't walk far. We can't. We're only a couple of blocks away when Kent says he needs to sit. His breathing is labored and his color has taken a turn for the worst. You'd think he'd ran a marathon rather than walked a few blocks. I listen for slurred speech as he apologizes for his poor condition and says he's not sure what's going on with himself. He promises me that he's usually a picture of health. I'm just trying to be sure he's not at the early onset of a stroke.

We settle on a bench across from a park teeming with kids on a play date. Living your life staring at an *iPP*, *VisiMon*, or laptop screen has become so much the way of the world for today's youth. Human interaction has become so nonessential and so "take it or leave it," that today's kids don't know what to do when faced with other, living, breathing, kids. Dates to play games have to be scheduled like business meetings: "Timmy naps from noon to one. Then he shits from 1:30 to 1:35. We can put you down tentatively for hopscotch at 2:00, baring no constipation." Friendships are arranged like antiquated marriages: "Timmy this is Johnny. Johnny this is Timmy. You two are best friends now. BEST FRIENDS! NOW!" Because of the dearth of natural interaction and the atrophy of social skills, kids when faced with other kids, just stare at each other bland, blank and confused like they're viewing some sort of extra-intergalactic thing.

The parents, however, show up to these play dates dressed in sweats, yoga pants, t-shirts, and sneakers. They run around playing kickball and tag until their sweat runs like an open faucet. They say they're trying to model the behavior for the kids, as they turn cartwheels. Grass stains their t-shirts and pants when their mid-thirty- and early forty-year-old bodies violently crash to earth like the meteor that killed the dinosaurs. They say they're trying to show them how it's done as they joyfully shriek and scream running from, or toward, one another. These are the things they say, the excuses they give, but mainly they appear to be doing it for the sheer joy of it.

Their adult lives have become so regimented and stilted that these play dates for their kids give them a chance to reengage with pieces of their happiness they've lost in marriages to the right person on paper but the wrong person in person. This is their chance to rediscover the parts of their smile seized by mortgages that rooted them to places they never thought they'd settle in, and to people they'd have never thought they'd settle for. In this park lives the space to remember the laughter repossessed by car notes that ask them to pay more than the car, or their time in it, was ever worth. It gives them a chance to try on the suit of youth again, to pretend there is nothing but this, nothing but kickball and "ready or not here I come!" No bills. No jobs. No affairs. No pending divorces. Just. This. They are olly-olly-oxen-free.

Their kids sit in the stands and watch like bored parents, checking their *iPP*s and playing online games with kids halfway around the world whom they'll never meet while ignoring the kids sitting to their left and right. It's Saturnalia. It's the world turned upside down. The children playing impatient parents and the parents filling the role of kids not ready to come in, not ready to take a bath, not sleepy, not ready to face the next week, the next day, the next moment.

I shout, "Lo, Saturnalia!" in honor of the ancient ritual returned to us. Everyone in the park looks around trying to find this "Saturnalia" that I've shouted "Lo" to. Heads turn and people point to one another as if to ask, are you Saturnalia? They finally decided that either I've got Tourette's or had a psychotic break, but whatever it is it's to be ignored and watched simultaneously.

One of the adults places his arm against a tree, closes his eyes, leans his forehead into the bend of his arm and says, "One Mississippi, Two Mississippi..." The other adults jump up and down giddily, scream and scatter, frantically seeking places to hide. The children in the bleachers check the time on their *iPP*s and roll their eyes in disbelief. Kent is rolling and turning the Aquarian quarter over and over again in his hand. He's hasn't said very much since leaving the cafe other than, "Midas," and, "I need to sit down."

Since sitting he's just stared at the quarter, just manipulated and stared at it; rubbed it and stared at it; stared at it and stared at it. It's as if he's waiting for a genie to appear and make sense of it all. The gilded quarter finally stops spinning between his fingers and he says,

"How do I know this isn't some con? some sleight of hand? some rather impressive magic trick?"

When the mind is faced with things it can't or won't accept they instantly become trickery or deception. It's easier and even safer in some ways to believe I'm Carpenter Blaine than to believe I'm Midas. It's always been this way with exceptional people in history. Joan of Arc was thought an evil witch. Jesus was thought a clever magician. The boxer Jack Johnson was once accused of being a human-bull hybrid. A minotaur of sorts. It was easier to accept that a bull and a person conceived a child than to believe a black man standing on his own two feet could not be bested in the ring by a white man. I've seen accounts of men who denied the ancient transatlantic slave trade, which they had all the evidence in the world to verify, but then readily advanced the idea of alien abduction to which there was no evidence at the time that they could point to. Of course it turned out both were true.

I finally take a breath and respond, "You don't, not until we walk past a *Goldilocks*. So extend me the benefit of the doubt at least until then. And also, it's all sleight of hand Mr. Kent. Everything. Everything you see and think you know, is misdirection and 'nothing up my sleeve.'"

"I haven't known you very long Mr. M but your propensity to wax philosophical grows annoying, quickly."

I laugh, loudly. The parents, their parental instincts still keen even as they play at childhood, look over again. I'm sure they're now sure it's a psychotic break I'm suffering.

73

"I apologize Mr. Kent. It's not my intention to grow annoying."

Kent begins to spin the coin through his fingers again before speaking.

"You screamed something about Saturnalia a couple of minutes ago. Funny, that's what I think of every-time I see these play date scenes too. You're maybe the only other person I've met who even knows what that is. You and... Kim."

"Ah! The lovely, curvy, feisty Kim."

"That now thinks I'm same gender, same species loving."

"But you know you're not *SGSSL* so what does it matter? You didn't have the heart or nerve, or both, to tell her you weren't interested. So done and done."

"You keep saying that like I should thank you for falsely outing me. I think you took some pleasure in it."

"Really?"

"Yeah. I'm a reporter Mr. M. I watch and read people for a living. It's also why I'm an above average poker player. I saw your eyes on her as she was walking, speaking, standing. The glow in your face. The way you stood a bit taller once you realized she wasn't an imminent threat, but a woman. A beautiful woman."

"Live long enough and you'll realize that being a beautiful woman and an imminent threat aren't mutually exclusive."

"I've already lived that long Mr. M. She is, as you described, lovely, curvy, and feisty. I noticed you noticing, and noting. I think the man in you found her attractive and the competitor in you didn't want me to have her. Though I don't know why. It's not like you can have her but clearly you wanted her."

I say nothing. I think about what he's said. My knee jerk reaction is to tell him he's being absurd and childish. I took something away from him that he didn't want and now not only does he suddenly seem to want it he's accusing me of wanting it too. Childish! His claim seems unfounded and petty but in my mind I can see her walking toward us, her hips doing the dance of the seven veils with every step, her high cheek bones pulled into greater definition by her pursed lips, her eyes sparkling like fireflies in the dusk as the green, orange and blue lights from the noise canceling headphones play off her hazel irises. I see her skin as close and dark as midnight is to tomorrow. Her hand is hidden behind her back. They always come with their hands behind their back. I watch her lips as glossed and full as the harvest moon parting to say, Clay? Clay Kent? His claim is baseless and I intend to tell him as much but, "... Perhaps." is what comes out instead.

I stop staring at the parents hiding behind bushes and trees, their heads on a swivel, their feet dancing, ready to run at a moment's notice, and look at him. His face says, I knew it.

"Have you ever been in love Mr. Kent?"

"Don't try to deflect."

"I'm not," I close my eyes and shake me head slowly from side to side. It has the opposite effect of the old etch-a-sketches. Instead of erasing, it brings the picture ever closer, ever clearer.

"The attitude, the walk, even the small things. The way she blinked slowly while you were speaking, and rapidly while she was. I... I know... or rather I once knew her. When I knew her, her name wasn't Kim it was Khadijah. This was, a very long time ago. Well before you, or Kim, or either of your parents were born."

"So, on this hyper-human Midas adventure of yours, if it's to be believed, you've known love?"

"How could I not? I'm still a man. I've known love, three times. Khadijah was the second."

I feel the tears welling in my eyes no matter how much I will them away. I can still feel her hand in mine and my face against her warm and soft thighs. My skin remembers. I can feel her eyes soft and loving watching over me as I sleep. I see me laying there, pretending to be sleeping.

"Tell me about her."

I could tell him everything about her. The way, first thing in the morning she yawned, her hands releasing yesterday and stretching into the uncharted newness of the day that lay ahead. How her tongue clicked and clucked as it scratched away at any harsh words that may have found a home in the back of her throat the day before. How she bobbed her head up and down as she yawned, clucked and clicked, her right knuckle vibrating like a hummingbird drumming a hip hop beat inside her right ear. Tell him about her? Where would I begin? How could I end? Could I even tell him the ending? Has it ended? I decide to start, somewhere else.

"I will tell you of Bes."

"Who is Bes?"

"Bes was the first."

Kent looks as if he wants to protest but simply nods as if to say, go on. And I do,

"I met Bes, quite a few years after I broke away from my parents. I had finally settled in D.C. It felt far enough away from Waukegan, the past, and Flint. A new place for me to hide in plain sight. Everyone was busy. Everyone was looking at everything but each other. It felt perfect. I was, in some ways, young and given to the desires of a young man. The only difference being that I had access to boundless wealth. As I've stated before, money can only expose character. This was true, even for myself. At the time I was not that much different than my parents I'm sad to say. If anything they'd given me a blueprint of how things..."

"I'm sorry Mr. M," He still calls me Mr. M although we're pretty far from prying ears on this bench. If not for me shouting earlier the parents would have probably never even known we were here. I wonder if Mr. M is his mind not wanting to wrap itself around me being Midas or has Mr. M in such short order become who I am to him now. I've heard it takes three weeks of consistently doing something to take that something from thoughtful routine to mindless habit. Perhaps Kent is a fast learner. I pause and he continues,

"I don't mean to interrupt but you said you were, young in some ways?"

"Excuse me?"

"You said you were, young in some ways, but you've also mentioned going to KCJH and that you're centuries old. Which is it? Old or young?"

I don't answer. Kent sees that my mouth is showing no signs of moving.

"Let me rephrase. What does young mean to you? I mean how old are you exactly Mr. M?"

"How old do I look?"

"Listen, I'm not feeling my best in this moment. I don't have the mental capacity to play Global Fair, guess my age, guess my weight, win a stuffed *Ursulus,* games. Just tell me okay."

I smile and say nothing. When you were a kid did you ever sit across from a sibling or a close friend, your fingers sticky from candy, your mouth blue from a Slurpee... did 7-Elevens even exist when you were a kid? Had they already been swallowed up by QT, and QT cannibalized by Starbucks, and... never-mind. As a child did you ever sit across from another kid, the both of you somewhere between a sugar

78

fit and a sugar coma, and just stare into each others eyes betting on who would blink first. Wagering with sweat on whose open eyes the air would sting like they were being attacked by a hundred bald-faced hornets. Laying odds that something somewhere beyond the control of one of you would force eyelids to bat and swat at the wasps? The both of you, still, hardly breathing, staring deep into each others eyes until you see something deeper, something different, something beyond? Something so wonderful, or beautiful, or frightening that it makes you happy or makes you smile or makes you recoil, but either way, makes you blink?

Kent and I sit in silence, the question hanging between us like a string with styrofoam cups at opposite ends. Parents are still disappearing behind trees in the distance. Two are fighting over a ball. I smile and stare at Kent. He sweats and stares. Neither of us seems to have any interest in moving beyond this point without the other conceding in some way. I could have waited a little bit of forever. Time is on my side, and not on his, in a way that Kent doesn't yet understand.

"265," I say without losing my smile or blinking.

"265... what?"

"I'll be 265 years old this year."

Kent begins to blink as rapidly as Khadi ... as Kim did when speaking. I win.

"... I would have guessed you were 45 tops. You certainly don't look a day over 150."

Clearly feeling a bit more free in the park, than in the cafe, we both laugh as loudly as we care to. Kent's laughter transforms into a coughing fit. He leans forward, his hand grasping my shoulder to support himself. I don't ask if he's okay. I try not to ask questions I already know the answer to. The coughing spasms nestle themselves calmly into the back of his throat, like a nest of vipers coiled and waiting to strike again. I put my hand on his back as he slowly regains control of his lungs. I feel like an expectant father telling a mother-to-be, *just breathe*. I explain myself as he begins to settle.

"In the way you think of age I'm actually 49 so 45 is still indeed a compliment. In the way you calculate years however, the earth making a full rotation around the sun, this will be my 265th rotation."

Kent wipes what spittle remains from the coughing on his coat sleeve.

"The 'gold'?"

I take his meaning,

"Yes. If one were to believe in such fairy tales then, yes my blood has altered my aging. My first thirteen years were like everyone else's but after that I began to age one year for your seven."

"Dog years? You age in reverse dog years?"

"I never thought of it like that," I smile broadly, "but I guess you're right. I'm a reverse dog age-er."

The children in the bleachers start to signal for their parents to wrap up their play date. The parents protest and beg for a few more minutes. Lo Saturnalia!

"So when you say you met Bes quite some years after breaking from your parents, how old were you?"

"In my years or yours?"

"... both?"

"In reverse dog years I was 20. In the way you count years I would have been 62."

"You were 62 years old before you ever dated... or... did anything with a woman!?"

"Time and age don't move the way you think they do Mr. Kent or rather time and age for you, move the way they do because of the way you think they move. Time is a construct that really and truly only exists in our minds."

"There you go with this Sufi existentialism again. If time isn't real why does my boss keep telling me that if I'm late again I'm fired? Explain that."

"If only we had the time, Mr. Kent."

I smile at the pun wrapped in the answer, as Kent shakes his head in mock disappointment.

"Suffice it to say for now that I was 62 of your years but only 20 of mine, and mine for me are what count, before I ever fell in love with a woman. I had... known women before that but moving around and fear of discovery kept my heart in a box. It wasn't until I was able to still myself, my mind and my heart, that I was able to avail myself to the possibility of love. Only then was the box able to be opened."

"And that possibility, the opening of this box you'd kept under wraps for 62 years, was with this woman Bes?"

"Indeed."

"Did it feel like Christmas morning? Were you excited to see what all was in the box? I mean it had sat under the tree for almost three quarters of a decade."

"It felt more like all hallows eve. Exhilarating, scary, a little anxiety producing. I was wearing a mask that I was anxious to take off. Love can be like that. Fill you simultaneously with so much joy and so much dread. I'm used to dueling emotions, however, Mr. Kent. You'll look in the mirror and not recognize yourself some days because of love; not know if you're looking at a costume or who you really are. You'll knock on someone's heart and they'll open the door and drop some part of themselves into your life, but you won't know what part of them you've received. The trick or the treat. Time tells. You'll reach down into your life and feel about for what you've got. Is it something sweet that will fill your days with unspeakable highs, or a lump of coal that will weigh you down and drag you to the deepest depths? Time always tells. Trust me on this though Mr. Kent, love is more Halloween than Christmas Eve."

"I know all too well."

Kent speaks these words to no one in particular in an almost inaudible whisper. His eyes are aimed at his feet. I wonder if his heels are grinding into his inserts as mine have. Is his *I know all too well* an unwitting answer to my earlier query about his ever having known love? His eyes lift, wide and search mine to see if I heard. I've enjoyed some playful sparing with Kent but this does not seem like the time nor the subject to playfully bandy about. I notice his, up until now, pasty wan skin go flush. This time it doesn't seem to be a result of his ailment but the product of embarrassment. A few seconds pass between us in silence and then Kent clears his throat and continues.

"So I'm going to guess Bes was probably in her early twenties, as I count years," he lifts his head and straightens his back giving himself a posture of confidence, "and had no idea you were cradle robbing ... or was it she that was grave robbing?"

Mr. Kent has emerged from his embarrassment with a playful attack, well done and noted. Kent may be one that when he feels cornered or exposed lashes out, but he's also one that can find a ready joke when needed. He also must be starting to feel better. His humor is certainly improving. He's still sweating but he seems to be on the mend. He smiles a playful but still weary I-used-to-play-the-dozens-on-the-back-of-the-school-bus smile before continuing,

"Tell me about her."

"About her and about myself because at that time the two certainly felt inescapably intertwined. Like I was saying earlier about money and character. The former only exposes the later. I discovered after 6 years, 42 years as you count them, of running from my parents, who were by then deceased, that I only had to look at myself to discover I hadn't run far enough."

"Your parents were dead by the time you were 62, 20, whichever. How? They should have been what in their early, mid, seventies? How'd they die?"

I hear the screams. I see my mom reach out, her arms stretching desperately, almost impossibly far. I can still taste the salt in the water. Our eyes locked. My dad's hand is on her shoulder. I pull away from that moment, that memory.

"I uhm. I'm not prepared to speak on that today. On their deaths. Just know that their lives, their lessons, impacted me greatly. If anything all those years of knives and razors and fists had given me a template to follow, a stencil to trace. It had shown me a path paved with gold.

"There were no hidden hands after I escaped them. No one came with their hands behind their back. There were only my own hands, trembling and holding razors. Me, holding my breath, counting to three and slicing my own flesh. Me, trading my own blood and pain at randomized *Goldilocks* machines in an effort to not draw attention.

There I was in a nice condo, wearing nice clothes, driving a nice car and working my way through the U-Street club and bar scene. I only appeared to be 20 at the time but enough money can get you anything, a fake driver's license, a fake passport, a real girlfriend.

"Can you imagine having to get an I.D. that says you're far younger than you truly are but older than you appear?

"Anyway, my father's way with words and my mother's love of finer things had found me. I'd always thought of myself as above them, as better than they were. I told myself time and time again 'I'd never...,' 'There's no way I would...' only to discover not only could I, but I would, and with little provocation."

"But you had to live and eat and survive, yes?"

"I did, but people do it everyday by going to work, or starting businesses. I was at home with a razor, an expanding tolerance for pain and a growing bank account."

"And that's bad? How many people in your situation would have done the same? Hell, I might have."

"True but I'm not how many people, and I'm not you. I'm a kid that suffered unspeakable abuse at the hands of his parents and swore I'd never visit such violence on anyone else."

"Promise fulfilled."

"How so?"

"You didn't do it to anyone else. You only did it to yourself."

"... touché Mr. Kent."

"Bes?"

"I'm sorry?"

"You were about to tell me about Bes."

"Ah yes, Bes." I hesitate. My mind is still wrestling with Mr. Kent's last statement. Have I spent all these years falsely persecuting myself? Have I been punishing myself for a non-crime, for just being a human being.

"Are you okay Mr M?" Kent asks. He clearly notices the wheels spinning behind my eyes. There is a bit of a smile hidden behind the, possibly feigned, concern in his eyes. I've been a step or two ahead of him all day. This is the first time he's drawn even, or possibly gotten a step beyond me. And he knows it. I gather myself and my thoughts.

"Yes, Bes. I met Bes in a spot called Bohemian reDEUxS. It was a rehash of a club that used to live on D.C.'s U-Street in the 1920s through the early 2000s called Bohemian Caverns. The more time moves forward the more people like to romanticize, revisit, recreate and live in the past. The Jordan LXXXIII's are just the Jordan XI's with a hover sole and nano-fit. They just put the 22nd remake of King Kong on *Kudzu* and *EyeSeeView* because for all of our advancement and growth as an interstellar society there are still those obsessed with the idea of the big dark animal stealing away the delicate white prize. A

Siriosian just released an Occ Imaging of his/her/their self dressed in lace, riding a gondola through space and singing the new universal hit, 'Like a Virgin.'"

"I love that song."

"Of course you do. Our obsession with the past and the constant remaking, reclaiming, re-imaging of it, is both an indictment on the present and a sometimes misguided love affair with times long gone."

I take a breath. I feel like an old man screaming, get off of my deeply loved, ancient, unable to be duplicated lawn. I look over at the parents in the park and notice that many of them are wearing Jordan LXXXIII's while their children are wearing Oxfords and Brogues. Lo Saturnalia.

I continue on with my story of Bes,

"Anyway, I was at reDEUxS and Bes was dancing late into the night, to Go-Go. Are you familiar?"

"With... Go-Go?"

"Yes."

"No."

"It's this percussion driven, call and response, thing of beauty that either you love or hate. There's no one that kind of likes Go-Go. You are either mad for it or mad it exists."

"It sounds like *Gamajan*."

"*Gamajan* is probably the closest thing to Go-Go. I wouldn't be surprised to find out it was birthed from the Go-Go sound and energy. Anyway, Bes was dancing, or rather, writhing to the Go-Go drums like she had no bones in her body. She was all white teeth, beaded sweat, and swinging locs. Her shoulders, hips and feet moved and undulated to the same rhythm but in differing directions. It looked, impossible. Like she might pull herself apart but instead it pulled the room all together. It was common for the entire club to just circle around and watch her dance. She loved it. She was a queen holding court. Her long, toned, dancer's legs would fall into full splits and then slowly pull her back to her feet as if she was a marionette being lifted by invisible strings. The entire time her hips would roll, rise and fall to the beat, as if she was teaching the oceans how to behave. All the while her hands and fingers twisted and turned just above her head, sometimes capturing her locs in their dance. She appeared to be casting an ancient enchantment deep in a forgotten bayou over a cauldron of eye of newt and *flanstel*'s breath; or claiming celestial gang affiliation with the gods local and universal. Her eyes were inescapable balls of light that demanded you stare at her, revel in her, worship her. She was perfection. If Gawd made anythin' fihner he kept it fuh himself."

I say that last part with an accent my father would have been proud of. Kent seems far less proud or impressed.

I continue,

"I'd watched her dance for weeks. I'd stood beside her at the bar and from time to time traded quips and bought her drinks. I felt like once or twice I'd found her eyes finding mine as she mesmerized the crowd with her movements on the dance floor. Then one night, as she stood beside me at the bar, I built up the nerve to ask her to dance. She said, 'buy me a drink.' Her accent had always been hard to place. It had a warmth that spoke of hot summers with her toes steeped in the red clay of the deep south. It had mixed into that warmth a ragged, jagged, jaded coldness that seemed born of the concrete walkways, glass store fronts and steel skyscrapers of the north east industrial cities. Her voice, which seemed to be half an octave above a whisper and as rich as oak barrel aged whiskey, was just loud enough to be heard over the music, if you leaned in. It made you come closer to the hypnosis that lived in her eyes. It made you gaze at those impossibly white teeth that must have been made just after God declared everything good, and just before he took rest. It dared you to try to ignore those locs that the Go-Go drums seemed to double dutch between as she danced. I could see my face reflected in the beads of sweat that covered her body like moving, bulbous, scarification keloids. I could smell her skin, musk mixed with sweat, but still somehow sweet. She felt like flame and moth, like spider and fly. Dueling emotions are nothing new to me. She, in that moment, went from queen on a throne holding court to a woman within arms reach. It made her so real she was almost surreal.

"I bought her that drink before she could walk away or ask twice. We sat and talked through three songs."

"Do you remember what you talked about?"

"I don't recall. I don't know if I could have recalled the day after or even an hour after. I was absolutely lost in the moment, lost in her, and so I just smiled and nodded a lot.

"That's seems like a dangerous place to be."

"ReDEUxS was no more dangerous than most clubs in those days."

"No, not reDEUxS. Bes. A person you don't know, seems like a dangerous place to get lost in."

"Where were you with this advice when I needed it Mr. Kent?"

"According to the proposed math of your life I was in the same place my parents were in. Not born yet."

"Ah, true! Well, in the absence of your yet to be born advice, I asked again if she'd like to dance. She smiled, licked her lips and said, 'buy me a drink.' I bought her another in prompt order. We sat and she talked as I nodded through five more songs. I asked once more if she'd like to dance. She looked about the room, at all of the eyes begging her to return to the dance floor, at all of her congregants ready to yet again worship at her feet and said, 'take me home.' I did... in prompt order."

My mind abandons Kent as I look off into the distance recalling that night. I see it as if it were yesterday but can't bring myself to share the intimate details of the night with him. I remember the silent drive to my condo, no radio, no conversation, just a stillness that seemed to have a weight about it, and her eyes staring out of the car window the whole time. I don't know why I didn't turn on the radio or neither of us spoke but it just seemed understood that's the way it should be. A silent reverence of sorts. The calm before the storm perhaps.

At some point my hand fell on her soft, toned, thigh. It landed there with a natural ease that betrayed the newness of it all. My palm had settled comfortably, as if this was a drive that we'd taken all our lives, her thigh home to my touch. I could feel the vibration of her muscles, beneath skin so dark that I appeared to have a handful of the night sky. Then she placed her hand atop mine and moved it higher on her thigh, her eyes still watching D.C. move past the passenger side window. Somehow I knew she was smiling.

My condo was filled with the trappings of wealth and success. It said a lot about the world but little about me. The furniture was what I'd been told was good furniture. The art was what was accepted as quality art by art brokers. The wine was what wine magazines swore had good legs, bouquet, and flavor. Bes seemed to suss this out immediately. She surveyed my condo and spoke her first words since leaving the club, "Where are you?"

I replied, "I'm right here. I'm behind you."

She waived her left arm, a sweeping gesture that took in the whole of the condo and said, "No. Where are you?"

I took her meaning and felt a tinge of shame. This woman that didn't know me, knew me in that moment better than most. My eyes settled on a chair that I had taken from my parents home when I left.

When I left I swept it up in my Exodus. Why? It had given me comfort during the dark days and had been with me ever since. A wooden chair with a high back and an orange velvet cushioned seat that I'd had re-upholstered at least twice at that point. Bes noticed my eyes on the chair, walked over and sat on it. She sighed and stretched, letting her back push against and slide along the back of the chair. She hitched her skirt up around her thighs and let her hips grind figure eights into the cushion. My heels began to nervously grind against the cushioned insets in my shoes. She threw her head back, her locs slapping against the wood creating a drumming sound that echoed through the condo. She sighed again then smiled her perfect smile at me through the dark.

"Ah, here you are."

Her eyes caught fire and invited me to come close to their warmth. I accepted the invitation.

In traversing the few feet to where she sat I felt like I had walked a city block. Once I got to her, she took my hands, warm and a bit sweaty, into hers and pulled me down gently to my knees. She parted her legs, wrapped them firmly around me and drew me even closer. Bes slipped a shoulder away from her top, letting the right side fall slack, exposing her right breast full and round, the areola like a dark ring of Saturn holding within its circumference a tumescent nipple. She placed her right hand behind my head and pulled me slowly to her breast. My breath, hot and labored, seemed to excite her as I drew closer. I took her nipple, soft and supple, into my mouth, and tasted the salt from her sweat and a sweetness whose origin I could not guess at.

The combination was, however, intoxicating. Her legs pulled me closer still and I could feel the warmth of her as I'm sure she could feel the weight of me pushing against her. Her body began to writhe much as she did on the dance floor. With a force that was unexpected she pushed my head away from her breast. There was a slight popping sound like a suction cup being pulled from a window. My tongue stretched trying to find its way back to her erect nipple. Bes looked me in the eyes as her hand began to push my head from her breast, to her belly and beyond. Her left hand pulled her skirt up so that it was entirely around her waist. She slid her hips to the edge of the chair, her shoulders resting against the back, allowing her warmth and moisture to hang free, begging to be caught. The hairs of my chin were the first to rub against and part her wetness. She maintained eye contact with me. Her legs found a home on my shoulders and her back arched in anticipation. My bottom lip found the very tip of, and brushed ever so lightly against, her pulsating clitoris just before both of my lips wrapped around it tightly. She moaned and threw her head back, for the first time breaking eye contact. Bes took my head into the palms of her hands and pulled my mouth more fully into her. My tongue began to dance quickly, ravenously against, around, above and below her clit. She whispered, her oak barrel aged whiskey voice snaking between clenched teeth, "Slow... slowly... taste me slowly ... know me."

I tempered my eagerness and let my tongue move slowly across her clitoral crura and urethral sponge. I could feel her bulbs of vestibule swelling as her hips then began to buck spasmodically against my mouth. Her hands held me in place while threatening to suffocate me.

Her legs, strong, firm, dancer's legs, began to squeeze my neck and shoulders just as she emitted a low pitched, almost guttural groan.

Bes exhaled the words, "I'm coming," before taking in a deep breath and introducing into my mouth a warmth, a taste and a delight I had never known before. Her hips rocked up and down my tongue now firm against her clitoris, which seemed full to the point of exploding. The back of the chair gave way just as her orgasm began receding. The seat split away from the back and we both fell gasping for air to the floor. There was a moment of quiet stillness that echoed after our fall as we both took inventory of our bodies. Finding no injuries, the moment of silence was instantly filled with laughter. Bes stood up and just as she'd used her hands to force me to my knees she now pulled me to my feet and said,

"Bedroom?"

I pointed to the lone room at the end of the hall and she led the way.

When I woke, her scent lived in my sheets and on my skin, the memory of the motion of her body was still causing mine to rock and sway like a sailor searching for his land legs. I remembered going into the bedroom. I remembered her sitting atop me, her eyes fire, her hands dancing in and out of her locs, her hips and legs moving in what felt like impossible ways. I remembered her mouth at times silently miming, her words later coming forth more as indecipherable chants than salient language. The next thing I knew I was waking up, never having remembered falling asleep. All of my thoughts of her were warm, and loving and light, but her side of the bed was cold. I jumped up and searched the condo. She was gone. I had no way of contacting her, not by phone, letter, or smoke signal. So I waited until the weekend rolled back around, which felt like it took a month of Sundays, and I returned to Bohemian reDEUxS.

There she was all white teeth, beaded sweat, and swinging locs. A queen holding court with her loyal subjects surrounding her, praising her, worshipping her. I walked right over to her in the middle of the song, a knight seeking an audience with her highness. I hadn't seen her in a week and felt that our sharing, the scent that still lived in my sheets and the motion that still caused my body to sway, gave me some privilege, some rights, some exclusivity where she was concerned. I was wrong. Before I could get close enough to catch my reflection in the beaded sweat disappearing into her blouse, to see God's perfect white teeth, to skip between her roped locs, she wagged her finger at me, no, no, no, like a child being admonished for climbing on the good furniture. Embarrassed, I receded to the bar less like a noble knight and more like a servile serf. After the song, after promising her worshipers that their goddess would indeed return, she came over and hugged me long and tight. Faced with the reality and truth of her presence, I found myself lacking words. At home I'd practiced what I'd say. In my room I was eloquent, I was romantic, I was clear in tone and intention. While waiting at the bar I practiced what I'd say. I was direct, I was incensed, I was firm in tone and intention. Standing before her all I could think to say was, would you like to dance. She licked her lips and said, "buy me a drink." Two drinks and a silent car ride later we were once again at my place.

She looked at the broken chair, laying exactly where we'd left it the week before. "There you are," the words came out with a sullen sadness. I reached out for her but she caught my hands and held me at bay. She walked over to the chair, gathered its broken and mangled pieces and gently and carefully laid them out like an archaeologist reordering the bones of a beast long extinct. The legs, the back, the cushioned seat. When the last piece was put in place and the chair lay in reposed perfection on the carpet, she then turned to me her smile returned and said, "there... there you are."

Later I laid exhausted, covered in her sweat, on the bed, fighting like a child on Christmas Eve not to fall asleep because I knew in the morning the magic, the gifts, the season would be ended. She pulled my head to her chest where the steady, rhythmic drumming or her heart's beat, repeatedly hummed my name and sang me a lullaby. The last thing I remembered was hearing her singing, saying, chanting ... something. In the morning she was gone.

Still with no way to contact her I had to wait until the weekend to see her again. As I walked into reDEUxS I saw other men asking her to dance and I watched her politely say no. I went to the bar and waited. I knew better than to be held in contempt of the queen's court again. She danced for another hour or so and then found me. We repeated our routine of offer, rejection, counter offer, rejection, exit, and sex.

As we laid in bed I asked Bes why she never dances with me, or anyone. She said because dancing is hers, it's sacred, it's intimate. I asked her what is making love? She said making love is sacred and intimate too. I asked her, then why do you make love to me but refuse to dance with me. Bes smiled her perfect smile and said, "I've never made love to you. We've fucked each other a few times and it's been nice but if I were to make love to you, you'd certainly know it."

I told her what I'd been struggling not to say since our first night together. I told her I loved her. She took my face into her almost too warm hands and told me that I was in love with the idea of her. She said I didn't love her I just wanted to own her, to tame her, to be able to say she's mine, and that those things would never happen. I told her... "I love you." This time the smile was accompanied with a laugh, "You don't know my last name, where I live, what my dreams are, what my mama and nem call me. If I were to leave now and never go back to reDEUxS you wouldn't even know where to find me." I told her I could give and get her anything she wanted. She told me that she could too; that my money could buy drinks but never buy her. She told me that I thought of her on some level, whether I knew it or not, as a prostitute, someone who could be easily had or bought just for the asking, but she was not. She was herself, all unto herself, unowned and unbossed. I told her, "I love you." She smiled, pushed me back onto the bed, took me erect and throbbing into her hand and eased down on top of me. She started saying the things she always says when the moon is high and her hips dip low and roll, but this time I heard some of the words. I can only remember a few: Bilqis, Kaizen, Bastet. Her body writhing, her

97

hands dancing like snakes above her head, her eyes aglow and staring into mine. I don't remember coming or falling asleep, just waking up, alone, again. I walked into the living room and discovered the chair she had so carefully put together, kicked about the room. In the empty space where it had earlier been reconstructed and in perfect repose, was a note that read "There you are."

The next weekend I found Bes once again, holding court. I was desperate to patch things up between us, to say whatever it would take to make it right. I waited at the bar, her drink already ordered and waiting. She danced for her congregants, as usual. This time there were no playful glances my way just intent stares. I followed her eyes as they took me in from head to toe and turned images and thoughts of me around and about in her mind. I felt like I was not so much being seen as studied. An hour later, the sweat beading again across the dark topography of her body, she walked over. I smiled, took her drink in hand and watched her hips, still moving to the beat, as she approached. A guy, nondescript, standing a few paces ahead me, between she and I, had been staring at her all night too. I thought nothing of it. Who didn't stare at her half, if not all, of the night? As she moved to walk past him, he said, "Excuse me, would you like to dance?" She exhaled, looked past him at me, expectant, anxious, with drink in hand and smiled, all white teeth, falling beaded sweat and shoulder length locs. She turned to him and said "... buy me a drink."

I watched as the ritual that I believed to be mine was played out with another. It was Preston Scott all over again but this time there would be no punch, no florescent lights in my eyes, no dancing *vmoji*, no blood turned gold in the hallways. This time I would pick myself up from the floor, tuck my hurt and disappointment deep into my chest, leave reDEUxS and never return. I'd offered my love, reached into my goody bag and discovered alas, I'd been given a piece of heart shaped coal in return. Trick or treat.

Bes taught me that day that you can't buy love. You can't even rent it. I tell Kent in part, what I just told you in whole. I leave out some of the steamier details. He can't miss what he doesn't know exists.

He asks, "She knew where you lived, right?"

"Yeah."

"And she never came by?"

"No."

"Not even just to say hi."

"That's how never-came-by works."

Kent smiles. His pale skin appears to be regaining some color or maybe it's just his feelings of gaining ground in our verbal sparring adding life to his complexion.

"You know Mr. M judging by your tort response and if I didn't know better I'd think you're still hurt about it. How many years ago was that? 203 by your math?"

"203 by your math. 29 years give or take by mine."

"But let me get this straight. You were in a club where I would imagine most of the people were in their early twenties?"

"Yes."

"And you're telling me you didn't feel like the old man in reDEUxS?"

I laugh, "No. Time moves differently for me. Although I've lived through so many years I don't actually physically feel any older than I appear. So when I appeared twenty I dated women in their twenties. Now that I'm almost 50 in appearance if I were to date it would probably be a woman in her 40's or 50's. I clearly can't date a woman that's 260. I think they call that necrophilia and there' are clear laws against it."

Kent laughs. The ice between us continues to break.

"Age and time are complex and intricate concepts Mr. Kent. Have you ever met a child that felt like an old soul. Have you ever met an old man that had more youth in him than a child? You ever spend a day doing something you love and it feels like only an hour has passed? You ever spend an hour doing something you hate and it feels like a day? Whose to say it's not? Time is an interesting, complex, and sometimes cruel mistress my friend. Khadijah taught me that."

"Ah, is now the time for the story of Khadijah?"

I know it is indeed time for the story of Khadijah but wonder if I can bring myself to tell it. Can I step back into a space that comes with

100

joy unspeakable and pain unknowable? I don't know, but I guess Mr. Kent and I will find out together.

"Yes, but let me tell it to you as we walk."

"I'm just starting to catch my breath Mr. M and my back feels, tight."

"Yeah, it's probably best we walk. I get stiff when I sit too long too."

When I mention walking and continuing our conversation I notice that Kent's body does not move an inch. He clearly has no interest in leaving this bench. He looks settled, in the way that wives accuse their husbands of a decade of being. His eyes move over the playground scenery and, the devil may care, plugged in children as they begin to gather their pouting parents. I hear pleas of "Just five more minutes," "Just one more game," "But whyyyyy!?!" from the adults as the kids explain that they're hungry and they have school tomorrow; and that the parents are also hungry and have work tomorrow. Heartfelt, tearful goodbyes usually reserved for summer friends that you fear you'll never see again are given out as grown-ups on the verge of full fledged tantrums tell each other goodbye. Their offspring don't understand what all the drama, fuss, and emotion is about as they take their parents' hands and pull them toward waiting cars, and lives.

It's hard to walk away from your youth, from a return to a time before debt, divorce, and taxes. The children don't understand because they're still standing in the middle of their childhood. When you're in the center of a swimming pool, your head beneath the water and your lungs filled with air and laughter that bubbles to the surface; when the water is not so shallow that you can't swim and not so deep that you fear drowning; when all is weightlessness and warmth and the sound of eternity muffled in your ears coupled with the view of the sun muted through rippling blue; you can't imagine what's on the other side of that feeling, of that moment. It's only when you're on dry land, when you're in a classroom, or in an office, or stuck in traffic, that you miss the sound of forever, that you miss life not being so heavy, that you miss the safety of being able to swim, or stand, but not drown in debt or divorce, or taxes. Only once you've left the utopia of the pool and you're shivering by a cabana chair do you really appreciate it; and when the day comes that you're allowed to return to it, to immerse yourself in it once again, you cherish it all the more. You watch the clock. You beg to stay. You plead for just another minute because on the other side of that minute is life, and life ain't no rippling blue, no bubbling laughter, no warm swimming pool. The parents know now what the kids will soon learn and so they fight to stay young, to stay weightless, to stay olly-olly-oxen-free. Lo Saturnalia.

Chapter 5 | Cut. Chase

"Mr. M, honestly my legs feel heavy."

"You sound like a child after a long day at the pool."

"... I guess."

"Come on let's walk."

I help him up. He's heavier than he looks but I manage to get him to his feet and we begin to walk through a neighborhood that was once one of the roughest in the city. They used to call the process of pushing the poor off of prime real estate and into hovels near prisons so they wouldn't have far to go when they were arrested; near cemeteries so they wouldn't have far to go when they were murdered; and near garbage dumps so they wouldn't have far to go to be reminded of what was thought of them, urban renewal. Urban renewal transformed into gentrification when I was a kid, and now it's re-branded itself as Metro UpRaising. The fighters of the good fight call it Metro UpRazing and say that it leads to metro uprisings. They paint clever slogans on signs. They sing songs older than the buildings they are fighting to preserve. They march in shoes that cost more than what many of those they're fighting for make in a week. They do all of this and still the buildings fall. The lives of the poor are pushed further into the margins and the metro is upraised along with the property taxes.

A woman jogs past, her baby stroller moving silently and perfectly balanced on automatically adjusting magnetic repulsors that use the natural metals in the earth's crust to elevate the stroller to the designated height from the ground. She stares at us a few seconds too long. I see her index finger go to her temple. I know she's using her *OccRecorder* to take our photo just in case she feels the need to report us to the proper authorities. I'm sure we fit the description. There has never been a time in American history when two black men walking together didn't fit the description. She's going to be sad when she gets home and looks at the stored blank images thanks to my ever present *Occ* and *AudBlockers*.

Kent and I walk side by side. Out of the corner of my eye I watch Kent's face, a mask of pain, as he continues to force his feet to fall one in front of the other. He's staring down at his legs as if they are new to him. Like a babe amazed by the miracle and mechanics of its own body. I begin the story of Khadijah.

"I met Khadijah when I was twenty-five, by my math."

I feel his eyes lift and find my profile. I don't look over at him. I look forward and continue to speak.

"She was thirty-five but like me also seemed to exist outside of time. Like so many black women she looked like gold had always coursed through her veins, like the fountain of youth poured from her pores, like her age could live anywhere between antiquity and eternity. When I met her she called me babyface because of the apparent decade between us. There was no way she could know that it was more like six decades, in my favor. I met her just after I'd enrolled in college, again."

"Again?"

"Yes, again. I'd get a few degrees under a name but once the age associated with that name grossly differed from my appearance I'd change names. I was studying Hematology at Morehouse College in Atlanta at the time."

"Wait, so you are a hematologist?"

"Who would claim to be such a thing that wasn't?"

"But in the cafe..."

"In the cafe we didn't know each other as well as we do now."

"So with you the truth is relative?"

"Close cousins. Everything is relative Mr. Kent and not just with me."

Kent's hand goes to his face as he shakes his head from side to side. With his palm still covering his mouth he asks, "So, not relatively speaking, how many degrees do you have?"

"Many. From many schools around the globe. Ivy Leagues, HBCUs, technical schools, IILs, Intergalactic Institutions of Learning. Whoever had the information I wanted at the time, that's where I went."

"So you're like a super, super, super senior."

"I have sometimes wondered if God is omniscient because he's just had the time and resources to get all the credit hours in the world."

"Interesting. So you're comparing yourself to God?"

"Oh no, never. I would have never made something as flawed as man and let it continue."

"Well he did try with that flood."

"Well maybe if he'd had a few more credit hours he'd have thought of something better than hard rain."

We both chuckle. Kent's already walking a bit better. I let him set the pace as I continue my story.

"Khadijah was getting her master's in business at Clark University. She'd already done eight years in the Navy just after high school. At 26, freshly discharged, she traveled for a year or so and then used the G.I. Bill to go to Spelman College. She finished up Spelman undergrad at 31, worked a couple years in Corporate America, and hit the glass ceiling quicker and harder than expected. So she decided to go back and get her master's. Khadijah was on the tail end of that when we bumped into each other at Ebrik Coffee Rooms and Emporiums. It was an overcast spring day in 2103 and I was going by the name Dashill. The barista inadvertently mixed up our cups, giving me the one that read Khadijah and her mine. Maybe all black names look alike too? As we exchanged cups I noticed her book *Financial Strategies and*

Assessments: Theorem and Practicum, and her eyes. It just so happened that I too, under a different name, had gotten a master's in business. I recognized the book but had never seen such eyes. They were brown in a way that would have made Crayola rethink what they thought brown to be."

"Crayola?"

"Right, I keep forgetting about the companies that have risen and fallen as I've walked this earth. What you know as *waxchalk* we knew as crayons and the biggest seller of *waxchalk* was a company called Crayola."

"No one really uses Waxchalk anymore. Now we have *Multichrome Children's Cerebooks* that allow children to color in their mind."

"*Multichrome Children's Cerebooks*. So many words for what is in essence a coloring book. Why use a sesquipedalian word when you can use a brachysyllabic one?"

"What?"

"Exactly. So, Ebrik was packed on the day Khadijah and I got our drinks and eyes mixed up. She took a seat at a table near the rear of the room. Sorry Mrs. Parks. The only other open seat was at the same table, across from her. Sitting there would put my back to the door, something I never did, but I have to say in the moment I didn't even think about it. I walked over asked Khadijah if she would mind if I sat with her. Without looking up she said, 'It's a free world babyface. Sit where you like.' She immediately placed her old school, can, headphones on over her ears and dove into her studies. I smiled but inside I bristled a bit. Her response felt so curt and dismissive. I know now this was my poor little ego feeling bruised. I think of myself as pretty progressive but in that moment I was little more than a man demanding a woman give him a smile. I was wounded but not enough to leave so I slipped my earpods in and began studying as well.

"My eyes seemed to have a mind of their own and kept lifting from the pages of my book and finding her face. She had round cheeks that I imagined she'd retained from childhood. Her eyes would shrink to slits when she was reading something that demanded her full attention. It gave the impression that she couldn't see well but I'd also noticed the contacts in her eyes. Her nose was keen and her lips full. She had her hair braided and pulled back, exposing her massive forehead."

"Whoa! Easy there charmer."

I chuckle.

"I was just making sure you were listening."

"Yeah, I'm listening. So her forehead wasn't massive?"

"Oh, it was huge!"

"What?" We both laugh, again.

"Listen Mr. Kent if you ever find a woman about 5'5", that smells like roses and honey, with round cheeks, full lips, her nose buried in a book and a massive forehead, marry her. Whatever happens ... whatever, it will be worth it, trust me. Let me be clear her forehead was huge in a Sade, not a Cro-Magnon Man, way. And yes I know that you don't know who Sade is. *Mersenne* her later."

"Noted."

"That day in the cafe I kept catching myself looking at her, and trying to demand my eyes stay on my own paper, like a teacher giving an exam. This would work for five minutes, maybe not even five, and then my disobedient eyes would sneak out, run across the table, hurdle her cup of coffee and land directly on her face, again. It was ridiculous and probably just a bit strange and annoying if she were to notice."

"Did she notice?"

"Of course she did. Women always notice guys acting a bit odd. They have to for their own safety and protection. She didn't tell me that she'd kept one eye on me the entire time in the cafe until years later."

"I decided to leave the coffee shop. I was too preoccupied and wasn't getting anything done. As I was gathering my things I glanced over and noticed two things, a few small scars on her right hand, and that she'd gotten one of the answers wrong on her study guide. I was torn as to whether to mention the wrong answer or not. I could still hear her voice, dismissive and curt in my head.

"'Uhm... Khadijah right?' Like I didn't know. She had the can headphones on listening to something that had her nodding to the beat and softly humming the melody. For a second I thought of Bes, there you are. I waved my hand in front of her to get her attention. She looked up and handed me the sugar sitting to her right on the table. I politely took the sugar and she continued head bobbing, humming, and studying.

"I sat for a second, wrote a number on a piece of paper and pushed it in front of her.

"She looked at the number, paused her music, took off the headphones and said, 'You have a very odd phone number babyface.'

'Dashill...' I pointed to the name written on my cup and tried not to sound irritated, 'the name's Dashill and that's not my phone number it's the answer to question eight in your study guide. If you had 5,789 participants in a tournament, how many games would need to be played to determine a winner?'

"She looked at question eight, closed her book and said 'You snooping babyface?'

'More correcting than snooping. If 5,789 represents the number of teams and not individuals broken into teams then the answer is 5,788. The answers to questions of that nature are always the sum of the teams minus one. Unless of course the professor isn't looking for a specific numeric answer, but for you to logically work through the thought process of individuals versus teams and what that means when applied numerically to the final answer. What you have written there, however, is wrong, no matter how you calculate it. Just thought you should know.'

"Where before I tried not to act irritated, now for some reason I was.

'How do you know that babyfa...' she looked at my cup and said, 'Dashill.'

"I continued gathering my things as I answered, 'I'm taking some business courses over at Morehouse, and I've done some studying on my own. A lot of that stuff lives in my head now, that's all.'

'You mad Dashill?'

'...No,' my lying lips said.

'You're slamming those books into that bag like you're mad. That bag said something about your mama? Tell me what it said and I'll beat it up for you.'

"I smiled in spite of myself.

'It said my momma's so black she crossed a cat and gave it bad luck.'

'Oooooh! That's messed up! I wouldn't take that Dashill! You're right to slam those books in there like that! That bag's got to learn!'

"I laughed, looked up into those brown eyes and was lost again."

'Sit down Dashill, please.' She reached across the table and grabbed one of my books.

My eyes went to the small scars on hers. She withdrew her hand and pulled her shirt sleeve down a bit. In doing that I noticed scars on her other hand too. I wondered if her skin remembered.

She held up her right hand. 'These I got fighting a West Virginia grizzly bear with a coat hanger.' She then held up her left. 'These I got rushing into a house to save a little girl from a fire.' She then sat both of her hands palm down on the table. I looked at the backs of both, cracked, scarred and marred like a river bed dried out by the summer's sun; and then into her eyes, soft as the clouds that will eventually bring the rain and restore the river. Something shifted in me at that moment. Something in me felt unexpectedly open toward her. I can't explain it. It just was.

She broke the growing silence between us with a loud laugh and said, 'It's just a skin condition boy, but people seem to like grand tales of bears and burning houses more than they care for stories of psoriasis. Listen, you clearly know your way around a business text. Help me study... or I'm not going to beat up that book bag for you.'

"We both laughed and decided to become study partners."

Through heavy breaths Mr. Kent interjects, "That moment has clearly stayed with you ever since. I mean, that had to have happened over 150 years ago, let you tell it, and you still remember it like it was yesterday."

"Time, as I've said, is a complex and intricate thing Mr. Kent. Who is to say how far away yesterday is? Is yesterday closer than

112

tomorrow? Are there things that happened five years ago that you remember better than things that happened five minutes ago?"

"Well five minutes ago I thought you were going to have to take me to a hospital, so I remember it pretty well."

"Indeed, and let me say you're looking much better. I think the walking is helping."

"Of course you think the walking is helping. It was your idea."

Kent jokingly pushes my shoulder. This is how camaraderie is born. I respond.

"Well, I'm not wrong. At least not about the walking."

"Well we'll see about the rest when we get to a *Goldilocks* Mr. M." There's something mocking in his tone. I'm not sure if it's on purpose or his natural reporter cynicism.

"So we still have a little time. The difference in age between Khadijah and I began to disappear over time. I wasn't 25 or 97 and she wasn't 35. We were just two people, two minds, two souls in college growing closer. After we'd finished studying one night and I had packed up to go she said, 'Alright see you tomorrow babyface... I mean baby... bae... I mean...' She blushed, put her face in both her hands. Hands that I found myself staring at more than she could ever imagine. Then she began to nervously chuckle. I took her hands from her face, kissed her fingertips, kissed the backs of her hands and placed them against my face. I looked her in those rain-making, Crayola-defining eyes and said, 'You can call me whatever you like.' We shared our first kiss that night.

"Khadijah and I weren't the raging gasoline fire that burns hot, burns bright, and burns out. Bes and I were that. Khadijah and I were the kind of fire that takes kindling and patience. The kind of fire that is slow to burn but once it catches it warms the whole house. The kind of fire that you fall asleep to and wake with the embers still glowing. With the hearth still throwing off heat. That type of fire only needs a small piece of dry wood to coax it to catch and burn hot again.

"We moved slowly. We got to know each other. We discovered in time we not only loved one another but we liked each other too. Bes once said to me, 'I haven't made love to you yet, once I do you'll know.' I don't think I understood it then, but Khadijah taught me the truth of it. I'd never been made love to in my life. I had not yet ever made love to anyone in my life either. Not until I laid down beside Khadijah. I understood that making love moves beyond the bedroom and into the small nuances of life. When she'd send me a *reading* that said, *have you eaten today*. When I'd *grip* her and say, *I had the oil changed in your car*. When she'd leave hand written notes that said, *I believe in you*, in my jacket pockets before an exam. When I couldn't find the words to express what I was feeling in my heart, and so I'd just stare. Bes was the first woman I loved. Khadijah was the woman that made me understand what love is, what it feels like, the shape of it, the depth of it. Khadijah."

My cheeks are wet with tears. Every moment I described to Kent I can feel myself reliving. My God I miss that woman.

"What happened? What... happened with Khadijah?"

I wipe my face on my shirt sleeve and take a deep breath.

"Everything happened with Khadijah. We lived. We loved. We argued. We made up. We made love. We did everything."

I feel the thumb on my left hand rubbing the base of my left ring finger. My eyes stare where once a ring rested proudly and I continue.

"And then when I was 32 and she was 85, she passed away."

I don't know what Kent's reaction is. I can't seem to get my eyes to meet his. I can still see hers in that coffee shop smiling at me.

"Oh, wow ... I ... I never even considered. Any person in your life will age and ... die ... while you will appear to basically not age at all. How... I mean, when did you tell her? She had to know, right? She had to look into the mirror at some point counting wrinkles and then look at you and see a man stuck in time."

I see her hand in mine. I couldn't meet her eyes on that day just as I can't meet his on this one. It was like a dark cloud hanging over our relationship. I was in love. I knew that she was too, and I knew I had to tell her. I had to tell her about Midas.

"I told her one afternoon. It wasn't a particularly special day. There wasn't anything pressing or significant pushing my confession other than my need for her to know everything about me. I loved her and I wanted to marry her, but I needed her to know not only who but what I was."

"Man. That's a lot to digest on any day, special or ordinary. Hell I'm still flipping a coin about it myself. How'd she take it?"

"She thought I was full of shit."

"Well damn! My name might be Khadijah too!"

I feel his effort to bring levity to what is clearly a weighty topic for me. He wants to push a ray of sunshine through this dark cloud I've introduced. I want to laugh. I want to bask in the sun. There are some things that have to be the full measure of what they are. You can't put your thumb on the scale to make it less or more than what it is because what it is, is perfect. It is perfectly heavy, perfect light, perfectly weighted and shaped to fit into your life. To try to make it something other than what it is, to try to give it an emotion other than the one it comes with almost feels like an insult. So I accept Kent's statement with respect for what it's attempting to be and do, and reply, "She thought I was full of shit ... until I pulled out a razor and proved it."

Chapter 6 | Bird. Prey

Khadijah and I spent that night pulling all of our skeletons from the closet. Telling the unabridged stories of ourselves up and to that very moment. I told her about Preston, about Waukegan, about my parents, about the many lives I'd lived. She told me about being raised in rural, racist, West Virginia; about joining the Navy at 18 to get away from a life that sinks its claws into you and pulls you down until you're six feet, buried, still, but still alive.

That night Khadijah told me the story of Raven, Bart, and Rose.

Time. Complex. Intricate. There are places in the world where time stands still. Where things don't grow toward tomorrow, toward the future; don't evolve. There are places like insects trapped in amber, never changing, stuck. I could tell you about places in 2160 that were still the mirror image of themselves from 1960. Two centuries of defiant stagnation. There are places that have chosen to save the worst parts of themselves. Places that have stared progress and growth both morally and socially in the face and said, *nah*. Khadijah, the most beautiful, brave, smart and forward-thinking woman I've ever known was born in such a place.

Khadijah had been born in a hospital near the West Virginia and Maryland border, of that much she was sure. The circumstances surrounding her birth, however, she'd later have to pull together from things she'd overheard, old *mind readings* and even archived editions of the print newspapers that still limped along in certain rural areas back then. As close as she could tell, it appears that Khadijah's mother, Fatima, was traveling along the winding and oft times dangerous West Virginia mountain highways when she either lost control of her vehicle, or was forced from the road. When Fatima's car was recovered from the bottom of the ravine, where it came to a rest after rolling and tumbling down the mountain side, there was green paint on the side panel of her maroon Ford. Local law enforcement never looked into it.

Fatima was pregnant and sustained injuries that took her last breath just as her baby girl was taking her first. The hospital was small and not equipped with the rigid protocols and safeguards of some of the more advanced care institutions. In the fuss, hustle, and bustle of trying to resuscitate the mother, the new born baby girl, who had just been sent down to the maternity ward, went missing. She hadn't had hand and footprint impressions made, a bar code assigned, or even a wrist band attached. Khadijah was in the world as an unaccounted for blank slate. She was off the grid.

She'd been born, cleaned up, wrapped in a warm blanket and placed in the maternity ward until all means and possible ways of saving her mother's life had been exhausted. By the time the chest compressions had stopped, the pads on the defibrillator had cooled, and the finality of the flatline's tone had been accepted, Khadijah was gone.

118

No one knew how or where. A nurse went to check in on this child that would never know her mother and, nothing, not even the blanket. Once the hospital realized the error of not following their post delivery protocols and the subsequent kidnapping, they panicked. And like most people do when they are panicked and in the wrong, they covered their own asses with lies.

They knew eventually someone would come looking and decided to get out in front of the situation. They used Khadijah's mother's driver's license to locate and contact the family. They told the family that the hospital had done all they could but it was with a heavy heart that they had to inform them that both mother and daughter had lost their lives in an unfortunate, but in those parts, all too common accident. The family was also informed that regrettably the baby was so damaged by the physical trauma and subsequent procedures instituted to save the mother and child's life that there was not enough of a body left to present them with. There was some push back from relatives but the sorrow was so deep that eventually everyone just wanted to get it all over with and begin the healing process. The following week Khadijah's father would bury beside Fatima, in Maryland, a small, empty casket. The grave stone read, "Khadijah Farooq, a flower forever in Allah's hand."

Raven Meade had been born in West Virginia with nothing and had managed to maintain most of it. She was white and poor in a town where almost everyone was white, except when they emerged from the mines covered in coal dust; and almost everyone was, to varying degrees, poor. In the world Raven grew up in, and even today in many

119

ways, tall, thin and blonde equaled beautiful. At five feet even, 140 pounds and with hair the color of the bird of her name sake, when asked about her looks most people said Raven had a nice personality.

Raven's life had been marked by almost getting what she wanted. As a kid she'd wanted Chuck Taylor sneakers but had been given *Tommy Tommy* knockoffs. As a teenager she'd wanted a Motoped Scooter and had been given instead a fourth-hand bicycle. At prom she'd wanted to lose her virginity to, and eventually marry, Ted Graves; but as the result of a cruel prank pulled in the dark, she ended up sleeping with his younger brother Bartholomew Graves. Ted thought it was hilarious when he flipped on the light switch, illuminating the dark bedroom just as Bart, his face inches from Raven's, screamed "I'm coming!" Neither Ted nor Bart could muster a chuckle three months later when Raven announced her pregnancy and the fact that she was keeping the baby. Raven and Bart's families, following societal rules as old as West Virginia itself, demanded they get married. They did. Regardless of the circumstance that led to her pregnancy Raven wanted her baby desperately, and so of course she lost it... and the ability to ever have children. She never got the things she wanted.

Amphetamines can't take the pain of loss away. They can only provide a heavy, expensive rug to sweep the pain under. Rural America in the wake of the death of coal, of mining, of fracking, of health care, of government outreach, of the American dream, had become a dealer in heavy, expensive rugs, and a rampant user of brooms. In an interview on *SeeAnEnd* a meth user was asked, just after smoking a bowl, if the drugs took him to a place where he felt no pain.

He replied, "It doesn't so much make you not feel, as not care," as he nodded out on a bare floor, his body sprawled out like a rug.

In her search for rugs and brooms and numbness Raven had become a known entity in her small corner of the world. Her fast half truths, and slow whole lies, told in a quest for scripts, were well documented in the halls and dispensaries of every local pharmacy and hospital. Raven's picture, alongside the words 'Do not listen. Do not sell. Do not resuscitate,' were taped to the inside wall of every pharmacy tech and nurse's station, in every clinic and hospital for five counties.

On the night of Khadijah's mother's accident Raven Graves had driven six counties over to visit the nearest hospital that might not yet know, not to listen to, sell to, or resuscitate her. Raven had just walked in to complain about a mysterious but excruciating back pain in the hopes of scoring some *Oxosets* when the small hospital exploded with activity. People running up and down the halls. Some already had blood smeared on their smocks. She sat and waited hoping the confusion would cause the doctors to just give her what she wanted in an effort to get her out of the way and attend to the truly important matters at hand. As she waited she saw a nurse run out of what appeared to be an operating room with a baby. The baby was small and crying, but sounded strong. The nurse placed the baby in the nursery, pulled the door behind her and ran back to the O.R. The door to the nursery swung slowly behind the nurse ... but never closed, never latched, never locked. Before she knew it, instead of *Oxosets*, Raven was driving back across the six counties, with a baby, small but strong.

Raven named the baby, that would one day be Khadijah, Rose Graves after her grandmother. Bart came home, pissed after a long day of searching for jobs that were few and far between. He came in the house rumbling and grumbling and grabbed an already open beer from the fridge. Before he could get into full bitch and moan mode Raven filled him in on the whole sorted hospital affair. He stood there, his mostly flat beer getting flatter, slack jawed and in disbelief for a moment or two. Bart imagined her in the throes of a drug fueled hallucination and conjuring from some needle, some pipe, some vape, the thing he knew she wanted most in the world. A baby. He grabbed Raven by the shoulders, looked into her eyes and saw something he hadn't seen in months, clarity. Just then he heard the wail of a baby coming from the living room. Bart tip-toed toward the constant cry like a man trying to sneak up on a burglar. He found, laying on a carpet that was in serious need of cleaning, a newborn baby.

Raven and Bart's marriage was a practical joke that had turned into vows, a cake, a miscarriage, and when neither of them could not find it anywhere or with anyone else, bad sex. Bart was stunned by Raven's story and the truth of it, but really he didn't care. He was glad Raven had something that would take her attention even further from him than the drugs. He cared so little he never even asked if she'd given *her* child a name. Raven for her part was relieved by Bart's willingness to be complicit, no matter if it was born from partnership or apathy. She picked the chubby cheeked baby up from the floor, stared into her huge brown eyes and sat down on the couch, which was as dirty as the floor. With *their* new born baby girl in her arms Raven asked Bart about his

122

day. She felt like she'd stepped into an old *Kudzu* family drama, *Leave it To Muskrat*, or something like that.

Bart pointed to the baby and replied, "My day!? Well Christ on the ark, it was nothin' compared to yours." The mixed metaphor spilled forth just as spittle mixed with beer fell on his already stained shirt. "Some crazy bitch side swiped me is all, or maybe I side swiped her. Either way nothing major, we just swapped some paint and ..."

Raven was so enchanted with the baby that Bart's voice was little more than the sound of a triangle tinkling against the symphony's roar that was the baby's coo. Finally, Raven thought to herself as she stared at the child. Finally! Raven was elated to finally and for once, no matter how it came to be, get what she wanted. She marveled at her perfect, chubby cheeked, happy, giggly baby. A white baby, that got browner with every day, every minute and every second it seemed. Baby Rose was, like a self rising roll with 350 degrees of oven hugging every inch of it, just getting bigger and browner. After a month it became clear to Raven that the woman who had died giving birth to this baby was either black or black adjacent. One evening while changing Rose, their ever browning baby, Raven looked down and thought, *Tommy Tommy* knockoffs... again!

A well-negotiated and managed disliking of each other aside, Raven and Bart had been raised on generations of hatred of anything that wasn't white, wasn't pure. Their bloodlines proudly traced back to soldiers that took up arms against the Union. The sheets that Bart had raped Raven on, with the aid of his brother, were covered in the stars and bars. While neither could sing worth a damn nothing would prevent them from singing Dixie as loudly as they could before every football game the local high school team played. Their parents had framed, in their childhood homes, postcards autographed by lynch mob leaders, of black men hanging by the neck from tree branches. Tree branches Raven and Bart would grow up climbing.

Now through the vicissitudes of fate, theft, and a quest for drugs they found themselves in possession of this, even though fairly fair, clearly black baby. Babies, however, have this way of smiling, of laughing, of reaching up with a strength that defies their size and gripping your finger, that melts the coldest of hearts. Day by day they thought of what they should do, how they could get rid of this black baby. Day by day they did nothing and Raven found herself becoming more attached, more enamored. She'd, in-spite of herself, found herself, over time, growing to love something she'd been taught her whole life to hate.

Raven was at war with her own emotions and familial history. She was raising the very thing she'd been told would lead to her, to their, downfall and demise. She stared at the cooing and gurgling baby and wondered how could something so small, innocent and pure be her undoing? What had her father and his father's fathers before him been so scared of?

The problem being though, that if her forefathers were all wrong, then everything she knew and believed might be wrong. Her whole world might be a lie. Hell, even Jesus might be black. It was a truth she couldn't psychologically afford, especially since her meth use had slowed almost to a stop. To protect her sanity and the sanctity of rural white living Raven decided this child, that she now loved, had to be bad in some way, had to be evil to some degree, and had to be treated accordingly. Raven loved and hated Rose, and that was hard for her to process and handle because dueling emotions were new to her.

Rose Graves had no easy life. She was created in love but born by way of accident. She was snatched from the warmth and security of her mother's womb and placed in a cold and harsh world that did not want her. From her earliest memories Rose was abused mentally and physically. She was told daily that she was worthless, trash, nothing. She'd been beaten viciously for just ... being; for reminding Raven of the few moments when her love and compassion had countermanded her upbringing, her heritage, her culture.

Raven and Bart had both been raised in a world built on a southern confederate foundation. A world that placed deep into the soil of their souls, pride and ritual. The ritual of the church. The ritual of the Klan. The ritual of rural living. Even Rose's abuse came with ritual. They always came together, Raven and Bart, they always came as a pair. They'd collect Rose from her room and bring her to the kitchen. She'd stand and watch as Raven fired up the gas stove and started frying bacon. Bart would sit on a backless chair, in his right hand he'd have the bible opened to Exodus 20:1-12, in his left hand, held behind his back, he'd have a coat hanger gripped firmly. He would read the scripture aloud, the sound of hot bacon grease popping in a non-stick pan they'd gotten from the Dollar Colonel in the background. He'd start out low and slow, "I am the Lord thy God, which have brought thee out of the land of Egypt..." His voice would get a little louder, and the pace of the recitation a little faster with each verse.

Bart's Sundays in his best t-shirt and jeans, swatting mosquitos and watching the red-faced traveling circus that was the southern tent revivals, all came flooding back to him in those bible and coat hanger gripping moments. The sweat, the fervor, the unwavering commitment to whatever meaning was ascribed to the text that day, it had gotten into Bart's bones in a way he hadn't realized. By the time he reached verse 12 he'd be shouting and frothing at the mouth, "Honour thy father and thy mother: that thy days may be long upon the land which the Lord thy God giveth thee!!" The coat hanger would be bent into a straight line from the intensity, strength and fury of his grip. He would repeat verse 12 as he beat Rose with the coat hanger, careful to never hit her in the face or anywhere that couldn't be covered with pants or a shirt, just in case she was ever out with them publicly. There were still a few liberals about that would not understand.

After the scripture laden beatings, as Rose lay crying and barely able to move, Raven would come over and rub the cooling lard from the bacon grease on the welts and cuts. A country remedy to encourage fast and blemish-minimizing healing. The beatings would have broken the average adult, let alone a child but Rose was her mother's child. She was not the offspring of the woman who was raising her, but rather that of the woman who'd died giving her life. Rose was smart, and strong.

Bart and Raven knew they couldn't keep the girl's presence a secret forever and had taken up the story of her being the daughter of a no-account wash woman and domestic they'd known. They told anyone who asked, that Rose's mother had lit out after having her. People were given the story that Rose had been left on the Graves' doorstep and that they had to do the Christian thing no matter the child's unfortunate color. If history has proven nothing it's certainly proven that you can do things both righteous and heinous that will be applauded by many, if not the masses, if you surround it with the right doctrine, the right scripture, the right religion, the right story. No one doubted their account. Who would make up such a thing?

Around the age of six or seven, young, smart, curious Rose snuck out of the house and to school one day. Raven had no interest in educating her. She was embarrassed that this dark mark on her life persisted, and was raising Rose to be no more than the domestic, the mother she invented for her was.

Rose had different plans. When she was five she'd made friends with Donna, a little white girl that lived not too far off. They both knew instinctively, in the way that children know the edges of things without having known those things, that their friendship would be frowned upon. So they played together in the woods, in the shadows, in the margins. They became best friends, in the way that children can love without condition, without being conditioned. Sometime later, a year or more on, Rose stole away with Donna to school. Stepped from the shadows.

Donna's teacher, Mrs. Thackery, walked into the classroom and found the two girls sharing the same seat and desk. She asked Rose who her mother was, why hadn't she been to school before now, and where she lived. Mrs. Thackery drove Rose home after school and informed Raven, who retold the no-count laundry woman story that she'd memorized and even improved upon a bit over the years, that she was in violation of state law by not having Rose enrolled in school. Raven always a bit leery of confrontations with the law enrolled her soon after. With school came a social security number and vaccinations, and suddenly Rose was on the grid. Rose paid for it, however, with a savage coat hanger and lard beating. The rule of not striking her where it would be visible began to fail as Rose began raising her hands more and more in defense of herself. This perceived defiance would make Bart roar like a Grizzly and beat her harder and longer. Afterwards Raven would always be there with the lard, and the soothing touch.

In school Rose started out behind the other students but caught up very quickly and soon was at the head of the class. Some teachers seemed to purposefully work to make it more difficult for her. She would still push her way to the front. A few even openly campaigned against her, but there were enough open-minded instructors to help her through. Some of the teachers that cared and turned a concerned eye toward her would ask about the scars that would appear and increase in number on the back of her hands, or the limp she would sometimes have. Rose would always give them an answer just good enough to allow them to drop it and sleep well at night knowing at least they'd asked.

As she moved into her teenage years, excelling at school and beatings at home were the ritual her life had taken on. Then one night when Rose was in her mid teens Raven noticed while applying the lard that Bart's beatings had become far kinder. It had become difficult to even find a welt on Rose. That's when Raven discovered that as Rose's body developed so had Bart's habit of finding his way to her room at night. Bart wouldn't even touch Raven, not even in disgust anymore, and would find all sorts of ways and reasons to slither out of their bed in the witching hours. Raven was soon jealous of the fact that Bart, a man she'd never wanted, clearly had a greater passion and desire for Rose, for this black ... thing, than he'd ever had for her. Now not only could she not get the things she wanted, she couldn't even have the things she didn't want.

Ted had rejected Raven, Bart had rejected her, but the *Oxosets* had never betrayed her, had never forsaken her. She once again found herself driving six and seven counties away, and reacquainting herself with her old constant and faithful friend.

Raven's *Oxoset* use and jealousy grew alongside Rose's beauty. Rough economic times in West Virginia seemed to be the default setting, and, for some, government welfare was a way of life. Employment for Bart, which was always in short supply, and money to support Raven's growing habit had become even more scarce. In Raven's addled and opioid-ravaged mind she hit upon a scheme that was equal parts money producing and revenge. She'd find men with loose morals and loose cash, and sell what Bart had seemed to find so much value in — Rose's body. Raven decided that if she couldn't have to herself what she wanted, or even what she didn't want, neither should anyone else.

Rose was her mother's child, however, smart and strong. She soon learned to take the throbbing member of these men, her adopted mother would sell hours of her night to, into her hand and instead of inserting them inside her, she'd clap her thighs, greased with some of the lard applied to her after beatings, around their member. She'd pull them close and whisper fantasy into their ears until they couldn't control themselves. It worked more often than not, but unfortunately, not always. Rose was fifteen.

Bart was at the local grocery when a friend told him about the good time he and some of the boys had with that no-count wash woman's daughter he and Raven were raising. The accounting was detailed: the touching, fighting, biting, slaps, pushing, pulling, the sweat, the tears, all the way down to how much they'd paid. Bart was livid. He found Raven, in the dark, sitting on a stool in their large kitchen pantry, in an *Oxoset* nod. Bart turned on the light, closed the door and confronted her. Raven, still in the grips of her high, admitted the truth of it and stood wobbly but defiantly in her decision. She stood, that is, until Bart knocked her fully into an unconsciousness she was never far from those days.

Bart's coat hanger beatings began to extend beyond Rose, to Raven. He'd seized on Ephesians 5:22 and would shout the verse to the heavens, his voice rising as the coat hanger fell on the retreating Raven. "Wives! Submit yourselves to your own husbands! As! You! Do! The

Lord!" He'd started pulling Raven into the pantry for the beatings so she wouldn't have much if any room to escape. After the beatings, when she was finally able to crawl out of the pantry and slowly get to her feet, Raven would fry the bacon and apply the cooling lard to her own wounds. She was a woman of ritual.

Bart never again snuck into Rose's room. He had become just as repulsed by her as he was by Raven. The fact that she was no longer his alone had unbalanced him further. That she was no longer solely his victim, had set him down an even darker path. Whatever energy he had left after beating Raven in the pantry he'd use to beat Rose, but still he could not deny the economic boon Raven had seized upon. He would take the money Raven collected for selling Rose and issue the sincere threat that if the money stopped then he could not promise that both Raven and Rose would not soon meet the Lord whose words echoed so loudly through their house.

No matter the threats, no matter the consequences, at sixteen Rose's mind and body could endure no more. She ran away. Into the shadows. Into the margins. Friends, that were not married to their parent's racism, would sneak her into their homes at night and hide her. She spent nights beneath beds and balled up in the back of closets. Her own personal underground railroad. She borrowed clothes and ate food stolen away from kitchen tables. She was homeless and often hungry, but still far happier than she'd ever been.

Raven and Bart eventually came to the school, found Rose and demanded she come home. They needed her back, and on her back, to make ends meet. Rose refused and ran. Finally in a fit of desperation Raven, who was always leery of the police, got word to her that if she wasn't home the following evening she'd have the police come to the school and forcibly bring her home. She was still after all a minor and *her* child. Raven knew that small town police and small town minds would probably not be on her side. She also knew she would face the reality of jail before she would ever be used by her "mother" or abused by her "father" again. Before push came to shove, however, the house that Rose had grown up in, the only home she'd ever known, burnt to the ground killing both Raven and Bart, who were trapped inside.

The scene was both gruesome and mysterious. Raven and Bart had somehow gotten locked in the pantry of the house. They always came together. After careful examination the lock on the pantry door appeared to have been jammed into the locked position with what appeared to be a piece of a coat hanger. Fire fighters had traced the origin of the blaze back to a grease fire, probably started by something cooking on the stove. No one in local law enforcement knew how that piece of coat hanger came to be in that door or who would have done such a thing, but they had a few ideas. Raven and Bart owed money to lenders, loan sharks, and drug dealers all over town and had made many enemies. The list of people with a reason to kill them read like the town's local phone directory. The officer in charge of the case said the person or persons responsible for jamming that door would have had to be very strong. Rose was her mother's daughter.

Rose finished high school in the top quarter of her class but she was still a poor black girl in West Virginia and felt like the only way out was in some branch of the armed forces. So when she turned 18 she enlisted in the Navy, traveled the world, and looked to find out who she really was. She eventually traced her date of birth back to the story of a black woman from Maryland and her unborn baby. Both reportedly died in a hospital six counties over from where she grew up. While on leave she visited Maryland and the grave site of that woman and child. There she was, staring at the tombstone of the woman who had given her so much strength and resiliency. Her name was Fatima Farooq and beside her was a small grave and the tombstone for her unborn daughter, Khadijah.

I tell Kent the story of Raven, Bart, and Rose—Khadijah's story —and his expression is equal parts disbelief and wonder. He's still trying to navigate the waters of what's true and false in our conversations. Surely this can't all be true. All of this tragedy and triumph and supernatural-ness can't be real. Kent is a newspaper man. He lives in a world of facts. In his profession even horrific endings are rooted in concrete beginnings. He opens his mouth as if to speak and immediately swallows the words. His lips purse and his eyes go to the sky as if asking some higher power for permission to speak his mind. I step in before God can answer.

"Speak your mind Mr. Kent." He sighs then tuns his gaze from the heavens to me.

"This sounds like an episode of *Black Cracked Mirror* and *Deranged* all rolled into some alternate version of *I Know Why The Caged Bird Sings*. I'm ready to call bullshit on all of this."

"Indeed. In a life filled with predictability and the mundane, the fantastic can seem like a flight of fancy, but you've been twirling that coin around in your fingers non-stop since receiving it. I imagine you're waiting for the gold to fall to the ground and prove itself cleverly disguised tin foil. But it hasn't yet. So some part of you is also starting to wrestle with the question, what if it's all true? What if Mr. M isn't spinning a yarn but knitting a rope that'll pull me into a world I didn't know existed. The stuff of comic books and late night *Kudzu Occ Streams*."

"Is that what you're doing? Roping me in?"

"I'm telling you the truth of me. I'm giving you what you asked for. I can just as easily step back into the shadows, into the margins and become again fairy tale, myth, and folklore. Wait another hundred years for the next Mr. Kent and see if he's better ready to receive what I have to give."

Kent stops spinning the coin. He looks at me his eyes surveying my face intently for I know not what. I don't think he finds what he's looking for and so his eyes fall to the coin that lay still in his open palm. We walk in silence for a few blocks his feet falling in step with mine, his eyes only on the coin. I feel like a seeing eye dog. If I were to walk over a cliff he would obliviously do so too. I must say though he is moving better than he has since we left the cafe.

What he can't find in my face he must have found in the coin. He blows out a large loud breath, begins spinning the coin between his fingers again and says, "I'd love to hear the rest of Khadijah's story."

"Khadijah would eventually go on to teach me what sacrifice looks like and the lengths to which love will go. I think I've spoken enough about Khadijah and Rose for now."

"Isn't Khadijah, Rose?"

"No, Khadijah is Khadijah. She was never Rose. Even when Raven and Bart were calling her Rose she was still Khadijah."

"Well... who is Rose?"

"Rose is Rose."

"Geez man, who's on first? This is some Kubrick's Cube stuff you're on. Bes taught you, you couldn't buy love, not even as Midas. Khadijah taught you what love is. Since Rose is Rose did she teach you anything?"

"Yes. Something I've never forgotten and been very careful not to."

Chapter 7 | Blood. Dust

Kent's health seems to be moving in the right direction. His color is returning with every step but his strength hasn't completely come back to him yet. His strength seems to wax and wane. One second I'm working hard to keep up because he's walking so briskly, and the next he's breathing like we've run a marathon after a few steps. We've walked and talked quite a bit. I can see the wheels in his mind turning as he juggles the Bes and Khadijah narratives. I also notice him struggling to keep up with the current clip of our stroll. If he was completely himself I'm sure he would have pushed me on the subject of Rose but it's apparent that the present moment is one of wane and not wax. I've slowed almost to a snail's pace when finally I ask if he'd like to rest for a second.

"Just a second," he says before the echo of my voice has finished reverberating.

His words are all determination but his eyes offer a sincere thank you for the respite. I point toward a bench but Kent flops down heavily on the grass, his chest rising and falling rapidly. A welcome breeze sneaks up on us, like a lover's hands cupped over your eyes before you can turn. The restoration and relief that the wind's currents wash over me, alert me to the fact that I too wouldn't be hurt by sitting for a second or three.

I survey the area before moving to sit down beside Kent. I'm just about to take a seat and begin the story of Emily when I catch sight of him. I hadn't noticed him before. It's almost as if he just appeared. There's something compelling about him. I can't seem to look away, like a rubber neck to a car wreck. He's sitting a block and a half ahead, in the middle of the block, on the sidewalk with his head down. His face is shrouded, hidden deep in the shadow of his well worn hoodie. His legs are crossed, lotus style, in torn, stained, distressed jeans. His back is as straight as that of a nervous applicant on an interview for a job he knows he's not qualified for. His left hand, a complexion somewhere between caramel and almond, is extended and ready to receive whatever change, food, help, anything, anyone can spare.

Something about his posture betrays his impoverished circumstance. He comes across as almost regal. The still urgency of his pose and the ironing board stiffness of his back remind me of Thich Quang Duc, subtract the hoodie, add the accelerant, and voila. I'm walking toward him without knowing I've decided to. He sticks out like tongues on teenage girls in the photos they share on *PhotoFriends*. There was a time when he wouldn't have. There was a time when this would have been his neighborhood.

Greater WoodLake with its billion *bytebill DomiCas'*, its "public" and yet still somehow private *Constitution Schools of Excellence*, and claims of "A Neighborhood Too Business Minded To

Be Hate Oriented," didn't always look the way it looks now. This used to be a N.N.N., a *Noir National Neighborhood.* It used to be part of Decatur, part of East Lake and on the border of Kirkwood. They all got put in a meat grinder, seasoned with an influx of interest and cash, cranked out with shiny new neighbors, a new neighborhood name, and wrapped in a whitewashed casing. That's how the gentrification sausage is made. Suddenly everything was bike trails and blonde ponytails. Everything was yoga pants and doggy daycares. Everything was gluten free and served with a side of mayo. Everything got avacado'd.

It used to be backyard BBQ's and front street brawls. It was freeze tag at the park and a job freeze at the plant. It was sweaty, hip swaying, brown liquor Saturday nights. It was sweaty, hand clapping, brown preacher Sunday mornings. It was wave your hands like you just don't care and hands up don't shoot. It was coded language and dap on the block, and can I touch your hair and you speak so well at the office. It was, you don't wanna go there after dark, and have you ever seen anything so warm and loving in the light of day. It was meant to be a punishment, a piece of land that no one wanted so let "them" have it. It was love, built one heart and one hearth at a time. It was a city project. A supposed monument of brown blight that black people turned into an experiment in overcoming. It was something out of nothing. It was supposed to be hell and somehow all that foot stomping to the drum beat, and kneeling in prayer put out the flames. It was, how did they make something so hot and unbearable, so cool and coveted. It was a Noir thing ... you wouldn't understand.

Then the *Ctrl Alt Rht* started pushing the idea that *Noir National Neighborhoods,* NNNs, were the new KKK. They had nonsensical talking points that they pushed ad nauseam on *Faux News.* Say anything loudly and often enough and you won't believe how many people will start to believe it, will start to repeat it. Ask Donald Trump. Suddenly Noir Nationals living in the marginalized spaces they'd been pushed into were deemed ... racist? This racism seemed to only exist, however, when Noir Nationals were living on land close to downtown or close to the next planned, zoned, and green-lit big budget Live, Work, Play Palaces. NNN's on the outskirts of town or in rural areas were never targeted, were never deemed unconstitutional or indicative of proving *retroactive race favoritism.*

Noirs were offered checks at, or just above, market value, to sell their *DomiCas.* Some did. Those that didn't often came home to find a mysterious fire had destroyed their living quarters or that imminent domain had swallowed up their place of residence. Others stayed only to discover they couldn't afford the rising property taxes on a *DomiCas* they had already paid off. The banks would auction off their homes to cover the tax debt leaving the now former owners penniless and homeless. Then they'd demolish the structures, making nothing out of something.

Noirs were pushed out of the city, many out of the state and a few even found themselves relocated to new planets where they didn't speak the language, know the culture or sometimes even biologically agree with the environment. *Amnesty Interstellar* stepped in but by then the damage was done. New laws had been written, land purchased, people sent to the four corners of the universe, families broken up never to be reunited again. When I learned of it I poured money into defending the rights of the Noirs. That's when I first learned of how much money could be marshaled by those dedicated to evil. Old money, ancient money, dollars that were made selling apples in the Garden of Eden, stood in defiant opposition to my efforts. The Noir Nationals openly, and me anonymously, fought against them in courts of law and sometimes on street corners. We won some and we lost some. This neighborhood, gutted and mutted, is one of the ones we lost.

I think about this as I approach him, his open palm extended as if hoping for a hand out or a hand up, or both. I'm sure he's passed by daily and viewed as little more than an extension of the sidewalk. I'm sure the police have been called early and often, and he's seen the back of more than his share of squad cars. I'm sure there are those that wonder why he won't just go home, never considering that this was his home. I'm sure.

I keep a few pieces of gold, and the number to an outreach program I fund, to give to the few refugees in their own nation, in their own neighborhood, that escape mass incarceration and have nowhere to call their own; not even the small piece of concrete or patch of grass or square of cardboard they find themselves sitting on with their hands extended.

He doesn't look up as I approach although I see his head tilt toward my footsteps. His face is still in shadow. His hand, palm up, moves toward me as if tracking my approach. I walk up, drop the gold pieces in his hand and just as I begin to tell him about the outreach program he drops the gold pieces on the ground and grabs my wrist.

"Two pieces of gold?" his lips don't move and yet his voice, easy and smooth, coasts up slowly from his throat like a car out for a Sunday drive. I go to pull my hand back and find his grip surprisingly strong.

"Where is the silver? The thirty pieces of silver?" He asks as he tries to pull me closer, finding me perhaps stronger than he'd anticipated. My adrenaline kicks in adding to my strength and hardening my skin. Is this a trap set by the Global Earth Government? By the government of another planet? How could they know I'd be here? I didn't even know.

"Isn't that what they paid Judas? Isn't that the going price for betrayal ... Midas?" Midas? I pull my hand away from his just as he pulls back the hoodie and reveals the maroon head wrap beneath. It feels like a shark's fin, smooth and purposeful, just breaking the surface.

"She wants to talk Midas. She didn't send us to hurt you this time, just to relay the message."

"You can thank God for that because the only one who would have left here hurt, is you," I reply as my hands form fists.

"Perhaps you didn't hear me ... she didn't send US."

I look around and watch as at least a dozen men and women stop what they're doing, face me, remove their hoodies, hats, hijabs and wigs to reveal maroon head wraps hidden beneath. They stand perfectly, deathly, still. When I turn back to face him, he's twenty yards away from me, smiling.

"We're ubiquitous Midas. Omnipresent like the God you pretend to love so much. You have no idea who is us and who isn't. How can you be sure your strolling companion isn't one of us?" He gestures over my shoulder, I turn and see Kent about fifty yards away, walking up, his eyes going to the people in maroon head wraps, still as mannequins.

"One thing you certainly taught her, and she taught us, is that you can never know who to trust. This is your last chance to do the right thing, to end this without... violence. You can give her what she wants or we will hunt you like the frightened deer you are, hang you by your ankles and bleed you. We will do what your parents wanted so desperately to do but didn't have the guts. Oh yes, you will provide us the answers we seek, must, and will have, one way or the other."

I take a step forward and he takes a step back. A car, so mint green it's almost glowing, pulls up slowly and careens to a stop just to his right. I recognize the driver from this morning. The rear driver's side door opens.

"You know where she is. She'll be waiting for you." The way he speaks without moving his lips makes it seem as if his voice is coming from the buildings, the tress, from all of the still people sporting their maroon head dresses.

"You have until the failing light of dusk. But Midas, once the full veil of night falls," he snaps his fingers and his dozen cohorts all cover their heads and disappear into alleyways, cars and homes, "we'll have a knife to your throat before you see us coming."

He steps into the waiting vehicle without ever breaking eye contact. The car pulls away slowly, smoothly, as if mimicking the sound of his ventriloquism. Kent reaches me, looks about confused by what he's just seen and asks, "What was that about?"

I look at the sun moving ever toward the horizon, ever toward the inescapable night and reply, "Blood and dust Mr. Kent. That was about blood and dust."

Chapter 8 | Fools. Gold

We walk and now I'm the one with the damp brow, both from a bit of worry and trying to keep up. It seems as if the rest did Mr. Kent well. For my every step his foot falls twice. Kent's sweats have stopped and the color returned to his face. The winter of his illness has if nothing else certainly given way to a spring in his step. He's well. He's better than well. He's a new man.

Feeling sickly and set upon by illness robs you of your ability to reason. All you can think of is, what on Mars' red planet is happening to me? What did I eat on Alexianium? Who did I touch at that Bajan bacchanal, and where? What do I need to do to remedy this? What do I need to take to fix me? In your mind you try to imagine who the patient zero or Typhoid Mary or LID monkey is that you've encountered. Who or what has saddled you with this plague. When that search comes up empty then all your energy is turned toward finding some magical, mystical, over the counter, generic if you have it, panacea to cure it.

When you're well again, the mind space and energy you were using to explore *Blanket* M.D., incorrectly self-diagnose yourself with Creutzfeldt, and cope with what feels like your pending doom, can all be reallocated to critical thinking and scrutiny. Kent is feeling well, again.

"So Emily..." I say with thoughts of Khadijah's smile and her face against mine. The memory of her touch, her hands softly massaging the nucha of my neck, causes the hairs to stand up on my arm. The sound of her voice in my ear, an inaudible morning whisper through vocal cords not yet fully awake, cause me to turn my head, almost expecting to see her there beside me. She's not there and yet she's always with me, just under the surface like a skipped rock just starting to drink in the pond as it loses momentum. Thoughts of her always make me smile, and break my heart. My emotions, dueling. Khadijah always causes tears to dance behind the curtain of my eyes, and threaten to come out onto the stage.

"Mr. M." Kent says. I register that he's spoken but can't make out the words. His, and all voices, sound like the garbled warble of Charlie Brown's teacher right now. His voice has to reach my mind which is hundreds of miles and years away. It's too great a distance to clearly hear anyone but myself right now. I wrestle with thoughts that I try very hard to keep pinned to the mat. Thoughts that hurt me to struggle against. I want to talk about something, anything to bring me fully back to now. Emily will do.

"Emily was beautiful..." I begin again.

"Mr. M." His voice a bit louder and more forceful cuts through the miles and the years. I look about and realize that we've walked several blocks while I was time traveling. I look over into Kent's eyes. They are clear, bright, and focused. The gold coin is revolving and rotating between his fingers like a kid with a fidget spinner, like a former drug addict begging you to notice his six months clean chip, like a magician just before he yells, tah-dah!

"... Yes?"

"You've told me a lot about yourself," his smile is wide but something in his now clear, bright, and focused eyes says mischief. He continues.

"Things clearly intended to take people's idea of Midas from cryptic myth to human being that walks amongst us, but I have a few questions."

His body language is different. He's restored the ice caps. The thawing between us that had begun has clearly been brought to an abrupt stop. His posture, previously relaxed, is now upright and stiff. His gait, the stride like that of two friends out for a stroll, now has, point the toe and set the heel, military precision. Things he'd clearly intended to cover in the cafe, before I implored him to grab some air, are flooding back. And here I am, Noah without an ark.

"Okay," I say preparing myself for whatever comes next.

"Mr. M in 2087 The NAAPC, The National Alliance and Allies of People of Color."

"Yes, I know what The NAAPC is."

"I'm sure you do. In 2087 when they were faced with bankruptcy they suddenly received a huge, anonymous, influx of cash."

"... if you say so." And so the verbal sparring begins again.

"I do say so, and In 2128 the Armed Marksmen of African American Nations whose position was, and still is, that every person of color should know their rights, know how to use a weapon and be armed at all times, had a mass weapons cache purchase, anonymously underwritten. This purchase allowed them to offer, for free, a weapon to any person of color that completed their firearms training course. The number of people of color who took those courses, secured a weapon, and joined their ranks made them a rival to the NRA."

"... I do indeed remember hearing about that."

"Do you? Because it was claimed that those two incidents, the funding and reopening of Morris Brown, then college, now university, and several other African American and persons of color led and driven ventures, that were only possible due to huge anonymous cash outlays, were funded by you."

"Who said that?"

"Right now I'm saying it and I'm also saying that I'm an investigative reporter and my job is to look at these lofty stories, these claims of mysterious anonymous donations and get to the bottom of them."

"Ah, a bottom feeder." He bristles, instantly recovers and hopes I didn't see it. But I did. "And at the bottom what did you find Mr. Kent?"

"I found out that there is no Santa Claus ... and no Midas behind these cash outlays. In 2005 Venezuelan president Hugo Chavez offered the black victims of Hurricane Katrina in New Orleans, Louisiana, 120 first aid and relief experts, 50 tons of food and millions of dollars in relief funding. President George W. Bush refused. In 2017 Venezuelan President Nicolas Maduro offered 5 million dollars to help the people of color that were victimized by Hurricane Harvey. President Donald Trump refused. In the 1960s the USSR and Cuba offered to help the economically depressed, overly policed, and openly abused people of America's ghettos. Their aid was refused by the provincial powers that be."

He pauses. I wonder if he's waiting for me to claim that I am in addition to being Midas also Hugo Chavez, Nicolas Maduro, the USSR, and Cuba. I continue to walk beside him and look straight ahead. He's either going to say what he's got to say or he's not. If his effort is to bury me then he's going to have to swing the shovel himself. He continues.

"The history of black and brown people in America is filled with offers of undergirding and assistance that they were not in a position to openly accept, from sometimes benevolent, and sometimes nefarious foreign entities. Somewhere around 2087, tired of getting the short end of the stick from their own government and waking up to the dire straights they kept finding themselves in, they created back channels, shell companies and offshore accounts where they could accept, secure, hide, and use these outpourings of aid that kept being offered and denied them. Tracing this kind of money back to its source is no easy feat and comes with its fair share of intrigue and danger. My life and reputation have been threatened more than once by men that don't make idle threats; but I was able to identify international Saudi terrorist Sadim Mai as one of the more nefarious characters channeling money from the Middle East into ventures that would eventually be attributed via urban legend to you. The same was true of Latin drug lord Dias Ven Muertes. His cartel was reported to rival that of Pablo Escobar, Joaquin Guzman, and Jorge Garza. In 2128 he began funneling billions into projects helmed by people of color in a clear effort to secure their loyalty and get an even stronger foothold into American interests. People whisper Midas in association with these mysteriously underwritten massive ventures but that's only because they're afraid to say the real names of the men responsible. They'd rather claim that an imaginary boogeyman helped them than to admit it was a real life villain."

I continue to walk. The silence is deafening. Kent continues. His voice is full, strong, and confident now.

"I haven't rubbed the gold off of this coin yet. It might actually be a gold coin. And if so I have no idea how you swapped it for the one I had in my hand. I've been spinning this coin around just like I've been turning over in my mind how you've pulled any of this off today. I mean you're a confidence man and a charlatan par excellent. We've walked. We've talked. You've ingratiated yourself to me. You've shown concern and opened up about your life, drawing me in. You've done the ultimate con man ruse, you've put the gold coin in my hand and said, 'Here you hold the evidence. You hold the proof. You prove I'm not who I say I am.' You've seized on this Midas myth and really run with it and I have to tell you that takes some balls, but this quilt you've woven before me is held together by the thinnest of threads and I'm tugging on the string that's going to pull it all apart."

I let him complete his thoughts. I let his words come to a full stop. I leave space and room to ensure he's finished. Then I say, "Can I tell you about Emily now?"

"Deflection? From Midas? Now that's unexpected. You've been all quick answers and Yoda wisdom until now. When you're backed into a corner with facts you turn quiet as church mice making love on a discarded Newport filter."

"So you don't want to hear about Emily?"

Kent throws his head back, laughs, turns his Aud Recorder off and tucks the coin into his pocket.

"Sure Midas." Midas. Not Mr. M. "Sure, tell me all about Emily."

His eyes look into the distance as if he's seeing beyond this moment, beyond this interaction. He's already writing the headline 'Midas Not,' 'Fool's Gold,' 'All That Glitters Is Not Gold.' The smile on his face is one of satisfaction. As I begin I'm sure he's not listening but it matters not. At the end of the day this part, the telling of the story of my life, has been more for me than for him.

"Emily was beautiful."

I begin again from the beginning, and just like with Bes and Khadijah I'm back in the moment. Her hands almost unnaturally warm framing my face as she tells me something she doesn't want me to miss or misunderstand. Her almond shaped eyes that are almost pushed completely shut by her high cheek bones whenever she smiles, look into mine. The toned, lean, dancer's muscles beneath her copper skin that always looks tan and decadent as if she's just come from the beach, undulate with her slightest movement. Her hair is in locs and held with a multi-colored, African print, scrunchy high atop her head. The ends of each loc died blonde. Her full lips are pouty, never without the proper amount of gloss and shining like the promise of a new day.

"We met at The Majestic on Ponce."

This seems to grab his attention,

"The Majestic Diner?"

"Yes? Why?"

"I've heard stories that much like you live somewhere between the truth and clear folklore."

"Really? Like?"

"Stories of the oddest and the most wonderful people in the world eating at a random greasy spoon."

"Whatever you heard ... is true. I once had chicken and waffles beside a naked woman that was wrapped in strategically placed blinking Christmas lights."

"Where were the lights plugged in?"

"Where indeed Mr. Kent. Where indeed. As I was saying we met at The Majestic Diner while Emily was pursuing her masters..."

"At Clark?" Kent cuts me off mid-sentence and steps in front of me, cutting me off. He puts his hand out, palm up, forcing me to stop walking, and speaking.

"You've already told this story Midas."

He's got me. He's captured me in a clear lie. His expression is one of satisfaction and disappointment, like a spouse discovering a *grip* that confirms that her husband is indeed having the affair he's been denying for three months. His eyes search mine for a reaction. He's not seeing what he'd expected. More than likely because, he hasn't caught me in anything. He continues.

"This is the story of Khadijah remember? Getting her master's at Clark?"

I remember better than most is what I'm thinking. When it comes to Khadijah I often wish I could forget. I wish that I could remove this boulder of heartache that lives in my soul, but like Sisyphus I must eternally bear this burden.

"Emily was getting her Master's at GA State."

"... GA State? Right? Was she also a great dancer that frequented some retro Atlanta nightclub?"

Kent shakes his head briefly, his eyes leave mine and look toward the ground in what seems like an act of utter disappointment. He lets out a heavy sigh, turns and begins to walk away.

"She did not! Meeting her the way I did, in a diner that felt like a coffee shop, Emily pursuing her master's, her height, her build, her brown eyes... it all reminded me of Khadijah. What sounds to you, like a lie conceived by a forgetful mind having a hard time managing stories, felt to me like God returning my love back to me. It felt like a second chance."

Kent just a few steps ahead stops. Something in my voice, the timber, the emotion, the how-dare-you outrage must have settled in his feet and pinned him to the spot. We stood there like that for a moment. His back to me. My chest heaving with emotion.

"Do you believe in God Midas? In reincarnation?"

I say nothing.

"You said you felt like God had returned your love back to you." He speaks to me over his shoulder like the adult in the park earlier, counting as other adults hid.

"That would imply you believe in both."

I refuse to talk to his back. I am Midas. There are places where I'm considered a king. There are places where I'm considered a God. There is nowhere, however, where I am a man that speaks to the backs of men. I've been as kind and gentle with Mr. Kent as I can but my patience is beginning to wear thin. He must sense that something is amiss. He turns and finds me closer than he'd realized.

"Mr. Kent if you have come completely to the conclusion that I am indeed a con man here solely to lie to you, to pull some sort of clever ruse, to defraud you and your readers then I suggest you terminate this interview and waste your time no further."

Kent shrugs and turns to leave. Halfway into his turn he stops and pulls from his pocket the coin and starts spinning it between his fingers.

"You have until we reach a *Goldilocks* ... Midas. You have until I can verify the true properties of this coin and I just happen to know there is *Goldilocks* Machine five blocks from here. So you've got five blocks to spin your yarn or rope or whatever."

I nod and start walking. Kent falls in to my right, step for step.

"Emily was damn near a genius."

"So she didn't need your help with classes?"

"She didn't need my help with anything and actually taught me a lot. It was the first time in a long time that someone had more information and intuition than I had. It was humbling really."

"I can imagine."

"You can't. To have lived for far longer than any one other than the pious characters of the bible. To have master's degrees and PhD's in hundreds of academic disciplines. I have traveled the world several times over and learned from mystics, prophets, kings, peasants, con men, and caliphates, and then to sit enrapt at the foot of someone who would be considered a mere child in the eyes of time. It's humbling in a way you cannot possibly imagine."

I can tell that Kent is half listening but mostly keeping his eyes open in hopes of seeing a *Goldilocks* that he wasn't aware of, that may be along the way. There was once a poet in Atlanta named Karen Wurl that wrote of her lover, 'I felt I could tell him anything... because I knew he wasn't listening.' I'd been speaking guardedly to Kent but his sudden mental distance and emotional disinterest opened me up to speak aloud things that perhaps I'd whispered to my soul by never vocalized.

"Emily was smart and beautiful. She was what most dreamed of but never thought they'd ever be able to obtain. To be loved for who she was, was the least anyone could offer her, and should have been on its face as easy as the Sunday mornings Lionel Richie once sang about. The problem was..."

I look over and see that Kent is walking beside me but he's not there. He's hearing but not listening at all.

"The problem was I wasn't looking for Emily. I was still looking for Khadijah. The things I loved about Emily were the things that seemed like they brought Khadijah back to me, if even for just a moment. The young lady you say I robbed you of at the cafe..."

I look to see if this will turn his head but no, his eyes dance as they scan the horizon for the lie detector he's sure must be just around the bend. I continue.

"Perhaps I did purposefully work to deny you her presence. The way she walked. Her smile. It was all Khadijah. It was all mine. Perhaps I couldn't admit it in the moment but the idea of any man possessing anything that is Khadijah makes my skin crawl. Gets my back up. Makes me work in the moment against their interest. So I apologize for that Kent."

I remember once when Emily and I had fallen out that I laid in bed beside her as she slept and apologized. I cried and lamented and poured out apology after apology for everything. When she awoke I felt released and resolved and she still felt angry and hurt. She wanted to talk but I'd already spoken my truth to the wind and sought absolution from the ether. My tears had dried and while she rested my explanation had bloomed, wilted, and fallen to chaff against her sleeping cheek. My apology was the tree that fell and no one heard. It had never happened. This conversation with Kent feels much like that, but this was in truth more me admitting to myself than trying to tell the world.

"Emily loved me and I tried to love her. I'd felt like I was in love with Bes and soon came to know that she was not in love with me. In truth maybe I never was never in love with her either. Khadijah and I shared a mutual, loving, nurturing, eternal love. It knows no bounds. Emily loved me, with her whole heart, and I wanted desperately to love her back. If I could have made my heart open, made my feelings grow toward her, I would have. The heart is an interesting thing. It doesn't choose based on logic and reason. It opens for those who awaken it, for those who touch it in places you weren't even aware it had."

Bes once told me that she'd never made love to me, that we'd had sex but never moved past that. I fully understood her when I was with Emily. We had our fair share of really good sex. But it was just sex. She once said after, 'I love the way we make love,' and I could see Bes, all teeth and glimmering sweat, staring at me, smiling and shaking her head from side to side.

"After about a year of trying to make it more than I could, and trying to will myself into being in love, I finally had to end things with Emily. We were back at the Majestic. Things had come full circle. We talked. We cried. She asked why. I explained as best I could. She was rightfully confused by it all. She said 'I'm in love with you!' in a voice and volume that made the restaurant come to a halt. It was a *Kudzu* playing out right before the eyes of the paying patrons. I saw people disconnect from the *Blanket* and give us their undivided attention. She repeated her statement, 'I said I'm in love with you!' Then her eyes filled, like a cup of coffee that you have to sip before picking it up for fear that it'll spill over with the slightest touch. Her voice, so loud and confident as it stood tall in its truth, fell to almost a whisper as she asked, '... are you in love with me?' I looked at her and then down at the table. I saw as she placed her palms flat against the formica table top. I heard the legs of her chair scrapping against the tiled floor as she slowly pushed her chair back away from the table. I heard her clear her throat, and her voice catch as she went to speak. I watched as a tear hit the table just to the left of her cup of tea. I saw her left hand rise from her side, go to her face and return wet. I heard her sigh deeply. She stood there another few seconds. I am a man who has faced time, and even death, but could not bring myself to face her. She left. I couldn't seem to lift my eyes from the table's top even in her absence. I sat there for another two hours before I was able to will myself to pay the bill and leave. Emily and I never spoke again."

I feel myself on the verge of tears just recanting the tale. Bes taught me I couldn't buy love. Khadijah taught me what love is. Emily taught me that you can't force, cajole, or recreate love. I was hurt by Bes' actions but Emily showed me that hurting someone can be even more painful than being hurt yourself.

Kent speaks and his voice catches me off guard.

"The truth is not always what we want it to be. The truth is autonomous. It stands alone. Many try to co-opt and manipulate it but at the end of the day it will stand at the mountains crest, solitary and undeniable."

Has he been listening this entire time and simply playing the role of the disinterested companion. This last leg of our trip I've viewed him as a passenger mindlessly staring out of the window but perhaps he's had his hand on the wheel the entire time. Perhaps he's given me his passive distant affect because he knew it would make me speak more freely, more openly, if I thought no one was listening.

"I agree with you Mr. Kent but what has inspired you to such a profound and undeniable statement?"

Kent points and just up ahead in the parking lot of a charging station that has known better days, is a *Goldilocks*.

Chapter 9 | Catch. Release

The first time I'd heard of a *Goldilocks* was back when my parents were bleeding me dry, literally. After I ran from them I became personally acquainted with *Goldilocks* machines as I began to leech off of myself. These machines have come to represent both my oppression and my salvation. Staring at it I feel like this must be what the cross represented to Jesus. A tool of punishment that became a vehicle of ascension.

Kent already has the coin in hand. He's doing everything he can to not fall into a full sprint as we approach the machine. He's trying not to seem anxious to get this over with, to expose me for the charlatan he's sure I am. I begin to walk more slowly, on purpose.

I've spent too many of my many years running from or to something. Running from my parents. Running from who I am. Running to ReDeUx. Running to class. Running to a *Goldilocks* machine. It took me well over a hundred years to learn to walk through life. To not be in such a hurry. Why would a man with several lifetimes to live ever run anywhere? In a way few could ever understand, time is on my side. Walking may even be too fast. In time I may learn to crawl.

Kent stands and waits for me to catch up to him at the *Goldilocks*. *Goldilocks* machines have a drawer that you pull out and deposit what you believe to be precious metals or gems inside. The machine then uses a cadre of lasers, x-rays and chemical tests to determine what's precious, precious-plated, or papier-mâché. Once the appraisal is done the estimated value of the item is displayed on the screen. The *Goldilocks* then itemizes what its cut will be and what you'll be receiving back via transfer. You also have the ability to reject the appraisal and demand your items back. Few people desperate enough to visit a *Goldilocks* ever choose this option.

Kent has the drawer pulled open and the coin in his hand hanging over the drawer like the sword of Damocles as I approach.

"Last chance Midas. You can come clean and spare yourself this embarrassment or I can add this unfortunate revelation to the story for my *mindreaders*. You already know that I know that you've done none of the things they've attributed to you. I have the proof."

"I understand," I say, now ten yards from where he's standing.

"You understand what?"

"I understand that for you it all comes down to proof and that's one of the reasons I chose you." Five yards.

"You chose me because you know I have a worldwide readership and you thought you could use me to pull off your clever little scam. Midas, or whatever your name is, and please know I will find that out too, this all ends here and now."

"Agreed," I say standing an arms distance from Kent.

Before he can drop the coin into the machine I pull a small knife from my pocket and swing it at Kent. With reflexes that I think even shock him he dodges and dances backward.

"Really? You think you're going to intimidate me? Scare me? You think you and that little knife are going to protect your lie? No! Plus you're clearly not even good with it!"

"Am I not?" I point at Kent's cheek. He himself can feel the warm flow of blood starting to trickle from the open cut. He reaches his index and middle finger up and wipes at the cut. He stares at his fingers and then at me. His jaw flies open and his hand begins to shake. He extends his trembling fingers toward me. They're covered in gold.

Chapter 10 | Symbol. Eyes

Kent is staring at his fingers in disbelief. He can't seem to get his hand to stop shaking. If you didn't know better you would think it wasn't his own hand his eyes were fixed on. His knees buckle and I hook my arm under his so that he doesn't fall. His weight throws me slightly off balance. We look like two drunks square dancing to a rhythm only heard in our minds. Kent grabs onto my arm as if grasping reality itself and leans heavily. He drops the coin as he steadies himself. His mouth is wide open, like a drowning man tasting his first breath of air after breaking the surface. His eyes, which seem as wide as his mouth, finally leave his fingers and follow the coin as it rolls away toward a drainage gutter. I feel his legs simultaneously wanting to chase after the coin, and accepting that it's gone never to return. The coin symbolizes this moment in his life. The past and many of the things he thought to be true are rolling away, never to return. There is no need in chasing after it, or them. I help him sit down on the edge of the curb. I remember doing this as a boy, sitting on the curb and playing that's my car with my best friend at the time. A time before Midas, and gold, and true folklore.

Kent touches the fast healing cut again and again his fingers coming back less and less gilded. He doesn't know what to say and so I say it for him.

"You want to know how? You want to know if this is another of what you perceive to be my clever tricks? You want to know if your eyes are deceiving you?"

He nods his head absently still touching the cut over and over.

"It's not a trick. Your eyes aren't deceiving you. And this is how."

I open my mouth and nothing comes out. The words are stuck, hiding somewhere behind my Adam's apple. Naked words in the garden of my mind ashamed to be seen. Adam's apple betraying me once again.

I had prepared myself for this moment. I'd even rehearsed the speech I would give, like I was sweaty palmed, dressed in pink and white, front and center beneath the blinding lights of the church Easter play. I had prepared for the possibility that Kent would be the one, and that I would have to tell him everything. He deserves at least that, right? So far in my very long life only Khadijah has ever known the whole story, and now when faced with there being two, my voice is cowering behind a fig leaf. 'Who told thee that thou wast naked?'

Out of the corner of my eye I catch a glimpse of Kent's fist just in time to move out of the way. The force of the blow and his lack of balance almost cause him to fall out into the street, not like a drunk dancing but like a drunk drinking. I'm quickly on my feet backing away, with my palms up facing him, a position black people usually find themselves in when dealing with law enforcement. Kent regains his balance, and begins to walk toward me. He takes two steps before his hands go to his knees and he's forced to sit again. I take this brief cease of not-so-friendly fire as a chance to speak,

"Mr. Kent have you ever heard of people making great strides of innovation in art, or math, or science, not because they were taught or trained, but because they were naturally gifted?"

I don't expect an answer but I see Kent turn his head in my direction which at least gives me hope that he's listening while gathering strength for his next punch. I continue.

"And since these naturally gifted people don't know the rules, they don't know that they're breaking them. Without knowing it, they truly understand what many learned and trained people never will, 'to a free mind there really aren't any rules.'"

This line seems to resonate with Kent on some level. I see his head turn to the side as if digesting what I've said.

"Children live in this space of, knowing but not knowing, better and more fully than most, Mr. Kent. You ever wonder what a child or for that matter an adult could or would do, if you never told them they couldn't do it? Maybe Jesus walked on water because he believed he could, and no one ever told him he couldn't. Perhaps Peter sank for the opposite reasons.

"When I was a kid, back when Midas was still just a story in a book, I had a friend that saw a ghost one night. He nervously told me about it one day after school. I don't know what prompted it or why. Maybe he just needed to tell someone, and I was the closest someone to him when the need to talk about it could no longer be denied. Whatever the reason I remember that when he began to speak his eyes looked off into the distance as if still in the moment, and goosebumps covered his skin. He described his experience in great detail. He was home, in the middle of the night, walking the hall from his bedroom to the bathroom. Something that even at our young age he'd felt like he'd done a million times. He'd dreamt that night, that he was in the bathroom relieving himself. Something he'd also done quite a bit, but with the occasional unfortunate result. His mother gave him a stern talking to, that was accompanied by a statement that was more threat than promise if he ever did it again. It was the memory of that threat, and not the dream itself, that woke him and had him traveling the well worn path to the bathroom that night.

"As he told it, it was summer and the hall leading from his room to the bathroom seemed much colder than it should have been. He said he remembered rubbing his arms with his hands to ward of the chill but being so tired and desperate to relieve his bladder that he thought nothing of it. He began rubbing his arms with is hands as he recalled the story. Watching him I imagined it must have felt like fall beneath the stars more than summer in the only home he'd ever known. The comfortable, soft carpet could have just as well have been a canopy of fallen leaves. He then said, his eyes began to squint as he looked into a light just up ahead. He assumed someone had left the light on in the bathroom but this light was different. The light from the bathroom wouldn't be originating from the middle of the hall, and slowly moving toward him.

"I asked him what the light looked like and he said that it pulsed as if it had, no as if it was, a heartbeat. He described it as a blue, that maybe even leaned toward purple, and as bright as a TV left on after everyone has fallen asleep. He rubbed his eyes and stared intently at the ever approaching light until his vision cleared he said. And then a figure emerged. A figure! He said he could see it as clear as he was seeing me. The figure was a man, well dressed and seemingly oblivious to my friend's presence. The man looked distressed. He moved slowly and steadily forward but his feet which were several inches above the floor, never moved. The figure looked around, shook his head, checked a pocket watch and continued slowly floating toward my friend. My friend was frozen, his feet were stuck to the floor like rodents on old sticky paper traps. His voice had done what his feet couldn't, it had run away and was probably hiding back in the bedroom beneath the bed. The figure floated to him, and through him with no hesitation. 'He never seemed aware of my presence and continued on through the closed door just behind me,' my friend said.

"He said he'd pissed himself right there in the hall, laid on the floor, pulled himself into a ball and was like that until his mother discovered him the next morning. When he told her of all that he'd seen, all that had taken place. She said he'd walked in his sleep, had a nightmare and pissed himself. She kept her promise/threat and spanked

167

him for dirtying her floor and soiling his underwear. He was told to tell no one about this ghost foolishness. He swore to me that day that it wasn't foolishness or fantasy, that it had really happened. He'd really seen the things he'd seen.

"When I asked him about it a week later he said he'd told his father and his father had reiterated what his mother had told him and given him a beating also, this time with a belt, for wetting the floor. He said he wasn't sure it was for wetting the floor or to drive home the point about what he hadn't seen. When I asked him about it two weeks after that he said the therapist his parents had him seeing told him he couldn't live in a world of make believe. Had told him the man in the hall was Alice's white rabbit, and the toilet represented the way to wonderland. Whatever that meant.

"When I asked him about the ghost in the hall a month on he said, 'It never happened.' He said he'd walked in his sleep, had a nightmare, and pissed himself. I could tell, by the tears in the corners of his eyes and the painted on Cheshire Cat grin, that he was trying to convince himself that this lie was in fact the truth. I'm sure if I'd have asked him about it twenty years down the road he'd have told me he'd never pissed himself, didn't have parents, and had never read Alice in Wonderland."

With a voice that seems desperate for a bottle of water or a shot of vodka or a little of both Kent says, "What the hell does this *Goosebumps*, Creepypasta, campfire story shit have to do with me?"

I don't know if I'm more surprised to hear Kent curse or to know that *Goosebumps* books, Creepypasta tales and even camp fires are still a thing.

"When I was a boy, Mr. Kent, my mother gave me the book *The Alchemist* by Paulo Coelho. Are you familiar with it?"

He says nothing, the cut is completely healed and so he lets his eyes rest in disbelief on his fingers again.

"It's a beautiful tale Mr. Kent and you should definitely read it if you haven't but suffice it to say the protagonist, a boy named Santiago, a boy chasing his personal legend, at some points runs into an alchemist. As I'm sure you're well aware, alchemy is an ancient science that lives somewhere between physics, the metaphysical, and magic. An alchemist can do many things, many wonderful things, but the thing they were most known and revered for was their ability to create a philosopher's stone. The philosopher's stone is a substance that can be used to turn base metals into precious metals. Mercury into silver. Lead into gold.

"As a kid I became obsessed with the idea I scoured the *Blanket*, it was called the Internet back then, for articles about the philosopher's stone. I was led to tales from Arthurian legend, artistic renderings by Joseph Wright, Zoroastrianism, Jabir Ibn Hayyan and his red sulfur, Saint Thomas Aquinas, and I even read tales of Adam receiving the philosopher's stone in the Garden of Eden from God himself. 'Who told thee that thou wast naked?'"

"I was a kid powered by belief, desire, and no knowledge of the rules. I set out, in my bedroom, to create the great work, the magnum opus. I wish I could tell you what I did. It was madness, mixed with mysticism, mixed with the most rudimentary chemistry set ever. Somewhere in the midst of it all, a few things that were clearly not meant to mix, like skinheads, Geraldo Rivera, and metal chairs, did."

"Who?"

"Geraldo Riv... Never-mind. It doesn't matter."

"Stop saying things that don't matter."

"Agreed, agreed Mr. Kent. Well, the result was explosive, and not just explosive in thought but there was an actual explosion. I was knocked to the floor and a fine red dust floated in the air above my head like a *vmoji*. It wasn't just over my head though, it was everywhere and covering almost everything in my room. I cleaned up and collected as much as I could, and told my mother a story that still got my ass beat. Parents were big on beating asses back then. The red dust though! It was what Jabir Ibn Hayyan had described. One day when alone I went to the kitchen grabbed a piece aluminum foil and covered it with the red dust. Nothing happened. I put the piece of dust covered foil over the eye of the stove and heated it. Nothing. I massaged it into the foil. Nothing. It hadn't worked. I hadn't created a philosopher's stone, or so I thought."

"Until the fight at school?" Kent balled his fists into tight and ready bludgeons." Until Preston punched you in your face!" I could hear in Kent's voice the menace and desire to, in this moment, be Preston. I ignored the tone, focused on the content and continued,

"Yes. Exactly. As near as I can surmise I had in my ignorance, and unbridled belief in self, achieved the magnum opus! It hadn't worked as I'd thought it would have though. Ain't that life? The explosion had filled the room with the red dust. It was on my hands, in my hair, in my lungs and in my stomach. I'd inhaled and swallowed the philosopher's stone."

"And?"

"The philosopher's stone turns base metals into precious ones"

"... This is like pulling teeth. Get to it already."

"Anyone that lived in or was born in Flint, Michigan after 2014 has a certain level of lead toxicity in their bodies. It's in their blood. That day playing around as a kid, I turned lead into gold, but not in the way I'd intended. The lead in my body and blood stream transformed itself, and me. You're from Flint too Mr. Kent."

"But I didn't..."

"Your coffee back at the cafe."

"... The cayenne? I didn't order any cayenne in my coffee and they didn't put any in it did they?"

"No. No they didn't."

Kent, his fists balled and trembling, starts to make his way to his feet. I keep talking while assuring I'm not within an arms length of him.

"I'm not immortal Mr. Kent I will live for a very long time but not forever. The Midas mantle must be passed on."

"What makes you think I want it!"

"Sometimes it's not about what we want but what is needed. People of color have always needed Midas. They haven't always had him but now that they do they, literally, can't afford to lose him."

With unnatural speed Kent crosses the distance between us and takes another swing at me. I easily avoid his untrained attack. By the time he swings again I'm already behind him. He turns and takes a third swipe at my face. When his fist reaches where my jaw should be I'm standing beside him almost as if I teleported. He punches and I evade several more of his blows. Preston he is not, nor am I still the little boy staring at the florescent lights. Kent finally realizes the futility of his efforts.

"How are you doing this!?"

"You can do it too, with some training. The gold not only gives me, us, long life and accelerated healing, it also augments our speed and strength."

He's breathing heavily. He grabs at his chest and begins to gasp as his lungs struggle for breath.

"You haven't been breathing properly. Your muscles and lungs require more oxygen when you accelerate your speed, energy, and exertion. I can teach you that too. While you're catching your breath, listen.

"I didn't know what was going to happen Mr. Kent. I admit that. I've only tried once before to give someone the red dust and it had unfortunate and tragic consequences. Consequences that have haunted my life every day since. I didn't truly understand how much the elevated levels of lead contributed to the making of 'Midas.' I thought back then that anyone given the red dust with normal levels of iron in their blood would transmute. Not true. You, however. You had what I believed to be the right make up; the right combination of lead toxin, immune system resiliency, and strength to endure the process. You were like *Goldilocks* in the fables, just right.

"And what if you were wrong?" Kent, clearly still laboring, takes a knee.

"If I was wrong this day would have ended with an unfortunate and tragic consequence, and my life would be doubly haunted."

"... so you stripped me of my choice and almost stripped me of my life!?"

Who told thee that thou wast naked?

Chapter 11 | Flint. Led

In 2011, ancient history for people today, the city of Flint, Michigan declared itself to be in a financial crisis, in the grips of a financial emergency and on the brink of bankruptcy. Just sixty years before, in the 1950s, Flint was an affluent city filled with industry, money, resources, and promise. Then the de-industrialization came, followed by business divestment. On the heels of those two major blows was white flight as Caucasians pulled up stakes and left for whiter pastures. The final nail in Flint's economic coffin was the closing of the General Motors plant.

Flint went from the homecoming queen, wearing her tiara, gown and push up bra while waving a gloved hand at all of the boys she would soon be rejecting in the bleachers, to a thinning meth madame, in ill-fitting daisy dukes, a halter top stained with vomit, offering two-for-one specials on blow jobs. In 2014 the Governor of Michigan, Rick Snyder, and his cronies, in an effort to appear to help Flint but mostly enrich themselves decided to save a dollar or two wherever they could. The place where rich and powerful people have always and historically felt comfortable saving a dollar or two million is at the expense of poor people, and especially poor people of color. So in April of 2014 a decision was made to move the Flint, Michigan water source from Lake

Huron and the Detroit River to the Flint River. This decision along with several severe acts of negligence resulted in the lead contamination of the water supply of a major U.S. City. Within nine months residents of Flint began complaining about severe health issues connected to using and consuming the tap water. People began bringing bottles of brown murky water poured straight from their home taps to city officials and asking if they'd drink it. None did. Some residents even filmed video where they were able to hold a match to the tap, turn the water on, and the water would catch fire. You needed water, to extinguish the water.

Remember that thing about white flight? Flint by then was a mostly black city though so the health concerns, and outcry over murky and flammable water, went mostly ignored. National health agencies eventually stepped in, Rick Snyder apologized, Flint's mayor Dayne Walling who drank a glass of, supposed, tap water on local television got his stomach pumped I would suppose. The damage was done. It was estimated that upwards of 12,000 children had been exposed to, and had their bodies compromised and contaminated by, the heavy metal neurotoxin.

So much posing and so much posturing and so much finger pointing ensued but the problem never was truly 100% rectified. If you go to Flint today you'll find traces of lead in the water and you'll also find a population of people that did the impossible; their bodies learned to mitigate and manage the lead. All reports said, there is no safe level of lead that can enter the body. Those reports were right. The history of black people in America though is a history of doing what is said can't be done; it is making gourmet meals out of Master's table scraps, or turning old dusty records into the most profitable music genre on the planet. The bodies of the people of Flint learned to process, store, and alleviate the effects of lead. Over 250 years ago I accidentally discovered how to turn that lead into gold.

Chapter 12 | Ruby. Con

I think these thoughts of history and discovery as I look at the sky. The sun is setting. The purple is pushing back into the horizon and the red coming forward like a midnight tide. When the ruby gives up its seat to the budding gold, and the gold dissolves to nothing, night will stretch, yawn, and begin to stand to its full height. We need to be inside soon. To be out and exposed once the moon's rays reach down through the clouds and crown the tops of our heads will bring with it its own set of problems. Kent is angry, and rightly so, but we have larger issues afoot.

"Mr. Kent let me help you. We should ... We need to make our way indoors. The adrenaline in your system is sapping your energy in ways that must have you feeling like you've just run a marathon. Let me help you up."

Kent lifts his head, his brow wet with sweat, and nods in the affirmative. His legs begin to tremble and give out. His eyes find the ground, which I'm sure must appear to be rising quickly to meet him. I cross the distance between us and scoop my arm under his. Just as quickly as I do this he spins using my momentum against me, pins my arm behind my back with his left hand and grabs me roughly by the throat with his right.

Thank God he's not at his full strength or he would have had a legitimate chance at crushing my windpipe. Even at what is probably a quarter of what his strength will be his hold on my throat is formidable. I could force his hand, flood my system with adrenaline and pull his fingers away from my neck. I could, in a display of dominance, assert my place as alpha, but I don't. The urge to do it is all ego, and all wrong. This moment doesn't call for strength, but sacrifice. I am the three Hebrew boys not bound and cast forcefully into Nebuchadnezzar's fire but willfully walking into the furnace knowing that another awaits me there.

I don't struggle against him. I relax into his grip, not like a man in death's grasp, but like a child falling into the fullness of his mother's life-giving embrace. I relax and feel the pressure of his grip growing. He too can feel it. His eyes go wide, and to his own fingertips as they push deeper and deeper into my flesh. I feel the hesitation in him. It's one thing to be so mad that you feel that you could kill someone. It's another thing to kill someone.

"You're right to be angry Mr. Kent. I have deceived you, but unfortunately we've crossed the Rubicon," I say, my voice compressed and strained.

"I used to be married Midas."

"I know..."

"I used to be married!"

He raises his voice and tightens his grip as a warning for me not to interrupt.

"I loved my wife deeply. Where you'd lost love, in the halls of KCJH, is where I found it. You know that box you said your heart was hidden in, until you met Bes? In my life that box was opened when I was thirteen. Lisa, my ex-wife, and I were in the same homeroom in 8th grade. I'd stared at her for what felt like half my life and finally worked up the nerve to say something. I shot at her heart with the clumsy musket ball of a boy in junior high and missed the target by a mile."

Kent's grip eases as he continues to speak. His eyes look like mine must have when I was telling him about Bes, Khadijah, and Emily. His body and voice are here with me but his eyes and mind are years and miles away.

"In the summer between 8th and 9th grade she ended up staying at her aunt's house which was only three blocks from mine. I ran into her at the park accidentally on purpose almost every day that summer. Fresh air and fireflies have a way of leaving warm friends where once stood cold shoulders and steely glares. We spent long days in what felt like the shortest summer of my life sitting in the grass, talking and laughing. The whole world had gone hyper-digital by that time and there we were, as analog as it gets. My first kiss was in that park, with Lisa. The sky looked much like it does now."

My eyes are already on the sky. Keeping tabs on the pure, menacing darkness that is just now beginning to stalk us from where the sky and earth meet.

179

"Summer ended as all eventually do. Lisa left her aunt's, went home, and I thought ... well I thought we had something. I didn't know what we had but we'd shared so much time, and fresh air, and a kiss. It felt like the beginning of things. A start. When school started and I saw her in the halls I quickly discovered that I was not playing the part of Michael in the play *Dream Girl Dream* with its happy ending. No, rather I was Sandy and she was Danny, from *Grease*. But there would be no *You're The One That I Want* or *We Go Together* sang as we danced arm in arm through the town fair.

"I tried again a couple of years later in high school and though I'd grown, my understanding of women and grasp of what to say to them hadn't at all. I stumbled over words and mumbled my affections. I then watched as boys with words as smooth as oil covered eggshells asked her out. She went on dates with those boys and later in the locker room they would tell half truths and whole lies about sweaty fumblings in the back seats of cars. I even fought one whose lies grew beyond what I could tolerate."

Kent's nostrils flare and his nose wiggles like Elizabeth Montgomery casting spells.

"Let me just tell you, everyone's nose doesn't bring forth liquid gold when broken. I can also tell you with great certainty that a broken nose, and a failed, unasked for, honor defense doesn't mean the girl you've been crushing on since 8th grade won't go to the prom with the asshole that challenged her honor and broke your nose."

He lets me go, and he flops down again on the curb. The sky transforms into a burnt orange as it mixes the fading ruby with an emerging gold, and the coming black. The desperate need to seek shelter dances in my feet but I calm my nerves, take a seat beside Mr. Kent and listen. My eyes can't help but peek at the ever darkening sky as Kent continues.

"Locker rooms have amazing acoustics. Did you know that?"

I don't answer. I assume the question is rhetorical and only after the pause lasts long enough to become uncomfortable do I understand that he's waiting for an answer.

"... Yes. I've certainly heard the stories of old music groups from the 1960s and 70s honing their signature sound in the echo of an empty locker room. For instance..."

Kent cuts me off, letting me know he wants an answer not a thesis.

"The walls, the tiles, the metal lockers they bounce sound around like it's that new game everyone is obsessed with on their *iPP*. Pong."

I would tell him how old Pong is but it seems beside the point.

"Bryant, the prick that broke my nose continued to break my heart with the tale of his prom night tryst with my girl."

"'My girl...' That's part of problem..." I interject.

I know my voice is taboo in this moment. My job is to listen, not to speak. I see Kent's hand reform into an open claw, that looks more like a mouth desperate to lock onto my throat. I tempt the fates and continue.

"The problem men have faced for time immemorial is thinking we can possess these women, these creatures of beauty, strength, and independence. The folly is in thinking they're ours and not their own. We try to rob them of their agency. The agency we look to steal may molt away for a moment, but it will over time grow back; and what grows back will undoubtedly be born of greater strength and independence. I know this because I tried Mr. Kent. I tried and I failed most miserably."

Kent continues as if I never spoke a word,

"I accepted my loss and moved on. I dated in college. Fell in and out of love. Fell in and out of women's beds. Fell into a degree in journalism and moved to Atlanta. I was at Lounge One Twelve Hundred drinking too much too fast when she walked in. She could have just as well been the ghost your friend saw in the hall. I thought I was hallucinating. I thought I was drunk out of my mind. Lisa? It couldn't be. She looked just like she did in high school, but grown.

"I ordered a drink and as I approached her found myself unconsciously rubbing the bridge of my nose where it had been broken all those years ago. You're right, the skin remembers.

"It was eighth grade summertime all over again. We were in the middle of a packed club, and in the middle of an empty grass field at the same time. The world dissolved and it was just us. The club closed and they eventually kicked us out. We spent the rest of the night sitting in my vehicle talking, catching up. Maybe it was because we were grown and had put away childish things, but she was the same in all the ways I liked and different in ways that made me like her all the more. We dated for a couple of years, told each other as much as two people could in that time and then married on a summer day much like the one we'd shared our first kiss on all those year ago. It was perfect. Then, summer ended, like all summers do.

"I hadn't been working at *Amazon World* for very long when Kim started."

I let my eyes leave the sky for a moment and find Kent. He is staring at the ground, this time not because he fears it will slap him in the forehead but out of what appears to be ... shame.

"Kim? Kim from the coffee shop?"

"The same. We both began working as journalists at roughly the same time. The truth Mr. M..."

Ah, I was Mr. M again. I don't know what to think of it. He continues his thought and I try not be lost in mine.

"The truth is there was a part of me that still felt like that discarded kid with the broken nose in the locker room. There was a part of that had never gotten over that, and was waiting for her to choose someone else, someone instead of me, again. I had never expressed that to Lisa not while dating and not while married."

"Why not?"

Now I abandon the sky completely and give Kent my undivided attention. We'll just have to deal with whatever comes with the night, when it comes.

"Why not? All the classic reasons, machismo, pride, all that shit that comes along with society telling you to be a man!

"One night while working late with Kim, all that shit found us in a *SharedBnB* in a sweaty heap. She told me she'd been interested in me since day one at the *Amazon World* and couldn't believe I was still single."

"Wait, she didn't know?"

"...No, and I'd never said. Unknowingly I'd... I'd .... well that isn't true is it because on some level I had to know. On some level I'd made a choice and lied to myself about knowledge of that choice. I'd never once spoken about Lisa around Kim or even suggested that I wasn't single."

Kent takes a deep breath, one because he is really dealing with some things he probably needs to be working out with a mental health professional, and two perhaps truly, unknowingly, he is walking alongside me as I steer us to a safe house, or as they would say today a *Clandestine DomiCas,* of mine. Right around the time of him calling me Mr. M I noticed that he was lost in the story. In being so absorbed his defenses were down and so when I stood he stood too, almost as if by reflex, and when I began to walk, he began to walk beside me.

I just keep listening and talking, and hope he doesn't notice until I've put a locked door between us and the night.

"But your wedding ring?"

"We never wore them. Lisa and I felt we were above such archaic signs of ownership. When people who knew we were married and didn't wear rings asked us, 'But how will people know you're married?' We'd always laugh and answer, 'We'll just tell them.' But I didn't. I didn't tell Kim I was married."

"Not even then? Not even when you're both in a sweaty heap on borrowed sheets and she's stating clearly that she believes you're single?"

"Not even then. Or the next time or the time after that. This is what they don't tell you about your heart and the box. There's not just one box. Your heart contains different boxes that can be opened in different ways. No one person can open all the boxes. Someone can open many, sometimes most, but not all. It's the unopened boxes that get you."

"What do you mean?"

"I mean, if your heart contains a dozen boxes and your wife, partner, whoever, opens 9 of them, then that's most of the boxes. Then one day someone opens the tenth box. It's just one box! But you've never experienced what's inside of it. It's shiny and new and the one box seems to be better than those other nine boxes that were opened so long ago. You'll forget the nine, because of the one, but in time the one will lose its luster and you'll remember how much you loved, wanted and needed that nine. And..."

"And?"

"The person who opened those boxes may have put the lids back on. May have put them back on the shelf where they were found with no intention of opening them again. Ever.

"Kim and I saw each other for almost a year. I lied to my wife, and my mistress, for almost a year. Opportunity after opportunity after opportunity to tell the truth presented itself and I lied to them, and myself, over and over again. I'd say, I can't tell them. I'm trying to protect them from the pain that knowing will surely cause. I love them both too much to hurt either like that. The truth is, selfishly, the kid in the locker room with the broken nose, wanted them both. He felt like he deserved them both. I was protecting nothing but what I wanted."

"How did she find out?"

"Who?"

"Whoever found out first."

"How do wives always find out? Too many late nights. Too many stories that don't add up. Coming home from a long night of working smelling like soap, too many times. You didn't have to be Maximus Platinum P.I. to figure that one out. All you needed were two fairly well-functioning eyes, and a nose for a brand of soap not found in the house. Lisa had those and then some. When she put all the pieces together and presented me with the completed puzzle. I, for once, didn't lie. I told her everything, all the way back to 8th grade."

"And she said?"

I can see the safe house we're only a couple of blocks away.

"She thanked me for my honesty and moved back in with her parents the next day. It was the beginning of the end."

"Did you tell Kim?"

"I did. She said I should have told her before the first sweaty heap. She said she was a big girl and could choose for herself, and that she may well have chosen me even with me being married. But now we'd never know because I'd robbed her of that decision. I told her that Lisa knew and had moved back in with her parents. Kim and I sat in silence for a while and then she said, 'Yes.'"

As we approach the door I figure I've missed some part of the story. I was so distracted I probably hadn't heard everything. Yes? Yes to what? Had he asked her a question and it gotten past me.

"Yes to what you're wondering," Kent says.

"Yes! Actually I was."

"You thought you'd missed something. In all your turning about and leading me to this door we find ourselves in front of, you thought your mind had wandered too far. I wasn't blindly following you Mr. M. I chose to follow you. I could see the real fear in your eyes as you looked at the sky, and from corner to corner as if the monster that lived beneath your childhood bed had come to life and was about to find us sitting on a curb. I'm mad, but I'm not stupid. I recognize real terror when I see it. So I chose, just like Kim chose that night. She chose to continue seeing me. She chose to, with full knowledge of my situation, continue to date me. The problem was I'd chosen too. I hadn't brought Kim there to confess and move forward with her. I'd brought her there to confess, end the almost year-long thing we had, and then see if I could get my wife back. That's why her *grips* go unhandled and why I never reach out or *slap* back. I've been doing everything I can to get Lisa back and leave Kim alone."

It's only after we enter the *DomiCas* and I lock the door behind us that I can begin to relax a bit. I lean my back against the door and breath for what feels like the first time in at least ten minutes. I walk to the window and look out through the blinds. The last of the caterpillar-ing grey dusk has butterflied into genuine night. I see the mint green car from earlier, the one that almost appears to be glowing, slowly round the block. I close the blinds and engage all security measures. I hear the fridge open and close and realize Kent has found the kitchen. When I walk in he's drinking water like a man newly rescued from a remote desert.

"Well... well at least she thinks you're SGSSL now. So crisis averted?"

"She doesn't. She's gripped me three times since the cafe to say, nice try Clay. Let's figure us out. Let's talk, clothing optional."

"Well damn ... what's her number again?"

Kent cracks a smile in spite of himself.

"You're no myth Mr. M. You're just a man."

"I've never said anything to the contrary."

"Where's the bathroom?"

"Down the hall and on the right."

Kent makes his way to the lavatory and I pull up the security cameras around the house. More cars have arrived and now red turbaned men and women are making their way to the front porch and back door. I see a flash of red move in the hall out of the corner of my eye. I sprint so quickly toward the movement I almost run over Kent who is standing in the hall, staring at the pictures that line the walls and drying his hands with a red hand towel. I don't remember having red hand towels here but then again I haven't been to this particular *DomiCas* in ... longer than I care to remember.

Kent pulls one of the pictures down from the wall and I feel a churning in my stomach. My every instinct is to snatch the framed portrait from his hand.

"Khadijah?"

"... Yes."

"She's certainly as beautiful as you described. On the way to the bathroom I peeked into what I imagine is your den. Excuse my nosiness but you knew I was a reporter before, and after all, you apparently gold roofied me. I noticed that there is a splintered chair, reconstructed and laid out on the floor like the bones of a dinosaur. That's the chair from Waukegan, the chair that Bes..."

"Yes."

"On your wall is a frame filled with what appear to be shorn off locs. Emily?"

"Yes."

"This isn't a *Clandestine DomiCas*. This is your, home."

"It once was. Now it's a museum to some of my greatest failures."

Kent looks at all of the pictures of Khadijah that line the wall. In some she's very young and others clearly much older.

"You lived here with, Khadijah. This where you two made your life together."

I say nothing.

"You've said a lot about her but you have been very careful not to talk about how she passed. I take it, it wasn't old age."

"It wasn't."

I take the photo gently from his hand, like its a priceless ancient artifact, and run my fingers across her face. That smile. That smile used to greet me in the morning and let me know everything would be okay.

"Whoever we're running from. Whatever drove us so desperately to this *DomiCas*. They or it killed her?"

I place the portrait back on wall. I see her crying, smiling, laughing, drinking tea, our backs against the floor staring at the ceiling and talking.

"No Mr. Kent," I carefully center the frame before turning, looking him in the eye and saying, "I killed her."

Chapter 13 | South. East

I walk past Kent, back into the kitchen, and sit down. Kent follows in silence, takes the seat opposite me at the kitchen table, and waits. It doesn't take long.

"I've said before that time is not what we think it to be. Well let me say now that time is simultaneously not what we think it to be, and everything we know it to be. It's doesn't always move in the straight line we imagine. When it does, however, it moves with all due speed, haste, and purpose. In my life time has had on its dancing shoes and waltzed forward and even moonwalked backward. In Khadijah's life, time was wearing track shoes and running straight ahead to an inevitable conclusion."

"Death. You mean that time was moving toward her pending demise."

"A demise that felt too soon for both she and I. She was tired of time running, and wanted to stand still beside me. She wanted time to waltz and moonwalk for her too. I did as well. And... and so..."

"You said you tried the red dust before and failed. Khadijah."

My face feels flush, feels hot. Time stands still.

"Don't tell me half the story Mr. M. I'm not here for the Cliff's Notes. I'm here for the novel. Did you try with Khadijah?"

"I didn't offer. She asked."

"Just because you don't offer a kid rat poisoning is it okay to give it to them if they ask?"

"Khadijah was not a child and what she was asking for was not poison. She was asking for what Ponce de León searched for, and what some report that Alexander the Great found. She was asking for the fountain of youth. We were in love Mr. Kent. We just wanted that to never end, or at least not end for a couple of centuries. I don't know if there is anything you love that much Mr. Kent. I don't know if you love Lisa like..."

"Don't!"

Kent slams his fists against the table and it almost splinters. His voice, forceful in a way I've not yet heard from him, seems to bounce off of every wall and shake the very foundation of the house. I proceed a bit more thoughtfully.

"All I'm saying is, if you do, if there is someone you could spend the rest of your life with, and know that the mutual happiness you'd experience would be just south of heaven and east of Eden. Wouldn't you risk everything for that? Didn't Adam risk everything for Eve?"

I watch as he genuinely considers the question.

193

"Khadijah and I did. We thought it was worth it. We risked everything."

Kent sits back and responds, his eyes hard and seemingly on the verge of tears.

"And how'd that go? Because from what I hear you killed her? That instead of extending your time together you cut it unnecessarily short."

"I didn't know."

"You didn't know what? You act like you know everything!"

"No one knows anything until they know it! You don't know fire is hot until you've been burned by it. I didn't understand the rare qualities needed to make the red dust work, until I knew."

"And when did you know?"

"Today Mr. Kent. I didn't know that Midas could be reborn until today."

"We'll get into how fucked up that is in a second. What happened Midas? What happened on the day you gave Khadijah the red dust?"

I look at the gold halo around Kent's grey irises and begin to tell him, and you, the whole story.

Chapter 14 | Grave. Decisions

"Making love to someone you care about with the entirety of your everything can be like a truth serum. It can make you speak of things you'd never thought you would. It can cause you to promise things you're not entirely sure you can deliver."

"Yeah, I once promised Kim a *DomiCas* on the beaches of Pisceria."

"That's a lofty promise. She must have..."

"She did. And also loft, *DomiCas*, I see what you did there Mr. M. Now, as you were saying."

"I was saying, that you can get lost if you find yourself in the right arms. One night as we lay in bed, after making love, I'd told Khadijah the story of *The Alchemist*, of Santiago, of the naïve invention of a child in Flint. I told her about the red dust and what it had done to, and for, me. I hadn't meant to tell her but I couldn't, or rather didn't, want to keep secrets from her anymore. I wanted her to know me. All of me."

"Did she believe you?"

"She didn't."

"Did you do the whole cut yourself and bleed gold thing?"

"I did."

"Did she wonder why you two were living in this, moderate at best, *DomiCas* when you were literally hemorrhaging money?"

"She didn't."

"She didn't!? She must have really loved you."

"She did. I explained to her why I was aging so slowly. I told her about the more-than-a-century I'd been alive, and that I had easily at least two more centuries ahead of me. She asked me if there was more."

"More truth? More to the story?"

"No. More of the red dust. She asked if she could walk beside me into mythology and lore. If she could be the Psyche to my Eros. At the time she was fifty but could have easily passed for a woman ten years younger. I was one hundred and twelve but only looked to be twenty seven and maybe not even that. Black don't crack is an idiom that has traveled the centuries and held true. More true for some than others. Today they say, 'Noir Don't Wrinkle Nor Scar,' it's clunky but I get it. Khadijah was fifty years in age but to me all I could see was that same woman I'd met in that campus coffee shop. The one that smelled like honey and roses.

"When she looked at herself in the mirror though, she saw a new wrinkle here, more grays there. Then I'd stand beside her in that same mirror looking no differently than I had fifteen years ago. And the truth was I'd look the same thirty years on, and she'd be nearing death.

"She had already begun to feel self-conscious when we went out together. Older women either looked at her gleefully like, 'You go girl,' for being out with this boy toy; or shook their heads in judgment and disapproval of what appeared to be a May-December romance. I mean it was, but I was December. Older men looked at her with great curiosity, their single arched eyebrow wondering, what is she doing to keep a man that young interested? Whatever the reaction it was clear that for Khadijah the movement of time had begun to feel like a train moving swiftly on a track she was tied to. She held me tightly that night in bed, and asked me to free her from the track, save her from the train."

"But you didn't know if you could."

"I didn't know, not for certain, but I felt confident that I could."

"If there is one thing the people of earth don't suffer from, it's a lack of confidence."

"We decided that in a week's time we'd do it. We'd usher her into my world."

"Why a week? Did you not have the red dust right there and then?"

"It is never far from me. It wasn't a question of attaining the materials but a matter of preparation. I told Khadijah of the many people and roles I'd played throughout history. I showed her where I kept caches of deeds, bearer bonds, gold, and currencies for different nations and planets. Some was held in safe deposit boxes, some in private safes and some buried in the ground like the pirates of old. I showed her as much as I could in a week."

"And what did she tell you and show you about herself over those seven days?"

"She spoke mostly of love and light. She spoke of joy, hope, and possibility. She also spoke of acceptance."

"How so?"

"... She said..."

I am rarely at a loss for words. I guess even now the words aren't lost just hard to find. I want to hide my face in the crook of my arm like the adults in the park counting to ten. I want to scream olly-olly-oxen-free to the words, so that they can know they are safe to come out. I find the words. They're like your misplaced keys, in the last place you look, but right where you left them. I continue.

"She said, we must accept what happens. We agreed to open this door into the unknown together and must accept what's on the other side of that door, no matter what. Whether it be her hand in mine for a piece of forever, or her hand in God's for all of eternity, we must accept it."

"So she told you to... she..."

"She said by the morning we'd either be together in this world or she'd be waiting for me in the next, but we must accept the outcome either way."

"Man, that's high stakes."

"The highest."

"... And then the week was up."

I close my eyes to stop the tears.

"Indeed. The week was up. I am a man with all the time in the world at my disposal and yet that week felt like but a day; but an hour. It flew by, and what we'd agreed to do was at hand. Mr. Kent my transformation was accidental, like Bruce Banner in the old Hulk *EyeSeeViews*. Khadijah and I decided that hers would have intention, direction, and ceremony. It was after all the birthing of a new life in many ways.

"Many cultures and religions believe in life after death, the ancient Egyptians, Buddhists, the practice of Hindu samsara, and so on. We borrowed heavily from their ceremonies and rituals, and those of other mystics, religions, and philosophies. We filled the living room, just through there, with candles."

I point just beyond the kitchen door.

"On the floor was a white sheet covered in symbols of life: the ankh, the cross, the Tao, the Yin and Yang. Symbols from Chinese heretics, Zoroastrians, Jewish mystics, Islamic Sufis and many more.

199

Khadijah entered looking as lovely, and as nervous, as a bride on her wedding day. She smiled at me, wide, her cheekbones forcing her eyelids into straight lines. She wore a red, sheer, floor length robe. The red symbolizing blood and birth. She walked to me and we embraced. We held each other long and lovingly. Then she took a breath, that felt like one of resolve, let me go and laid down on the sheet. She began to laugh when she looked up and noticed that I'd pinned to the ceiling a picture of two coffee cups with our names on them sitting atop a master's level business text. I told here that those things were there when we'd first met and they should be here for our reintroduction.

"She reached out for my hand and pulled me down on the sheet beside her. The room was filled with her favorite things: foods, music, books, letters, clothes, and pictures. We laid there in that womb of love and life, and just talked."

"Talked about what? About what might happen?"

"The things, positive and negative, that could happen were known. That night we let them be unspoken outcomes that lived in the breaths we held just a little too long between words. We didn't give them voice, or shape, or possibility. No, we talked about what our life together had been up to that point. We laughed at inside jokes. We cried about times we'd hurt each other, accidentally and on purpose. We were just being, us. Das and Khaj."

"Was she scared? Were you?"

"Terrified, the both of us I think, but trying to be strong for each other. I wanted to tell her that she didn't have to go through with it. I wanted to tell her that this could just be a weird night of sacrilegious sex, while surrounded by enough candles to burn Atlanta to the ground again. I wanted to tell her she was perfect and didn't need to change anything about herself. I'd take whatever time life allowed. Be it another hour, another year or another fifty years. I'd happily take it."

"Why didn't you tell her?"

"Because ... it was the truth but not the whole truth. The whole truth was that I'd have gladly taken those things but what I truly wanted was her by my side into a time beyond time."

"And you were willing to risk her life for that?"

"We both were."

"Yes... but you specifically. You had the red dust. It was your call. She couldn't make you give it to her so ultimately the choice was yours. You, were willing to risk her life for that?"

"I ... I ... I was."

"...what happened next?"

"Neither of us knew how much of the red dust was needed. So we went with what black grandmothers still use to dole out medicine, two tablespoons. We mixed it into a green tea with honey. She drank it and laid down, her head resting near the ankh. We talked until she drifted off to sleep. Her breathing was a steady note that you could tune

201

a piano to. Her chest rose and fell, like day into night. I watched her lovingly, and closely. Then, after about an hour, she woke with a deep gasp and sat straight up. Her eyes, wide and filled with tears, met mine. There was now a gold halo around her brown irises. A gold halo! She was like me. We'd done it.

"She said she felt different. The world looked different. I told her I couldn't wait to show her how different the world was truly. I was ready to show her the world as I'd seen it, through a lens that didn't fret over time. In my life I'd learned to stop running. I'd learned to walk. With her I'd learn to be still. I'd learn to be motionless in her love. She grabbed my face and kissed me, longingly, passionately. There were now tears in my eyes too. I couldn't help it. I couldn't hold it. I was overcome with emotion. We sat there with our foreheads pressed together and our hands framing each other's faces. I was just about to take her hand and lead her to the bedroom when I first noticed it."

"It?"

"Yes, it. The gold halo around her eyes was changing colors. She must have seen the concern in mine because she asked what was wrong. I didn't say anything. I didn't know what to say. I just watched as the halo went from gold, to rust, to a fiery red."

"... What does that? What did that mean?"

"I didn't know. I'd never done anything like this, or seen anything like that before. She began to sweat profusely and said that something felt, wrong. Then she let out a scream that, to this day, chills me to the bone to remember. It was a sound I'd never heard before and haven't heard since. She collapsed into my arms. Her eyes were on the poster on the ceiling when they rolled back into her head. I'll spare you the details of the convulsions, the spasms and the seizures that followed. I did everything I knew to do, but, I couldn't save her. I couldn't save her."

"Did you call for medical help?" Did you call a *MediDrone*? Did they have *MediDrones* then?"

"No they didn't. They had ambulances, and no, I didn't call."

"You, you just let her die there on the floor?"

"No, I didn't let her, anything. We'd agreed before hand. We'd agreed Mr. Kent."

"Damn that! Damn promises made in the light of day when the woman you love is dying in your arms in the dead of night. You loved her and you could have called for help! You, you might have even been able to save her. If it was Lisa..."

"It wasn't Lisa! I couldn't! It's not what she wanted!"

"I'm not sure any of this is what she truly wanted! She clearly just wanted to love and be loved. Was it what you wanted!? You said you'd take whatever time you could with her, a day, a year, fifty years."

"Or... an hour."

There is a long silence between us. Kent is fuming but composes himself. Kent asks his next question without looking at me,

"How did you explain her death to the coroner, to the authorities?"

I let his question wait. I see Khadijah's last moments, again. The tears, the pain, feeling her body go limp and then cold in my arms. Sitting there cradling her for hours. Screaming at the heavens, at myself. Then what happened next.

"I didn't explain her death to anyone."

Kent still doesn't look at me. I can still feel the white hot judgement and anger radiating from him. He could probably heat this whole *DomiCas* right now. He's so incredibly mad because though he's hearing my story, he's seeing Lisa and himself.

"You didn't tell anyone. How is that possible?"

"I have extensive land holdings Mr. Kent. I had Khadijah's body discreetly and carefully brought to a 10,000 acre, 15 square mile private nature preserve I own in south Georgia. It was there that I buried her with my own hands, in the center of the property."

"What in the entire fuck. This is..."

"Crazy. I know."

"I was thinking criminal."

"Crazy and criminal are first cousins."

Where before he wouldn't look at me, now he won't take his eyes off me. He's eyeing me like a kid that jumped the neighbor's fence only to discover a growling pit bull. He appears to be keeping a relatively safe distance and an inventory of where my hands are. Neither of us knows what to say now. We sit opposite each other in the kitchen, with more separating us than just the table. He shakes his head and briefly drops his head into his hands as if to say, I can't believe this. Which is exactly where we were at the beginning of our meeting. I sigh and continue.

"I visited her grave site often, almost daily, the first year. There were weeks when I wouldn't leave. I'd set up a tent and just be near her."

Kent straightens his back and I notice that while his head was in his hands he took the time and opportunity to turn on his AudRecorder. I've become newsworthy again, but this time as a murderer it seems. He's still clearly upset but also back in news reporter mode. Instead of introducing Midas to the world, I suspect he's now solving a cold case.

"Would you drive into the nature preserve? I mean how did you visit your wife's grave. Your wife that you had a hand in killing. Were there roads? This sounds very remote. Would you take a *HeloLyft* in? I mean the center of a 15 square mile nature preserve in south Georgia is not something you enter into without a plan."

He's repeating things I've said when he didn't have the recorder on. He's purposefully using phrases like, *had a hand in killing*. He doesn't want his readers, or the authorities, to be lost or confused. He's after a recorded confession.

"No Mr. Kent I'd hike in. I'd fill a backpack with gear, set aside the time, and hike in. It gave me time to think and reflect. It gave me moments to honor her spirit and arrive at her grave with the proper reverence. As I said, I did this with great regularity the first year. Then life has a way of making you live it. People needed my help. My visits went from less frequent to not at all. I felt guilty about it, but then realized that she had permanent residence in my heart and I didn't need a gravesite visit to be with her."

"I didn't need a gravesite visit to be with her, that's the stuff of *MindReading Greetings.* That's the stuff people say to forgive themselves, and free their conscience. Just be honest, you just stopped going to visit the grave of your wife because you didn't want to go. Maybe it was too hard. Maybe you'd met this Emily person by then. Whatever it is, name it, and spare me the placating platitudes."

His face is flush. I don't respond to his accusation. I continue.

"For a while, for the reason stated, I stopped going. Then on the four year anniversary of OUR decision, and her death, I went back to lay flowers on her grave. My intention was to lie down on the ground beside the flowers, look at the night sky and speak some of our favorite inside jokes to the stars."

"And?"

"And when I got there the grave had been desecrated."

"Desecrated? How?"

"The grave lay open. The body gone."

"Jesus!"

"Not quite."

"The body had been taken? Just when it seems this can't get any more insane, you pull another crazy rabbit out of the hat. What do you imagine happened? Animals? Did you not dig the grave deep enough? And animals had, I hate to say, dug her up? Do you think someone did it? Perhaps an enemy or rival group did it to hurt or threaten you?"

"No. It was nothing of the sort."

"Perhaps..."

I cut him off, "When I looked more closely I discovered that nothing, and no one, had as you say, dug her up. It was clear that someone, or some thing, had dug their way out."

"Wait, what?"

"Her body was gone Mr. Kent."

"I heard that part. Are you saying what I think you're saying?"

"What do you think I'm saying?"

"There's this old movie, you can watch it on Kudzu, it's called *Pet Cemetery*."

"I'm familiar with it."

"Are you saying she Pet Cemetery'd her way out of the grave?"

This attempt at humor is for his *MindReaders*, and in poor taste in my opinion. He wants to seem clever and witty to his audience when they sit down and explore their download over breakfast tomorrow.

"That's an incredibly insensitive way of describing what happened Mr. Kent. If you're asking me if Khadijah's body re-animated, the answer is ... yes. Somehow, at some point, she came back to life, and clawed her way out of the grave."

Kent lets out a scream through clenched teeth, squints and grabs his head. He's in clear pain. I know this look. It's usually what happens when an AudRecorder feeds back into the frontal lobe. There are cases where it's caused brain aneurysms. He taps at his temple desperately trying to turn the recorder off.

"Fuck! Did you do that!?"

"I didn't, but I should have."

"You agreed to be interviewed, Midas."

"So finally you believe! And this moved well beyond an interview some time ago. You know that."

Kent shakes his head furiously from side to side, and flexes his jaw as if he's been on a long flight that just landed and he's trying to get his ears to pop. His voice sounds exasperated and annoyed,

"You know this morning I was getting dressed to meet with you and as I was pulling on my shoes, through the window of my place, I saw my neighbors in some crazy, pretzel-ed, yoga, tantric, sexual position. There was a cat running feverishly around them and a small dog licking the woman's feet. Some sort of vermillion colored whipped cream was involved. Don't ask. I felt certain, that was going to be the oddest part of my day. Then I have a cup of coffee and it's you bleeding gold, then it's me bleeding gold, it's you killing your wife, and now your widow is an unaccounted for zombie roaming the land!?"

The hairs on the back of my neck stand up as a smell reminiscent of roses and honey and earth wafts into the room. A smell I know all too well. The honey sweet, but the flowers dead. Adrenaline floods my system. I flip the table, grab Kent, lift him from his stool and place him on his feet behind me, in one motion. I'm holding Kent tightly by the collar. I can feel him struggling but he's not strong enough yet to truly challenge me. I'm sure my true strength has come as a surprise to him. He knows he's much stronger, but now knows I'm stronger still. The kitchen table is on its side in front of us, like a barricade, facing the kitchen door leading to the living room. A voice drifts in slowly out of the darkness beyond the door.

"Unaccounted for Mr. Kent? Not at all. I'm here and everywhere, always."

She emerges slowly from the darkness, head first as if the shadows are breech birthing her before our eyes. Kent stops struggling, his gold haloed eyes go wide. I set him down and stand firmly between him and Khadijah.

Chapter 15 | Moon. Queen

What I didn't get to tell Mr. Kent, before we were so completely interrupted, is that four years after her death, when I returned and found the grave empty, I'd felt, no known, I was not alone. There was something else there. Something in the woods, in the brush, in the trees, in the shadows, in the black dark. Something watching me, studying me, stalking me. Something that smelled like honey and flowers and earth; that smelled like something sweet that had gone old. I ran after this feeling, this scent, this shadow, but as fast as I was it was either faster, or not there to begin with. If I was simply chasing my imagination made wind, or an uncatchable fragrant nothingness, then I was certain that the nothingness of my imagination was surely watching me. I stayed there, in the preserve, every day for the following seven months, only leaving to resupply. I stayed there searching for Khadijah's body, and whatever lived in the dark. I had to know if the two were the same.

Somewhere in the seventh month the feeling of being watched went away, the faceless movement in the shadows grew still, and the smell of something sweet that had gone old, no longer lived on the wind. I knew whatever it was, Khadijah or not, was gone, and so I left too with every intention of returning to suss it all out. Life has a way of making you live it, however. People needed my help and I stepped back into the world of Midas.

Time moved. A generation, for most, can feel like barely a fortnight to me. I blinked twice and a century had passed since Khadijah's death. In that time I'd underwritten revolutions, bailed out developing nations, and leveled playing fields in games where the odds were never supposed to be remotely even. I hadn't visited her grave since leaving all those years ago. I'd thought of her often but busied myself with the work of the world. Here, however, on the centennial of her passing I felt drawn to her, called to her grave.

I gathered my supplies and began hiking to where I knew her grave to be. The way time slows for me is nothing compared to the way it comes to a halt for Gaia. A century later, presidents had come and gone, business had boomed and burst, people had been born, married, divorced, married again and passed on, and the landscape of the preserve was unaffected and unchanged. They say an eon is but a full breath for mother nature, and she hadn't even begun to inhale since last I was there.

Something had changed though, and changed drastically. As I neared the center of the preserve I could see light, hear voices and smell food being prepared. I thought surely I must be imagining things. I wasn't. Where there had been nothing one hundred years ago, there was now a small village. Huts and tents, well defined dirt pathways and, people. People busying themselves with the stuff of life; raising children, raising livestock, raising crops, raising their voices in anger, laughter, and song.

I watched and studied them from the shadows for a long while, just as I felt I'd been watched and studied a century ago. The inhabitants of this fledgling village were all wearing red head dressings of some sort. Some also wore red sashes and others were adorned with red tassels or ribbons. Were these differences signifiers of rank, delineators of status, or was it just personal choice. They all appeared to be buzzing about readying for something important, like your mom cleaning spaces and places on Christmas Eve that wouldn't be cleaned again until next Christmas Eve. Their movements were not unnecessarily rushed but purposeful as they attended to various tasks in the village. I could see that there was a definite order established, perhaps a hierarchy. From what I could tell, this order didn't seem to be based on race, gender, or even age. There were men, women, and teenaged children clearly giving and receiving orders. I felt like an anthropologist peeking behind the curtain at an emerging society. It was curious and engaging. When I'd seen all I needed to, and felt no imminent threat or danger, I emerged from amongst the trees and entered the village.

All conversation ceased. A place that was buzzing a moment ago fell perfectly still and quiet.

A young, caramel-complected woman wearing a red sash, approached slowly. She stopped in front of me, a few steps to my left, folded her arms across her chest, bent at the waist and bowed until her right knee rested on the ground. This was a clear signal to the others.

Everyone wearing a red sash, slowly approached, and either stood to my right or left and genuflected. This action repeated until two phalanxes of kneeling people with a clear path between them was created. The villagers, as they bowed, had all oriented their bodies so that the crown of their heads pointed toward, what I could only assume, was the direction I was intended to walk in. I moved slowly, unsure of what any of it meant. Was this the yellow brick road, or the green mile? There was a feeling of reverence wrapped in it all, but why would that be? Were all strangers greeted in this way? Was this a precursor to some sort of aggression? I couldn't know, and so I proceeded as carefully as I could.

I approached, what seemed to be the center of the village, and the scent returned. Honey and flowers and earth. Something sweet that had gone old. And there it was, the point that the entire village had seemingly been built around, the fulcrum, the cornerstone. Khadijah's grave.

The grave had been built up as a dirt mound. Surrounding the small earthen heap were lit torches leaned inward. It had the effect of illuminating and focusing all who came to watch and listen's attention on whoever stood atop the hill. Draped across the crown of the mound was a sheet of white covered in symbols of life.

"Do you remember it?"

A voice came out of the very shadows that just moments ago I'd been tucked away in. The same shadows I'd chased for seven months, almost a full century ago. The voice was familiar but, different. Like that of an old friend that you haven't seen or spoken to since high school. I knew it, but I didn't. My heart, with every beat whispered, it's Khadijah. My mind screamed back, but how!? The voice now seemed to descend from the tree tops,

"You do remember don't you? The black night. The white sheet. The red dust."

The cadence and inflection were hers but the tone and timbre were not. Then a figure emerged. It was as if the person had been there, perfectly still, the entire time. Someone so conjoined with the night that only their movement would reveal their presence. It was a woman, clad from head to toe in red. She wore a turban, a high collared billowing robe, beneath the robe a top reminiscent of a karategi and flowing pants long enough to cover her feet. She appeared to leave no footprints as she made her way. It reminded me of a framed picture on the wall of the Waukegan apartment I escaped from as a young Midas. A painting called Footprints in the Sand.

The way she moved, and oriented her body relative to that movement, kept her face obscured by the robe's collar. Just when her face seemed about to appear it would tuck back and hide behind the stiff fabric. I knew that walk however, its cadence and gait. I'd wanted that walk beside me for all time. The woman continued speaking to me from beyond the collar, never turning her face toward me, but I knew.

"I wondered if you'd return. You haven't in more than nine decades now. This year is special though isn't it? The centennial."

She walked between the torches, and climbed the mound, her back to me. Once at the center of the white sheet atop the mound, two figures approached from her left and right flank. They wore red turbans, white robes and red sashes. Priests? They walked to her, their heads lowered, and removed her robe. The person on the left folded the robe and presented it to the person on the right as if it were a flag that had draped a loved one's coffin. Then the two walked to the edges of the sheet and sat facing me. One was a black man, he appeared to be in his forties. The other a Latin woman, possibly in her mid twenties. The red clad woman, atop the mound, turned and sat, her legs in lotus position. She lifted her head, looked at me and smiled. Her eyes. Her sclera was more than three fourths black with a red halo surrounding a brown iris. Khadijah.

She continued, "It's been exactly one-hundred years since you killed Khadijah."

She referred to herself in the third person. I didn't know why. I didn't care. I wanted to run to her, to take her in my arms, ask her how any of this had happened, but something in me knew better. She sat still, nothing about her obviously threatening, but danger radiated white hot from her. It's difficult to explain but something was off, not right. It was like seeing Khadijah reflected in a fun house mirror. It was her but askew, angled oddly, like a doppelganger or a twisted twin. Still, it was ... her. That night in my arms when the halo around her eyes went from gold, to rust, to red, her sclera had been white. Now it was mostly black. I didn't know what that meant. What would happen when it was completely black. I found my voice,

"Khadijah?"

"Don't call me that."

"It is you? Tell me what happened love. How?"

"How? I'm my mother's daughter Dashill!" My name which had always felt at home on her tongue had come forth like an unwanted invader, "I'm smart and strong. Your tomb couldn't hold me."

"It wasn't meant to. Had I known."

"Had you known you'd have done what?"

I felt more like a defendant being cross-examined than a husband, through means magical, mystical or both, being reunited with his wife. For every ounce of rancor in her voice I responded with a pound of tenderness.

"Had I known, I'd have moved heaven and earth."

"I don't know about heaven but I moved earth, six feet of it, pressing down on me for three years. I clawed through mother earth's womb until I was standing free beneath the new moon. Reborn."

"Let me help you. Khadijah..."

"Do. Not. Call me that. You buried Khadijah! My father buried Khadijah! Let her finally rest in peace. She wasn't meant for this world, wasn't built for it, wasn't enough. I have finally become who I always was!"

I turned and realized the entire village had gathered at my back. Their eyes were fixed on the illuminated figure sitting atop the mound.

"If you aren't Khadijah, the woman I knew and loved, the woman who knew and loved me; then who are you?"

She stood to her feet, her hands never touching the ground. The black man and Latin woman stood also and moved hurriedly toward her. She extended her arms and the robe was once again wrapped around her, the collar raised obscuring her face. The man and woman instantly fell to their knees, their arms extended forward, their foreheads pressed to the ground.

With the voice I knew but didn't know, a voice that once again seemed to be emerging from the shadows and descending from the trees, she said, "What was killed in love..."

The entire village joined in, completing her thought in unison, "Was reborn by faith!"

She continued.

"What was born of flesh..."

Their voices rose with each response to her call.

"Was reshaped by the dust!"

"What was planted in the earth..."

"Was born again by the moon's light!"

"And in the third year she..."

"Rose!"

"And in the third year she..."

"ROSE!"

"And in the third year she..."

"ROSE! ROSE! ROSE!"

Their voices which had risen to the heavens as one, stopped in unison. The name Rose bounced off the moon, skipped across the lakes, settled into the earth and echoed across the land. Even when it could be heard no more, you could feel it. She folded her collar down so that it draped her shoulders and addressed me directly,

"That's who I am Dashill or should I say, Midas. I am Rose."

There was a collective gasp and an energy moved through all those gathered. Rose addressed the crowd,

"Yes! Midas! The one foretold. The one who buried me, not knowing that I would not accept death. The one who holds in his hands the red dust, and in his blood eternal life. This is the one that will usher us into eternity either by his will, or ours."

"What have you told these people Khadijah?"

The man and woman to her left and right stood, and exposed sheathed blades beneath their robes.

"Address me by that name again tonight, and you will not know another tomorrow. Yes I know what your skin is capable of, but even you have your limits. How long can the adrenaline live in your bloodstream? What happens once it's gone?"

I felt the crowd at my back pushing closer.

"What have I told them you ask? I have only told them the truth. You have the red dust. It is never far from you. In the red dust lives eternal life. You will give it to us willingly or we will exsanguinate you and find the secrets in your golden blood ourselves. The choice is yours but I assure you it will be one or the other."

"Kha..."

I watched as the muscles in the arms of her priests began to twitch, and their blades eased slightly away from the sheaths.

"I don't have the dust, and even if I did that's not how it works. I know that now. You know it too. Look at your eyes. Do you know what happens when they go completely black? I don't know but I can venture a guess."

"Then give me, give US, the red dust!"

"I can't. I won't."

With those words, and a speed that caught all off guard I ran for the woods. I folded myself into the night, into the brush, into the trees, into the black dark. Khadijah gave chase. As I had suspected all those years ago the red dust had augmented her strength too. That's why I'd been unable to run her down. I moved and evaded until I found a space that I felt confident would shield, conceal, and protect me. I heard her feet moving around, past, and even over top of me. I remained still as the grave. Khadijah continued her search, and began speaking to the night,

"This is how I alluded you, you know. When I was lost and scared and confused. When I first emerged from the grave I had no memory. I didn't know who or why I was. For a year I just moved aimlessly, never far from the grave, the womb of my new mother. Then you came. I didn't know who you were but I knew to keep away. I knew you were danger. Then the memories started coming back in pieces. You. Me. Coffee. A *DomiCas*. A coat hanger. The smell of men's breath. The feels of men's hands. Grease. Running. The Sea. You killing me. YOU KILLING ME! Then I remembered the red dust. The promise it offered. I remembered gold and money buried and stashed. The memories were out of order but they were there. I left, and the memories took me to some of this hidden wealth I recalled. It was as I remembered. Cash and gold. A wealth that I used to walk the earth and speak the truth of how I was made from the dust, born again and could offer through the blood eternal life. People heard and believed. I led them to my birthplace and we built our village, waiting for your return. It took decades. Some passed on to the next plane, new souls joined our ranks, babies were born and so on. It took many decades but here you are, as promised."

With her last words she flipped over a downed tree that easily weighed a few hundred pounds. She tossed it like a tooth pick. I wasn't hiding there though. She turned and rushed around furiously reaching into dark spaces hoping to find me. I remained still. Her hand coming closer than she knew at least twice. Finally she stood and looked at the sky. Daybreak was nearing. She took a deep breath.

"I will find you! If not now then soon enough. It's just a matter of time."

With that she hurried off in the direction of the village. I laid there, still, until daybreak and then ran as fast as my legs would carry me out of that piece of forest, never to return.

Rose and her followers who claim the title Thorns have been hunting me ever since. They search and track me by day, but she only hunts by the light that greeted her when she was reborn. The light of the moon.

Chapter 16 | Das. Rose

I stand in the kitchen between Kent and Rose. I hear movement in the other rooms. Thorns. Rose's eyes only have a sliver of white left in them now. This would explain why her hunts have become more frequent and desperate recently. She's nearing the end, and she knows it.

"Is that Kha..."

"Don't! Hold silent," I shout before Kent can finish.

Rose smiles and I can still see the woman I used to love in there. Four of her Thorns silently enter the kitchen and stand between her and the table that separates us.

She looks at Kent puts her index finger to her lips and says, "Ssssh. The immortals are talking," then her onyx eyes fall on me.

"I see you still know the rules. Excellent. Do you remember the other part too? Red dust or gold blood? We will have one or the other."

One of her Thorns enters and stands to her left.

"You'll have neither," I say my eyes searching for a way out. "Neither of us is immortal. Your time is drawing to a close. I can see it in your eyes."

"If you can see it in my eyes then you know I will most certainly have one or both! My Thorns stand ready in ways you don't yet know, and your fledgeling is not matured."

I feel Kent push against me ready to assert his readiness but I hold him firm. Two more Thorns enter and stand just behind Rose.

"This is where you killed me and ushered me into a life eternal with the red dust." Rose makes a sweeping gesture with her arms, signifying the *DomiCas*. "This is where the dust lives. Give it to us and let's be done with this foolishness once and for all. No one has to die here today, but many, through your sacrifice, can live a life eternal."

"That's not how it works! You know that. It's not how it works for me and not how it worked for you. The red dust is not the key to eternal life." I say this as much to her Thorns as to her.

"Not in your hands, but let me try mine. You told your fledgling here that perhaps God is omnipotent because he's had the time and resources to get all the credit hours in the world. Well time has been on my side as of late. I've studied and stand ready to show myself approved."

Kent breaks the silence imposed on him,

"How could she ... She couldn't know..."

224

"Oh Mr. Kent. Mr. Clay Kent of Flint, Michigan. Do you remember a woman jogging past you with a stroller this afternoon? Did you note the red tassels hanging from her shirt? The man with his arm against the tree, counting one Mississippi, two Mississippi, did you notice his red baseball cap? How about the moment when all the FauxFillment birthday revelers' noise canceling headphones blinked red, red, red as you were rushing out of the cafe with your gold Aquarian quarter? No?"

I feel an undeniable shiver go through Kent's body as Rose continues.

"Of course you didn't. You didn't even know you should have been looking. But he knew," Rose gestures toward me, "and even he didn't see, so obsessed with telling you his fairy tale, fable, bedtime story. Spoiler alert," she leans in and whispers, "most of it is lies AND the woman comes back in the end."

I can feel Kent's eyes on me, not knowing what to believe. Khadijah continues.

"I could have had you killed at any point today. I just wanted to see if he would kill you with his little experiment first."

"Bullshit!" Kent is scared but not paralyzed by the fear. Good. Hopefully a moment will present itself soon when we will have to both move, quickly, through our fear.

Rose chuckles, "Your neighbors this morning, what color was the whipped cream again?" As she says this the couple Kent watched through the window while dressing this morning walks in wearing red turbans.

"We are everywhere Mr. Clay Kent of Flint, Michigan, mediocre writer for *Amazon World Solar Times,* mediocre lover of women, and mediocre ex-husband to Lisa who as we speak makes love to a beautiful woman of Mediterranean descent wearing a—what was the word you used? Ah yes, vermillion. Wearing a vermillion-hued negligee."

Kent is not at full strength but it's still difficult to hold him back. I have to turn and grab him with both hands. I pull him to me and look him in the eye. I can see the rage and hurt that lives there. I learned earlier today that Kent when he feels attacked will strike back, even if it's a clumsy attack. I speak to him as a friend.

"Don't let her get in your head Clay."

It's the first time, since we've met, that I've used his given name. He stops pushing against me. Rose steps on the moment.

"Why not? I'm in your head, and heart aren't I Dashill?"

"Fuck you, Khadijah!"

I say it, my back to her, before I can stop myself. Talk about clumsy. I take a deep breath and take note of the horizontal knife block on the counter. I turn to find a grimace on Khadijah's face and the room filling with Thorns. Just the mentioning of the name Khadijah gives her pain. I reach behind myself, just past Kent and grab a knife from the block. I hold the knife in my hand, behind my forearm, behind my back, obscured. Kent sees me, and does the same. Whatever happens next we're in it together, our hands behind our backs.

Khadijah, her voice like a bullhorn, says, "What was killed in love..."

The Thorns reply in chorus.

"Was reborn by faith!"

I can hear voices coming from the other rooms in the *DomiCas*. The place must be full at this point.

She continues shouting, "What was born of flesh..."

"Was reshaped by the dust!"

Voices flood from outside the house, through the windows. We're surrounded.

"What was planted in the earth..."

"Was born again by the moon's light!"

The voices are everywhere now.

"And in the third year she..."

"Rose!"

"And in the third year she..."

"Rose!"

"And in the third year she..."

I shout at the top of my lungs,

"ROSE!"

Her jaw sets. Her lip trembles. A black tear rolls down her cheek. She wipes it away, nods, and her Thorns begin to slowly advance. She recedes back into the shadow of the living room and I hear her whisper,

"... My Das."

<End>

Haint (a short story)

Chapter One

Pulled closely around her shoulders was a small genuine, imitation, Persian throw rug that had known better days. It had once been a prized and treasured possession, given to her by her boyfriend, Bradford, back when she moved into her first apartment in Atlanta. It was 3' x 5', multicolored, faded, weathered, and ornamental. Bradford had told her all about the rug's cost and provenance over sushi, edamame, and green tea the night he'd gifted it to her. The story involved at least one person, long long ago, losing their life in the weaving of the rug, and a subsequent historic desire and lust-driven chase after the floor cloth that sounded like something out of an Indiana Jones movie. The early Indiana Jones movies, not that *Crystal Skull* madness. Bradford said he'd spotted it in a thrift store. The owner, a shrewd man, according to Bradford's account didn't know what it was, or what it was worth, but still charged more money than Bradford said he was comfortable disclosing. He said despite the cost it was worth any expense, if it made her smile. Later that night they'd made mediocre love atop the ancient piece of carpeting, beneath the iridescent glow of a television playing *Temple of Doom* in the distant background. Being in love can make a mediocre lover seem like the clitoral and climax king of your dreams, and Bradford, if nothing else, had certainly stolen her heart. Kali Ma!

A few weeks after receiving the expensive gift shrouded in intrigue her friend Monsour came to visit. She couldn't wait to show off the thoughtful and extravagant gift. Monsour took one look and without touching it said, "Fugazi." Fugazi? She was not familiar with the term and could have assumed it was Arabic for, "Amazing rug that you recently had sex on." She could tell, however, by the furrowing of his brow, the pursing of his lips, and his refusing to touch it as if it were rug patient zero, that it didn't mean that. "What do you mean by, fugazi?" she asked. Monsour was a young, well traveled, graduate of Georgia State. That's where they'd met. He'd tutored her in Economics and they'd become friends. Whenever she spoke of not being capable of being racist because she had a "a black friend" she was talking about Monsour, who wasn't really black in way that people in America think of black. He was a darkly complected Persian, not an African or African American, but she didn't really know the difference. Monsour had grown up in a family of international rug dealers and distributors. When he told people this he made sure he slowed down his speech and enunciated the word RUG, loudly and clearly. He did this because due to his accent people often heard "family of international DRUG dealers and distributors," and then the conversation would quickly turn illicit and illegal.

Monsour's father, uncles, and cousins could identify a rug's origin down to the township just by looking at the stitch and weaving. He wasn't as skilled as they were but having grown up around rugs his whole life, he wasn't that far off. Monsour sighed, flipped the rug over and said, "It's fugazi. It's fake. It's not even a good fake. Look at this,

this is machine stitching. See this spot here on the back? Where it looks like a tag was removed? I'm sure it's where a tag was removed and that tag said Target, or Walmart or something else equally bargain basement-y, discount cellar-y, savings hell-ish. All I'm saying is don't get it too close to any heat source. It's probably made exclusively of matches soaked in gasoline, Monsanto GMO seeds, and things China would deem too toxic for production. And not for nothing, it smells like someone had sex on it."

She didn't care, however. She loved Bradford, Bradford had given her the rug and so she loved the rug. It was an ad hoc fallacy of the heart. In the end, the rug had been realer than, and had outlasted, her relationship with Bradford. It kept her feet warm long after his had grown cold. It kept her company long after he'd abandoned her for Khristine. "Who but a whore spells Christine with a K?" she'd ask herself between tears and spoons of Rocky Road while watching *Raiders of The Lost Ark*.

Rugs are interesting things. You can become so used to them that you forget that they're there. You forget the cold hardwood reality that lives just beneath the warmth of the soft, expansive, floor covering. You might even, while standing on a rug, begin to imagine that you have sure footing on solid ground. An even more interesting thing happens when the rug gets pulled out from under you. When all of the ugly things swept under it surface.

It looked more like a weather battered shawl than a rug these days. It was a very talented and versatile throw though. It served as a blanket, a bed, a jacket, a poncho, a shelter, and a reminder of the life she used to have. A life before, well before, any of what follows.

Chapter Two

Her fingertips had gone from red, to white, to blue as the full bite of fall's frigid evening air continued patriotically nibbling at her extremities. She blew her breath, warm and stale, on her fingertips and tucked her partially gloved hands into her armpits, which hadn't known a hot shower in more than two weeks. Her well-worn gloves, picked out of a "Take what you need. Leave what you don't," box set outside of the West End Goodwill, no longer had fingers. She'd angrily torn them out one evening after a five dollar bill, given to her by a stranger through the window of his car as he sat at a red light, had Houdini'd from between her gloved fingertips. She'd watched in horror as the wind took the bill, blew it across the street, beyond the sidewalk, over a fence and down into the highway 85 rush hour traffic never to be given by a stranger through a window ever again.

Her face and heart sank faster than the five had, as she mustered the strength to look back over at the giver of the bill. The bearded man looked tall even while seated in his warm and comfortable Lexus hybrid. He was drinking free trade coffee from the latest, greatest, greenest, no-gluten, no-gmo, no-flavor boutique coffee house. Without even being aware she was moving, she stepped close enough to take in the aroma of the coffee, and the man. He smelled like a corner office with a nice view, a not-so-nice wife in Alpharetta with a great ass, a web browser full of Porn Hub bookmarks, an inexpensive "real" mistress in Bankhead with a greater ass, a fantastic promotion on the horizon, an expensive, fabulous, male lover in Midtown with the greatest ass... and a pricey sandalwood cologne.

He too had watched the five-dollar bill David Copperfield from her hand and do a Greg Louganis into an eight lane meat grinder. Her capsizing heart filled her eyes with tears that carried in them an inherent plea and an apparent, "please sir may I have another?" Her quivering chapped lips, however, never found the words hiding just behind her rotting teeth. He looked at her from the comfort of his heated, hand-stitched, soft as lard in a tin can of grandma's hot stove top Italian leather seats. He looked at her damp tired eyes, at her trembling cracked lips, at her dice roll of rotting teeth and shrugged as if to say that's the way the Lincoln gets assassinated. He rolled up his window, turned up the trap music that seemed to betray the Trump Pence bumper sticker on his car and sped off the second the light turned.

The social, political, and economic climates were, then and now, volatile. They had been since a property blowhard turned reality star turned politician had turned into president. Talk about a David Blaine. Getting a fiver from a stranger was no small feat no matter the weather but seemed extremely hard now that the economy was, doing so well. For a homeless person, being handed a random five was like hitting the transient lottery. It meant you could get one thing from the Mickey D's $1 menu at least four times. If the cashier let you slide on the four or five cent tax you could get five things! Five things that

235

would surely kill you slowly, but hunger on the streets of Atlanta came with the certainty of a quick death. Life on the streets meant you had to pick your poison while some clown told you it was okay, literally.

She'd caught her own reflection in the window of the car before the driver sped off. She didn't recognize the person looking back. When she raised her hands to her own face it was the feel of the gloved fingers against her skin that alerted her to the truth. She indeed was this haggard woman captured in this mobile mirror. The lines in her face had gotten long and deep. There were so many now. They looked like the Marianas Trench running the length of this ocean of skin that used to be her face. Her reflection reminded her that time is a parade; it keeps on moving whether you're watching or not. She hadn't been watching and time had gotten further down the road than she'd realized. Who was this rotten-toothed, matted-haired hag in third hand rags, and where had the woman she knew herself to be gone to hide? Had she gone to hide forever? Olly-olly-oxen-free! She ran her gloved fingertips along the endless, bottomless wrinkles as if tracing state roads of circumstance and struggle back to the main highway of pain and regret. She followed the map closely and found, herself then and there. It was no illusion. She discovered what all wicked witches do, mirrors tell the truth of who is and who is not the fairest of them all.

Chapter Three

She stood in the dust and exhaust of the driver's low emission vehicle after he'd sped away. Her small genuine, imitation, Persian throw rug hug heavy around her shoulders as she looked down at her gloved hands, at the gloved fingers that had touched the hard truth of now, at the gloved fingers that had let five things from the dollar menu escape. She removed the gloves and tore the fingers violently from them. They'd felt too little when touching the five and felt too much when touching her face. They'd not betray her like that twice. As she pulled the now fingerless gloves back onto her hands, which seemed more bone than skin, she still had the scent of his cologne, expensive and thick in her nostrils. Scent and memory walk hand in hand, like all married couples do before divorcing.

She inhaled and remembered back to when she smelled like a newly renovated apartment in Kirkwood, a new job at a start-up in Grant Park, a stupid break up with Bradford because he pronounced La Croix as Le Quah, student loan debt through the glass ceiling, and a vibrator with new batteries between a box spring and mattress that needed to be replaced. This was back when showers were taken often and for granted, and new clothes arrived at her apartment door in a brown box with a blue label on the top and a smiley face on the side.

She recalled vividly a time when she was the one sitting tall and comfortably in her car blasting Taylor Swift when she wanted to seem young and with it, and Rihanna when she wanted to seem edgy and in touch with what The Blacks listened to. That's what she thought of most people of color as back then, The Blacks.

The Blacks were good at dancing... and basketball. They were dangerous for reasons she couldn't put her fingers on. They were loud. They could really really sing. They were not allowed to use restrooms in convenience stores without buying something first, and they were always complaining about slavery. The Mexicans were all non-"The Blacks" but still brown people. The Mexicans were good at dancing... and soccer. They were dangerous for reasons she couldn't put her fingers on. They were loud. They were really really good at cutting grass. They were not allowed to walk the streets without proving citizenship and they refused to not speak Mexican. Any non-"The Blacks," non-brown people with almond shaped eyes were The Chinese. The Chinese were not good at dancing and not good at sports. They were not dangerous for reasons she couldn't put her fingers on, gloved or not, but they were also not to be trusted. They did your nails, talked about you in Chinese (even if they were Korean), played Mah Jongg and engaged in unfair trade practices.

Those were the wide nets she cast to capture any and all people who were not readily identifiable as white. She hadn't even realized that she'd become such a stereotyping fisher of men. If you'd have asked her if she was racist she'd have said, "Absolutely not! I have a good relationship with The Blacks, I have a friend named Monsour, and I have certainly hired The Mexicans." What she couldn't know was that soon life would teach her more about The Blacks than she ever wanted to know. She would discover that being one of The Blacks wasn't what she'd thought. It wasn't just about, color.

Chapter Four

The same life on the street that had carved deep crevices into her skin, robbed her of showers and forced her to sleep under the stars, had also taught her what it meant to be one of "The Blacks." As a poor, white, homeless person she found, that to many whites, she was now one of The Blacks, possibly one of The Mexicans and would be treated accordingly. In a world where once her entering an establishment was met with smiles, her purchases concluded with pockmarked teenagers declaring it was their pleasure to serve her, and police letting her off with a warning, again and again, she was now invisible to whites passing her on the street and hyper-visible to law enforcement. She was always on guard and never felt safe. Cafe's she'd once upon a time run in to quickly use their restroom while out shopping with friends, now pointed to the "No Public Restroom" sign, that she'd never noticed before. They would then tell her that she needed to buy something before she'd be allowed to use the restroom. When she'd inform them that she used to frequent the establishment and use their restroom all the time, they'd inform her that she hadn't. When she'd ask them if they remembered her, they'd inform her that they didn't. She'd then be asked to leave in a way that let her know it was more an order than a request. It was no longer their pleasure to serve her.

She'd also found out that some of her best protectors on the streets had been the very people just a few years ago, if caught with them on an elevator alone, she'd have clutched her purse tight to her body and bungee jumped through the emergency escape door if possible. Some of her closest confidants in these dark, blind corners and back alleyways were people that, before, if she'd have seen them standing on a curb while stopped at a red light she'd have quickly locked her doors, her windows, her gas tank and her pants pockets if possible. She'd have turned up Rihanna and stared straight ahead like the Statue of Liberty after reading their signs pleading "Hungry please help," stating "Veteran, anything welcome," or humorously declaring "Why lie? I just want a beer." These protectors, confidants and friends she'd made on the streets were not who she'd thought them to be... but also they were. A few weeks of living on the streets and seeing purses snatched out of desperation and cars broken into for the loose change in the ash tray taught her that there were times when she'd have been wise to clutch, bungee, and lock up.

Chapter Five

The Blacks of varying races had noticed how helpless, lost and inept she seemed when she first found herself with a concrete mattress and a small genuine, imitation, Persian throw rug wrapped around her shoulders for warmth. They'd taken her under their wing. They'd shown her which churches offered free meals and when. They'd taught her how to turn cardboard into memory foam. They let her know which cops would let you sleep in the park and which cops wouldn't even let you stand on the sidewalk. They'd pulled back the veil and showed her how the people she used to act like she didn't see, and act like she couldn't hear, survived in a world that had let them slip between its gloved fingers and float away to nothing. They made her family. That is until they recognized her. Until they figured out who she was. Until they remembered what she'd done. Once they realized that, everyone's generosity dried up like a midday summer's rain on a Decatur sidewalk in June. Everyone except Florida Jenkins.

For the record no one called her Florida Jenkins she was Flo Jean or Jinx on the sidewalks and side streets of Atlanta. Jinx was five foot, six inches of laughter surround by 250 pounds of take no shit. She was as dark as the seam on brand new Jordache jeans, with pitch circles around her eyes so dark they could have sucked black holes in. Jinx played straight spades in the park for two dollars a game and sold loosey cigarettes on the train for fifty cents a smoke. She had a sharp wit and sharp blade on her at all times. She laughed loud whenever she took a notion to and fought hard if you thought about trying her. Jinx wore flip flops on her swollen, cracked feet in the summer and flip flops and socks on her frozen, swollen, cracked feet in the winter. She walked slowly as if contemplating the meaning of life on a bright spring day, but really she was almost always in pain and trying to mask it. She sported a red wig that served as a hat and ear muffs when the weather turned cold, and shade and protection when the sun grew brutal. Her floral patterned dress was a bit too small and her pink, used to be red, leggings were crotchless. Jinx's newly blackened friend found out later the crotchless leggings were not an accident or a mistake, but to ensure ease of access when the sometimes necessary sex-for-ten-items-on-the-dollar-menu trades were agreed upon.

If you took a deep breath while standing next to her you'd discover that Jinx smelled like marriage to the wrong man, hog maw, concussions and stitches that came with his promise never to do it again, a deep knife wound to the stomach in his sleep that made him keep his promise, potlikker, an attempt at being a lesbian that didn't stick, an undiagnosed bipolar disorder that made keeping a job impossible, resignation to her current situation and an encyclopedic knowledge of the streets of Atlanta. Jinx told her she knew who she'd been the first time she'd laid eyes on her. She asked Jinx why hadn't she shunned her like everyone else and Jinx said, "I looked at you and knew you wasn't her no more. You can't live on the streets and be who you was. The streets is a test of fire. If you survive it, who you was is burned away and all that's left is who you is now. You think I always been Flo Jean? You think I always been Jinx? At one time I was Florida Jenkins. Not no more though. Florida Jenkins would have never survived half this shit, but Jinx... Jinx built for it. And you? You better leave that old bitch behind. You can't be her no more. Ain't no latte's out this motherfucker and ain't no days off. Yeah, you been through the fire and you almost who you is now, but you gotta do what you gotta do to let that last bit burn." She asked Jinx what she meant by, let that last bit burn. What last bit? Jinx looked her in the eye, turned and pointed at the little boy standing a few feet from them, with his hand out. "You gotta settle up with him. That's what I mean. That's the last bit."

Chapter Six

He never changed. He was eternally ten years old, dressed in old worn jeans and fresh, just out of the box, Jordans. His short sleeve red polo was unbuttoned far enough for you to see the top of his white-as-the-Republican-Party t-shirt just beneath. He wore a backpack that had sponges, jellyfish and sea snails all magically come to life, wearing pants, and saying semi-lewd things in comment bubbles just over their heads drawn all over it. The comments in the bubbles seemed to change and always seemed to be directed at ...her. Whether he was a country mile or a few feet away she could feel his presence and smell his omnipresence. He had the aroma of what becomes of a dream deferred, pop rocks, new clothes on the first day of school, sulfur and saltpeter, hands up don't shoot, and the Nae Nae. What he really smelled like though, what he smelled exactly like, always, is a tomorrow that never comes.

He'd been with her for the last three years, following her closely at times, just appearing up the road a bit at others, but always with his hand out, and with a distended almost painful smile. A clown's smile complete with its joy and sorrow mixed message. A crocodile's smile with it's inherent hunger and danger. His smile was certainly the last thing the canary saw before being devoured by the crafty, ravenous cat.

His eyes always seemed too big, too brown and to brim with imminent tears.

She first saw him, this version of him, while driving her car to work. He was suddenly there, in the middle of the street, directly in front of her car with his hand extended, his eyes and smile wide like Jack Skellington come to life. She swerved, narrowly missed him, but lost control of the car. As she skidded past him his eyes, the brown of carpets made to hide stains, met hers and the world began to move in slow motion. His body stayed perfectly still but his head turned and turned until it could turn no further, and then it turned some more. His head, almost too big for his body, rotated to an impossible degree. His eyes, the brown of bottom shelf liquor, were locked with hers; his wide, wide, wider, joker's smile ever present. By an act of sheer will, she loosed herself from the grip of his stare just in time to lay on the horn and warn the woman her car was quickly careening toward.

LaToya was also known as La La or Toy Toy, her life had a thing for repetition. She was a middle aged employee of Mickey D's if her hypertension, uniform, and bank account were to be believed. La La was the complexion of a Mickey D's ice cream swirl after it had melted. She had broad shoulders for a woman and her legs had a tone that only running for buses, hurrying for trains, walking miles to work, and standing all day taking orders could create. She was five foot nothing. but when she put her whole attitude on she seemed at least 6'3". La La was waiting for the #21 bus after just having been approached by a gentleman suitor with cornrows to his shoulders, a t-shirt to his thighs, and his pants to his knees. He looked like he was melting. He looked like people do in Sci-Fi movies once they've been accidentally zapped by a shrink ray. Except he'd done this to himself, on purpose. Baggy everything man saw her sitting at the bus stop, walked over and said, "Shawty what yo name is?" His right front tooth was gilded and his left front tooth was missing, as were a few others. His mouth had the appearance of a picket fence with a few pickets missing. The hit or miss nature of his teeth also meant the aroma of the beer on his breath didn't have much to keep it from hopping the fence and running unencumbered into the world. La La didn't respond to his query and so in his best attempt at mimicking the classic romanticists such as, Byron, Keats, and Wordsworth, he proffered, "You smell like French Fries ... and pussy, bitch," before walking away.

In truth La La gave off the scent of, three unexplainable miscarriages, a useless associates degree from Bayer College online, two all beef patties, a two parent home, why is this damn ice cream machine broken again, a recent text from her ex asking if they could try again, special sauce lettuce cheese, budding diabetes, a monthly MARTA card, lettuce pickle on a sesame seed bun and French Fries... sans the pussy.

It was an exhausted La La, sitting at the bus stop thinking about texting her ex back, that the honking, sliding, sideways car was fast approaching. The sound of the screeching tires growing louder and louder pulled her out of her thoughts and exhaustion. She stood so fast that when she looked back she almost expected to see herself still sitting there. La La, like a child bouncing lightly on the edge of the public pool diving board, contemplating their first plunge into the deep end, held her breath and jumped. She lept with an agility that only adrenaline and the threat of imminent death can give to a woman as tired as she was after working a double d. That's what double shifts at Mickey D's were called back then.

La La used to dance all night at Club Kaya in her youth, DJ Banksy would spin down southern hip hop classics and La La would Scrub the Ground and Yeet the night away. Men would always comment on how toned, long, and strong her legs looked. This observation was usually followed by some lewd comment about wrapping those legs around their back. Back then she thought those legs would jump her from Peachtree and all the way to Broadway. They didn't. They had at one time, more than thrice, slid down a silver pole on a narrow stage at Club Peach. Now she just needed them to jump five yards to her right. She had been on her feet, at the register, at the front line, at the drive thru, restocking the ketchup, and cleaning the bathrooms all day. Her feet, her legs, her everything was tired but she found a reservoir of strength and lept with all she had left out of the path of the vehicle. She almost made it. Almost making it, felt like the story of her life. Her right leg, the one that remembered those Kaya nights and silver poles the best, was a sesame seed too slow. The only thing louder than the sound of the impact was the sound of Latoya's ricocheting, echoing screams.

The car was still shaking from the impact, as was its driver, as she registered La La's screams. Her trembling hands grabbed the pair of shades that had fallen from the top of her head onto the floorboard, and pulled them on. She reached back over her shoulder took a hold of the hood on her sweatshirt and pulled it down and low over her head. The car had just stopped rocking and the woman was still screaming when she backed the car up, freeing the woman's leg from the pin between the car's front bumper the back wall of the bus stop stand. The screaming woman crumpled to the ground as people rushed over to help. She stayed in the car with her shades on, her head down, and her door locked, her window locked, her gas tank locked, her everything locked. She wanted to run. She had to put her trembling hands on her trembling legs to keep them from running while she waited for the police to arrive.

She hadn't been on the streets without shades, or purchased a shirt without a hoodie in over a year. That seemed like a lifetime ago. She was remembering her pre-hoodie, pre-shades life, and that strange, familiar kid in the middle of the street with his hand extended and eyes locked to hers when the officer knocked on her window, startling her. She was asked to exit the vehicle. She sat perfectly still for a few seconds, as if hoping her stillness would render her invisible, as if hoping the officer had the visual acuity of a T-Rex. He did not. The officer asked again that she exit the vehicle. She felt like Buckner walking back into Shea as she stepped slowly from the car. Her legs were still shouting, run! The screams of the arriving ambulance's siren mixed with La La's screams until it all seemed deafening. The responding officer asked her, How had she lost control of the car? What happened exactly? The flood gates to her mouth opened and what came out what a steady stream of semi-coherent ramblings about a little boy in the middle of the street. She left out the part about the Jack

Skellington smile, and the one-eighty his head did while his feet stayed rooted in place. The officer asked her to remove her shades and hoodie. Again stillness. Again a repeat of the request. She acquiesced. With a deep breath she pulled back the hoodie, took a deep breath, removed the shades and looked the officer in the eyes. There was something teetering close to recognition on his face as he gave her the "don't I know you?" eye squint. He looked at her, looked away, shook his head and looked again. Whatever name was on the tip of his tongue never made it any further. He asked her to submit to a breathalyzer. She agreed and passed it. Witnesses to the accident were staring at her now too. She kept her head down and evaded their eyes as best she could. She asked the officer if she could give her statement about the accident at the precinct. He'd never seen anyone so happy to be put in the back of a squad car in his life.

None of the eyewitnesses to the accident could remember seeing any little boy in the street. Not a single person corroborated her series of events. When the traffic cam footage was retrieved and reviewed, it revealed that there was indeed no little boy present. What there was, was a clear image showing what every eyewitness seemed to agree to seeing. The video showed her driving and then suddenly and purposefully targeting this poor innocent, black, woman.

The footage somehow leaked to the web, Black Twitter dubbed her #TrafficRageTammy, and the Internet did what it does. The posts, the memes, the gifs, the blogs, the op eds, the vitriol and the death threats came faster than a teenage boy on prom night. A self-proclaimed psychologist and ancestry expert, known on Youtube as Dr. Hotep

Ahkenaton Nation King, without knowing her name said he had conclusive, probable, possible proof that her great great great great grandfather single-handedly started the transatlantic slave trade. He was certain that it might, could, have happened, in theory. @ICUCinMe_Bitches, an Instagram specialist in virtual behavior, whose pronouns are They, Them, never We and sometimes Us said that They could tell by watching the video that #TrafficRageTammy was predisposed to running down black women with her car due to unconscious bumper bias. Then Sean Prince, champion of the wronged, got his hands on the police report and revealed her real name, her government name, to the world. It was a name that the world was already familiar with. It was why so many at the scene felt like they already knew her. It was a name that many had strong polarizing opinions about. Exactly one year prior, to the day, #TrafficRageTammy had been given a different moniker and was at the center of a separate race-driven media frenzy. It was why she'd worn the shades and hoodies for a full year, and would never go outside without them readily handy.

Chapter Seven

One afternoon, a year prior, the woman that would be #TrafficRageTammy ran out of Riesling, and desperately had a taste for it. She'd thought of having Scoop 'Em Up Eatz deliver her a bottle but figured there was a Pic N Pay convenience store right on the corner of her Kirkwood block. She threw on some jeans, a t-shirt and flip flops, all of which had been delivered a week prior in a brown box with a blue label on the top and a smiley face on the side. She stood for a second on her small genuine, imitation, Persian throw rug debating as to whether she really needed or wanted a drink this badly. The answer came back yes and so she made her way to the store. Walking through the neighborhood was always interesting. She was a white woman in what had historically been a black neighborhood. As she strolled the sidewalks she was always met with black and brown faces that seemed to say, intruder, Christina Columbus, colonizer and of course, gentrifier. She was also met with just as many white faces that seemed to say, welcome to the resistance, thanks for increasing the property value, and kudos on ushering in the increased police presence. The walk to the store was a gauntlet of menacing smirks, welcoming smiles, and everything in-between. It was exhausting. She was halfway there and Scoop 'Em Up Eatz was looking like it would have been the smarter choice.

The corner Pic N Pay was a holdout from the old neighborhood. The store's owner hadn't been bought and forced out by a Sprouts or Whole Foods, yet. The Pic N Pay, like a Cheshire Bridge adult store, was just clean enough that you didn't mind it and just dirty enough that you didn't stay long. The store never seemed to have enough staff and always seemed to have in the ceiling, at least one, flickering, damn near seizure-inducing, about to blow out florescent light. The Pic N Pay smelled like, you gone buy that or not?, halal snacks and malt liquor, you can leave a penny but you can't take a penny, Biggie and burkas, we fix phone screens too, Evian and tap water, I said we're closed, As-salamu alaykum, and Oscar Meyer Bacon.

The owner of the Pic N Pay was a man of Middle Eastern descent that left the day to day running of the store to his three sons. His son's were third generation Arab-Americans who idolized everything culturally black. They wanted to be niggas but didn't want to be niggers. They would even refer to each other as, my nigga, when white people were around but never in the company of black people because, well... black people. For all of its shortcomings the Pic N Pay did, however, sell a five dollar Riesling that was as good as you could get for the price of five items from the Mickey D's dollar menu. The taste of the Riesling was just north of turpentine but as far as turpentine goes it went down smooth enough.

The store was bustling the day she decided to brave the gauntlet of smiles and glares and purchase a liquid lunch for the Pic N Pay. The line at the counter was so long you imagined that there had to be more than the TJ Maxx of Rieslings at the other end of it. It felt like a Six

Flags line that ended with a rollercoaster of a hangover and possibly a merry-go-ground of bad sexual choices. She endured the line because, well... wine. She was bumped and jostled as people moved in and out of the busy, tight corner store. There were no excuse me's or beg your pardon's. It was mostly either hard stares, as if she'd done something wrong just by existing, or people completely oblivious to the idea of personal space. She finally reached the counter feeling like she'd gone a round with Zab Judah and all he'd thrown were body blows. She put her wine on the counter and it rang up as eight dollars. Eight dollars!? It was barely worth five and definitely not worth six. She informed the clerk that it had always been five dollars. The sign by the bottles said five dollars. The taste said five dollars! The clerk told her she could step out of line if she liked and that one of his niggas, would resolve it after they'd checked out a few customers and gotten the long line under control. Pissed she took her wallet out of her back pocket, grabbed a ten from it, pushed the wallet violently back into her pocket and slammed the money on the counter. Just then she felt it. An anonymous hand from the crowd on her ass.

She was simultaneously stunned and enraged. A hand on her ass? On her ass! She remembered the stupid little boys in junior high always brushing up against her in the halls. Their greedy little hands, like kids reaching into Halloween bags as they walked home in the dark, busy, grabbing whatever they could. She remembered those boys and their wide lustful grins, and slightly bulging trousers pointing at her as if choosing her in a police line up. She remembered the stupid big "boy" in college inviting her over, promising that nothing was going to happen, and then explaining to her how she wanted it as he pulled his shirt and pants back on. She remembered lying in a ball on the edge of the bed trying not to cry as he hurriedly left. She hadn't visited those hallways or that dorm room in decades, and she'd thought of those memories, like the hairs standing up on her neck, as behind her. Here they were though, a sarcophagi freshly excavated, opened, and carrying the curse of the pharaohs.

She turned her head, a violated vehicle of rage, so quickly she almost did a complete one eighty without turning her body. Her emotions unbalanced, on edge, at a tipping point. She turned fully, to give a piece of her mind to whoever had stolen the feel of her ass. She turned to find him looking at her smiling with his brown hand extended. He couldn't be anymore than ten. Close to the age the "boys" in the halls had been. He'd probably grow up to be the "boy" in the dorm she thought. In his outstretched hand was her wallet. He was smiling and holding her wallet? He'd grabbed her ass, stolen her wallet, and thought it was all some kind of game? Some kind of joke? She snatched the wallet from his hand. His smile disappeared and his eyes, large and brown, the color of his mother's love, seemed to almost instantly fill with tears. It was clear that he could feel her rage. He knew something had gone wrong.

She asked where his mother was but before he could answer his mother appeared at his side almost as if by magic, talk about Houdini. She told the mother what her son had done. The mother looked at the boy, looked at her and then asked the little boy if he'd done that, if he'd stolen her wallet and touched her inappropriately. He shook his head no. Perhaps it was her residual anger from having walked the gentrification trail of tears. Maybe it was her annoyance at being bumped and prodded as she waited to purchase the Dollar General of wine. It certainly could have been the headache she had from the strobing florescent light or the freshly resurrected rage from boys-will-be-boys long gone, but whatever it was it left her not at her best. She looked at this brown boy, denying what she knew to be true, saw red and said to the mother, "I don't care what this little lying black fucker says! That's what happened!" The rest was a blur.

Threats were made by both parties. Cries of, how dare you, were directed at her from people of color in the store. She didn't remember pulling out her cellphone but suddenly it was in her hand and she was on it telling the police she'd been sexually assaulted and was being threatened by a black mob. Now not only was her phone out, but everyone in the store had their phones out too. They were all pointed at her. Recording.

The police arrived, and she felt safe. She didn't know why but she knew they would protect her, she knew they'd be on her side. The crowd knew it too. The police took statements, dispersed the crowd as best they could and made sure she made it safely home. Home, safe, and feeling much better after her second glass of ten dollar wine. She realized after the first glass that in the midst of the melee she'd never gotten her change. She rubbed her bare feet across her small genuine, imitation, Persian throw rug and let it soothe her. She felt herself relaxing, calming, breathing. She decided to forego the change and also that she'd call the precinct and drop the charges. She pulled out her phone but it was frozen while the Scoop Em Up Eatz app updated. She resolved that she'd call in the morning. What she didn't know, what she couldn't know, was that it was already too late.

Chapter Eight

The incident had instantly gone viral. Black Twitter had dubbed her #PicNPayPatricia, and they were demanding she be run out of Atlanta. "Dr. King didn't die so that #PicNPayPatricia could threaten a priceless child over cheap wine!" one post read. "The soul of Emmett Till will rise up and pull her body down into Georgia's red clay," an op-ed insisted. Faux News, Fair and Un-Balanced had red-faced, red-necked, red-white-and-blue-flag-waving anchors calling her the new face of the #MeToo movement. It was Faux that first introduced into the English lexicon the term, Sexual Super Predator Children, to describe the young black boy that had allegedly felt her up, and those that looked like him. SeeNN sent a gender fluid, transgender, bi-racial reporter to do on the scene reporting. BeNextNWellSee did hour long video editorials on the effects of climate change and GDP on sexual assault in economically depressed areas. She missed it all. The Scoop Em Up Eatz app update didn't complete until well after she was asleep.

The incessant pounding on her door woke her the next morning. She was right about the hangover that lived at the bottom of that bottle of wine, but wrong about the merry-go-round of sex. As she dragged herself to the door she thought, well at least I didn't throw up. Whoever was knocking was knocking like they were the police. She wiped the crust from her eyes and looked through the peep hole. It was the police. She opened the door. An officer said, "PicNPayPatricia?" She looked over her shoulder hoping to see the Patricia person he was talking to, and to ask her to leave. Another officer answered for her, "Yeah, that's her. Ma'am please get dressed and come wit us." She imagined that this is when they'd rip off their pants and reveal that they were really strippers. Then the promised Riesling sex might show up. Their pants stayed on, their faces remained serious and the Riesling sex was still nowhere in sight. "What's this all about?" she asked. The officers looked from one to another, confused. Surely she knew. "It's for your protection ma'am. Now please get dressed and come with us."

"For my own protection? From what? No. Why?" One of the officers pulled out his phone and showed her a meme with over 25,000 comments and a million shares. It was a picture of her holding her phone to her ear with the hashtag PicNPayPatricia written across it. "Is this a joke? Because of yesterday? PicNPayPatricia? It couldn't have gotten that serious? Listen I'd like to drop the charges." The officer that she'd really and truly been secretly hoping was a stripper put his hand on her shoulder, "Ma'am you can certainly drop the charges once we get to the station but right now, for your safety, we must go."

"What's happening!? Please, tell me what is going on!?" An officer that looked too young to be protecting and serving anything or anyone said, "He's dead ma'am... the little boy from the incident yesterday. He was killed."

Chapter Nine

Jonah smelled like, his mother's first born, be in this house before those street lights come on, now-uh-latahs, sweet behind his left ear, a stolen piece of penny candy from the Pic N Pay, excited and nervous to start sixth grade, now I lay me down to sleep, and the horizon on the first day. Jonah was dead. Murdered. He'd been kidnapped in the night and found the morning following the Pic N Pay incident, down by the Chattahoochee. The You-look-too-young officer informed her and she felt the floor coming up fast. The Please-be-a-stripper officer caught her before she slammed face first into the small genuine, imitation, Persian throw rug. She looked at his trousers, noted they were definitely not tear away pants, and vomited.

She was dressed, in the car, and headed to the station when she was told about the three men from Walton County, Georgia, that drove up under the cover of night. One of the bombastic a.m. conservative talk radio hosts had "accidentally" revealed the address of Jonah and his mother's house on the air. He'd told his rabid audience, made up of loaded guns passing as people just looking for a target and direction, what he would, hypothetically, do if he were in their shoes. What happened next pulled the hypothetical ramblings of a blowhard into stark, irreversible, reality.

The home Jonah shared with his mom was broken into at roughly one a.m., according to the police report. Jonah's mother tried to fight off the men but was beaten within an inch of her life. This young man who had just recently made it to double digits, who had been labeled a Black Sexual Super Predator for radio ratings, who was accused of having the nerve to assault with impunity a white woman, was taken. He was bound and thrown into the back of a pick up truck and driven to the Chattahoochee. There he was shot, tied to an old car transmission, and an attempt was made to throw him in the river. The perpetrators were discovered before they could complete the crime. They ran off leaving the truck but didn't get far before being apprehended.

The You-look-too-young officer looked at her through the rearview mirror and said, "They said they did it for you."

"For me!?" She responded.

He looked forward and continued, "They said, The Blacks have gotten too free with their hands and their thoughts and what happened to you was the last straw. It gave them the courage they needed, and they don't care if they're put to death because it was the white thing to do." She listened to the officer while simultaneously, from her phone, she ordered hoodies and shades that would be delivered in a brown box, with a blue label on the top and a smiling face on the side.

Sean Prince got his hands on a copy of the police report, the one with the charges that in all of the madness, she'd forgotten to drop, and let the world know the real name, the government name, of

#PicNPayPatricia. The Internet did what it does. Memes, gifs, and vitriol flowed freely. Death threats were issued. Marches were organized. Old civil rights leaders with perms, permanently stained shirts from lunch counter sit-ins, and scars from police dogs that ached when it rained, sang, spoke of non-violent resistance, and urged everyone to gather at a community fish fry that would be held the following Friday. Fish plates would go, one for seven dollars or two for ten. Hot sauce would not be provided. A young freedom fighter whose pronouns were Reparations, Freedom or Death, and No Justice No Peace, went live via Face-A-Gram to warn of the dangers of conservative talk radio, and fish cooked too closely to hair perm chemicals. He then accidentally Face-A-Grammed out a pic of his penis prompting people to suggest his pronouns be changed to she, her, and hers. A loc'd Dr. Petoh Halla insisted all people of color shed the shackles and citizenship of their white oppressor immediately and return to Africa as he would be doing by month's end. His plan to become an ex-pat raised the eyebrows of his three baby mamas, all of them white, who immediately filed for child support and drained his return to Africa fund. And in the midst of all of this the security camera footage from the Pic N Pay went public.

She saw the video for the first time along with the rest of the world. There was no audio but she could hear it. The sounds and smells of the Pic N Pay came flooding back to her. The loud bustle of the day, the jostling, the one flickering florescent light. All of it. There she was at the counter. There it was, her overpriced wine. There they were, the selective my nigga brothers, asking her to step aside. There she was reaching for her wallet, pulling out the ten, slamming the wallet into her back pocket and slapping the ten on the counter. There he was ... eternally ten years old, dressed in old worn jeans and fresh out of the box Jordans. His short-sleeve red polo was unbuttoned far enough for you to see the top of the t-shirt just beneath. He wore a backpack covered with sponges, jellyfish, and sea snails all magically come to life, wearing pants and saying stupid things in comment bubbles. His backpack bumped her rear as he was walking past. It knocked her wallet, that in her anger and haste she hadn't put into her back pocket fully, onto the floor. The footage clearly shows her, and the world, that it isn't his hand but his bag that touched her ass. He bent over, retrieved the wallet, smiled and extended it to her. She watches herself turn around ... and watches herself become #PicNPayPatricia.

The revelations of the video push race relations in the city to the edge. Atlanta hadn't burned to the ground since Sherman's visit in 1864 but the video from the Pic N Pay was like a match to a city already covered in the kerosene of racial tension. What followed were talks amongst community leaders and politicians during hopeful days. Skirmishes during anger filled nights. I-85 was brought to a halt by protestors more than once. Drug dealers turned rappers, using words valued at the price of Pic N Pay Riesling, seemed to be making more sense than the property blowhard, turned reality star, turned president who claimed to have the best words. #PicNPayPatricia got a lawyer. She made a tearful, on-air apology,

"I'd like to apologize for what I said and what I did at the Pic N Pay. I was wrong. I know that now. I'd like to apologize to the young man and

263

his family. My apology can't bring him back or right the wrong but I'd like to extend it to you."

SeeNN aired the apology on a 24 hour news cycle loop. Faux News refused to air it calling it Fake Blues. BeNextNWellSee did an hour long video editorial discussing the effects of climate change and GDP on apologies and remorse in economically depressed areas. People of color including the family of the young man had heard these empty declarations of remorse before and wouldn't, couldn't, accept the apology. Angry whites who had named her their Virgin Mary reborn were too married to their reverse racism revelry to even begin to understand what she could be apologizing for.

#PicNPayPatricia moved out of Kirkwood leaving everything except a small genuine, imitation, Persian throw rug. She cut and died her hair and tried to hide in plain sight behind shades and hoodies. She used a pseudonym most of the time, ordered in a lot, watched tons of WebFlicks movies and just wanted all of this to blow over. The worst was the week after the murder of Jonah when the funeral was held. All of the networks came with cameras rolling. When they asked Jonah's mother if she had anything she'd like to say to #PicNPayPatricia she gathered herself, looked into the camera, and let out a moan, that turned into a scream, that turned into a roar. It lasted longer than most people would have thought possible and chilled to the bone any and all that heard it.

Then the world did what it does. An unarmed young black man was shot by an Asian cop in Youngstown, Ohio. A Latina citizen was shot by a white security guard for trying to enter a building, and work a shift, at a job she'd had for over a decade. A middle aged white woman accused a prominent politician of sexually assaulting her, and several other women found the courage to make the same allegation. Then the Internet did what it does. Memes, gifs, and vitriol flowed freely. Death threats were made. Before you could digest one tragedy, there's another that you're told is more important, and then another, and then... It was like today's pain being overwritten before ever having a chance to resolve yesterday's anger; and tomorrow's tragedy standing ready to erase today's miscarriage of justice completely. Before you could fully remember #BoyKilledInYoungstown's name or that his black life mattered you had to immediately Face-a-Gram about #MeTooPoliticalScandal or you were anti-feminist, but not before you drop everything to write a lengthy post about #SayHerNameLatinaWorker lest you be labeled Xenophobic. It was an ouroboros of tragedy. A snake of responses to civil and social unrest and crimes constantly devouring itself.

#PicNPayPatricia got lost in the Face-a-Gram stream. She became last minute's villain. She kept her head down, her hoodie up, her shades on, her brown boxes with smiley faces coming, and lived her life quietly in the shadows. Until, there he was in the middle of the street, a year to the day after his death with his hand out, his smile wide as the horizon and his eyes a levee trying to hold back Katrina's rains.

Chapter Ten

When it became known that #TrafficRageTammy was indeed #PicNPayPatricia there rose a call to label her a serial killer and the accident a hate crime. Sean Prince let the world know that the traffic accident happened on the same day and in the same hour and minute that the Pic N Pay incident occurred. The traffic cam video showed she clearly drove off the road and targeted La La, that poor, black, woman. #TrafficRageTammy got a lawyer and while they easily beat the serial killer label and barely beat the hate crime charge in criminal court, the civil suit ruined her. It financially stripped her to the bare bones. She soon found herself homeless, out of doors with just the clothes on her back and a small genuine, imitation, Persian throw rug around her shoulders.

On top of that, through it all, Jonah wouldn't leave her. He'd been standing in the court room beside the judge during her trial. She used to find him every morning in her closet standing beside her hoodies. He'd stood, smiling, his hand extended in the corner of the bathroom while she showered. He'd been behind her in the line at the grocery store his hand nudging her in the back. He'd ride shotgun with her Lyft drivers, the whole time his head turned 180 degrees and staring at her in the back seat. Her employer, who had been under great pressure to let her go, called her in to talk about her future with the company one day during the trial. When she sat and looked up, Jonah was on the other side of the desk beside her boss with his hand extended almost to her chin. Her boss had said to her, "I don't know what to do here," trying to be honest about his position and her prospects. "Get your hand out of my face! Get the fuck outta here! And leave me the fuck alone!" Her reply was intended for the apparition standing just to the left her employer. The apparition that her boss clearly couldn't see. She was fired immediately.

They say we're all just one paycheck from homelessness. She proved it. She was broke, and broken. A social pariah cast to the wolves and the streets. Even the homeless, society's omnipresent outcasts would reject her when they discovered who she was. For people with no television or Internet she found them to be incredibly well informed. Thank God for Jinx, the woman formerly known as Florence Jenkins, who now pointed at the little boy that no one but herself had seen for three years and said, "You gotta settle up with him."

She couldn't believe Jinx could see him too.

"You can see him!?" she asked.

Jinx replied, "Fuck yeah he's right there with his damn hand out."

"I thought I was going crazy Jinx!" she blurted out, tears now welling up in her eyes to match his.

"Who the fuck said you ain't?" Jinx said as she slowly eased down beside her on the sidewalk. They both stared at him as he stood still as a statue, his eyes glistening with the water held just beyond.

"Listen girl, I don't often mix into people's business but since you've been coming round here he has too, with his hand out smiling at you all wide mouthed on some Colgate shit," Jinx gestured toward him.

"I know. He's been with me for three years now. Three years ... but I don't know what to do."

"What to do? Shiiiit! Why don't you give that motherfucker what he want!"

"What he wants!? I've given him food, money, candy. I've given him everything! I've got nothing left to give!" She shouts angrily at him.

"Yeah? Have you though? Have you ever apologized?"

" ... What?"

"Have you ever given him an apology?"

"I went on national TV and apologized."

Jinx sucked her teeth loudly and chuckled sarcastically, "That bullshit? I remember that. After looking like you had been forced to eat a shit sandwich you said, if I remember correctly, and I always remember correctly, 'I'd like to apologize for what I did.'"

"Yeah. I apologized!"

"If I walked up to you right now and said I'd like to beat your ass does that mean I beat your ass?"

"...No."

"Right! It means in the future I perhaps have intentions on beating your ass. You saying, I'd like to apologize, ain't apologizing. It's saying one day in the future perhaps I have intentions on apologizing." Jinx let that sit in the air for a moment before she continued,

"Maybe he just wants an apology. Fuck if I know though. My last husband apologized to me after hitting me in the mouth and I stabbed his ass in his sleep with a steak knife so... it could go either way."

She sat, feeling the regret of the last three years in her bones, staring at him and thinking about what Jinx had said. Then #TrafficRageTammy shrugged the small genuine, imitation, Persian throw rug from her shoulders, stood and walked over to him. Then #PicNPayPatricia sandwiched his outstretched hand between hers and said in a soft, forgotten voice, "I would like to... No, not I would like to. I ... I am sorry. I'm so, so incredibly sorry."

She felt a drop of rain hit the back of her hand and looked up into the clear sky. She then realized it wasn't rain, it was her tears... and his.

<End>

Handsy (a short story)

Handsy

I used to think it was corny when couples talked about celebrating their one month, or three month, or six month anniversary. It seemed to signal to me that perhaps they'd never had a relationship that lasted longer than one, three, or six months, and thus this was truly a cause for gaiety. I imagined these people as bacchanal buddies, or euphoria addicts just looking for a reason to eat, drink, drug, and be merry. I mean honestly, I've got mold on cheese in the fridge that's thirty days old. I'm not proud of it, but I do! I thought these relative strangers, merrymaking due to thirty days of knowing their semi-significant other, to be exaggerant, extravagant fools. I thought that, until COVID-31.

Now every day feels like an anniversary, a need to celebrate, a cause for jubilation. No one, with any sense, takes tomorrow for granted anymore. Few even take the next hour as a given. All it takes is a slip of your mask, a hole in your gloves, forgetting to put in your nose filters, ear screens, or microbe blocking contact lenses. All it takes is forgetting to wash your hands and then touching your face, eyes, nose; or neglecting to follow home decontamination protocols. The smallest mistake or lapse in vigilance and, well. The homeless used to carry signs that said, The End Is Near. Those that are left now they carry signs that say, The End Was Yesterday, You Can't Hand Sanitize The Past, You Can't Wash Your Hands Of ... Us.

Us. I got us, Celia and I, reservations at *Table for Two*. It's our three week anniversary. Don't judge me. I read somewhere that anything you do for three weeks straight becomes a habit, and anything you do habitually, you can do forever. Celia and I are exactly twenty-one days into what might turn into a lifetime together. Albeit a lifetime isn't as long as it used to be.

We matched and met, like most people do these days, on *hAPPy Dating.* Digi-dating has become the only way people meet. No one bumps into anyone anymore, figuratively or literally. All of the typical gathering spots, where singles used to mingle - bars, clubs, malls, even offices - closed after the CDC advised against groups larger than 250, then 100, then 25, now three or more, coming together at any one time, in any one space.

Concerts are now held virtually. The band members all stand in front of green screens in their homes and are electronically edited and commingled together on a virtual stage. The concertgoers buy a ticket, log in and watch; or if they have Virt-You-All's (Virt for short) contact lenses, glasses or goggles, and a Virt-Life Suit, they can have an experience almost like being there. Which also happens to be Virt-You-All's latest slogan, "Like Being There." Which is better than their original slogan, "The Only Thing Realer Might Kill You." Accurate but not as catchy.

What is true for concerts is also true of sporting events. Once the NBA, MLB, NCAA and every other major, minor, college, and high school sports league suspended play indefinitely, the players began to stand in front of green screens on omni-directional treadmills in their homes. Their movements are recorded and combined in real time on a virtual field, ring, court, or what have you. You can buy floor seats, mid-level, or nose bleeds and have an experience that directly aligns itself with your spending. No matter what, however, everyone, the patrons and players, do everything alone, in their homes, in an effort to avoid contracting, and to work toward stopping the spread of the virus. So the chances of meeting someone outside of digi-dating is somewhere between nil, no, zero, and none.

The hAPPy Dating algorithm said Celia and I had a 72% chance of possibly marrying, coupled with a 28% chance of definitely succumbing to COVID-31. So there was no time to waste. We got online and talked, laughed, cried, wined, and dined via SkyMe. She told me about her greatest triumphs. I told her about my greatest fears. She told me about her darkest nights. I told her about my brightest days. We understood and bonded with each other instantly. We sympathized and empathized via SkyMe every night, for a few hours, for an entire week. We discovered that we were what the young folks call Sole Mates, people willing to Heli-Car a mile in the other person's shoes.

I told her I loved her after that first week. She told me she loved me after a week and a half. We went to second base virtually in Pear's xxX-Box on the night we said I love you at the same time. Jinx! It seemed written in the stars, or at least gave us a superstition fueled excuse. We both put on our skin thin, ultra-absorbent, intimacy undergarments, our Virt-Life Suits, and touched and held each other across the miles, from the safety of our own homes. This is how intimacy is done. No one can risk skin-to-skin contact, or the exchange of fluids. That's like playing Russian Roulette with a Derringer. No, no one does that. You either sit in the seclusion of your homes and wear gloves, goggles, absorbs, and a Virt-Life Suit; or you sit a safe distance across the room from each other, usually with a flexiwall between you, and describe what you'd like to do to the other person while that person, with a gloved hand, engages in auto-arousal until completion. That is unless you're rich. The rich have twin, hermetically sealed beds, separated by a micro-thin, body compliant, e-lastic sheath. It allows them to get close enough to feel each other's warmth, and even enter each other, without ever touching skin to skin. It's a very, very, expensive condom.

As you might imagine, due to all of this, birth rates are down. All fertilization is done in labs. All babies are gestated in tech giant Cadabra's Womb-Manned Machines, or as they are called by people keyboard squawking on Noir Chirper, Faux-Lopian Tubes. The babies are emerged after nine months. The mother's can't breastfeed because their bodies aren't producing milk. They were never pregnant. The children are instead given a vitamin enriched, steroid infused, nutritional supplement. Cadabra keeps the children in a sterile environment for at least two years, so that they are immunized, some say indoctrinated, and prepared for the viral dangers of the world. Parents can visit, daily if they'd like, but aren't allowed to touch the children with their bare hands during that time. It's for everyone's safety. Unfortunately there is a high infant mortality rate during the first year. No one is sure of the cause. Some speculate it's the lack of a mother's touch, human warmth, mother's milk, a warm voice, mother's love. Scientists have ruled that out and dubbed it ludicrous.

Tonight at *Table For Two* will be the first time Celia and I have met in person. It's risky. Some never chance it. Some couples date, marry, and divorce without ever once having been in the same room. There are even those who have developed debilitating anxiety when faced with the prospect of having to leave their homes and interact with people live and in-person. Those folks used to be called agoraphobic but are mostly referred to today as Innies. Then there is digi-dating phenomenon known as Puffer-Fishing. This is when someone blows themselves up to be someone they're not. They use software to present online as far more attractive than they are, or as another race, or gender. A Puffer Fish will never want to do a face to face. I think Celia and I both want to ensure we're not being puffer'd, and so we agreed to dinner.

I arrive at *Table For Two* a few minutes early. I look at the sign affixed to the door that reads, No Mask, No Gloves, No Nose Filters, No Service. More and more places seem to be posting these gentle reminders. You're expected to wear a mask to the restaurant, remove it to place the food in your mouth, and replace it before you even begin to chew. My cousin Vincent celebrated his one week anniversary with Anika here. He didn't replace his mask after every bite. He actually waited until they were about to leave to put his mask back on. He received an in app message later letting him know he was no longer welcome to dine at that location. Anika broke up with him two days later. He celebrated his one week anniversary with Brooke last week, at a different *Table For Two*. He put his mask back on after every bite, almost before the fork could deposit the peppercorn crusted Salmonlapia into his mouth.

I do a retinal scan at the door to confirm my identity. There's a small red light flashing just to the right of the scanner to denote that the room is still occupied. I look through the window at the front of the restaurant and see the couple that had the reservation before ours leaving through the rear exit. Once the door closes and locks behind them a fast drying disinfectant mist is sprayed over the entire room via a sprinkler system. An employee, dressed in a safety suit (what was once called a Hazmat Suit), quickly enters and removes the previously used table and chairs. A new table and fresh chairs are peeled from the their plastic wrappings and placed in the center of the room. The employee quickly exits behind what appears to be an airtight door, the light beside the retinal scanner goes green, the door unlocks, opens, and I enter.

The entire room is off-white. In the center of the room is a beige table and two red chairs. *Table For Two* has revolutionized the dining out experience. A couple reserves the restaurant, arrives at the agreed upon time, dines, leaves, and another couple arrives and does the same. The food is ordered via an app on your phone and delivered to the table via drone. The couple interacts with no one but each other. *Table For Two* is open, and booked, twenty four hours a day, seven days a week.

I hear a buzz and Celia enters just as I'm about to sit. I stand up straighter than I know possible. I feel a trickle of sweat run down my back. Here she is, in the flesh, and I'm not sure what I'm supposed to do now. None of us get much real world dating practice these days. I have a better idea of what do do when landing on the moon, than what to do when confronted with a living breathing woman. Hugging her is out of the question. Shaking her gloved hand with my gloved hand, making physical contact, seems forward. So I fold my right arm across my chest and bow down to one knee as if about to engage her in a martial arts death match. It feels stupid. I saw it done in a movie once. What am I doing? When I stand from my genuflection I can tell by her eyes, she's smiling. She does a curtsy, just like the woman in the movie! She walks over to her seat.

Her hips rise and fall like the Dow Jones in her mustard colored pleated trousers. At the bottom of her pant legs is an elastic hem that seems to give her a good solid seal against her leopard printed, block heeled, Louboutin, red bottomed boots. The crimson of her mock-neck blouse echoes the sole of the boot. Celia's jacket is made of a transparent biopolymer. When she moves you feel like you're looking at her shirt through a basin of rippling clear water. When she's still the jacket almost seems to disappear. Her Louis Vuitton mask and gloves are leopard printed to match the boots. She looks stylish and amazing by any metric, but it's her eyes that catch mine and won't release them.

It's all the rage for women, and men, to adorn and makeup their eyes. I was thirty when COVID-19 arrived, and thirty four when COVID-23 ran roughshod through the world. I remember clearly everyone, everywhere, beginning to wear masks in public, and sometimes at home. It seemed ironic that here, in a nation that suffered from such severe Islamaphobia, everyone began to basically wear a niqab.

Since the only thing that could really be seen on a person's face was their eyes, it became what people began to accentuate. And accentuate they did. Eye lids became the peacock feathers of the world. A brand of eyeliner for men, Guyliner, and colored microbe blocking contact lenses became very popular. There were even subtle, and not so subtle, eyeshadows that came into vogue for the gentleman that wanted to raise eyebrows. Not for nothing, I have on a clear coat myself this evening. Women, however, had full color pallets and elaborate techniques for lids, lashes and brows. Brow beating tutorials dominate ViewTube to this day. Fake rhinestones, real diamonds, Lidoplasty, whatever can be used to enhance the area just beneath the forehead and just above the nose, can and will be used.

Celia however has gone with the less is more approach. Her lids have only the faintest wisp of orange playing across them. It gives the effect of a sunset. Her brows are neat but not beat, tended but not busy, and she wears no color in her contacts. Her eyes are clear, full and round. They are a brown that seems to almost exactly match her complexion. I can't take my eyes off of hers. She has the kind of eyes you can take home to mom.

It's only after she sits that I notice that I am still standing. I take my seat across from her and smile a smile I hope she can see in my eyes. We pull out our phones and order. The conversation is a bit stilted at first, muffled through our masks, but the more we eat and drink the more we become the people we know each other to be on SkyMe. Perhaps we can love each other in real life and not just through screens, monitors, and fiber-optics. Perhaps.

I look at the time and notice we're almost out of it. Our reservation is fast drawing to a close and the next couple will soon have their eyes to the scanner. I want to ... go somewhere with her and continue talking. This is better. In person is better in a way that I had not anticipated or remembered. I haven't done it in so long that I didn't realize how much I've missed it. It is this, the sitting across from one another, talking, looking into each others eyes, this is the human part of human being. I've just been, being. I understand that now. But I have nowhere to take Celia. We'd have had to have made reservations to go to *Single Serve Coffee Bar*, or *One Diner*, but I hadn't thought that far ahead. I should have, but I hadn't. I feel very unpracticed at something that I'm sure should come natural. That I'm sure once did. As I'm having these thought my phone lights up with a new message, from Celia.

The message is all emojis, a peach, a pair of eyes, an eggplant, and a gloved hand. Does this mean what I think it means? Is she inviting me, back to her place? I look across the table. Her eyes smile wide, and look away bashfully. I respond with 100, and a percentage emoji. I think there is one that combines the two, but whatever. I watch as she reads my message. I watch as she swallows hard, pushes her chair back and stands. It's not until she's standing that I notice that I'm still sitting. I stand so quickly I knock my chair over. She laughs as she puts her invisible coat on. I place my eye in front of the retinal scanner just beside the rear door. I feel my phone buzz, which is probably the receipt being sent to me. The door swings open, and Celia and I step into the night.

We both order a single passenger, self navigating, Heli-Car to take us to her place. We stand a respectful and safe distance away from each other in silence until her ShareCopter arrives. She steps inside, gives me a wink, and is whisked away in an instant. A wink ... a wink. I smile broadly and look down at my phone. The app says my Heli-car is still six minutes away. I'm thinking about her wink, what it means. Was there just something in her eye? Was she just blinking slowly, with one eye? I replay it over and over in my mind. That's when I see them. Really I hear them first, laughing loudly, their voices bouncing off of the buildings like fireworks against the night sky. The sounds coming from them are unencumbered by the muzzle and muffle of a mask. They're ... not wearing masks. The woman is tall, her legs look like they extend back to where God began. She's darkly complected, and her hair is in an afro that shakes as if answering in the affirmative with her every step. She's wearing a skirt, her legs bare, a tank top, her arms bare, and out of nowhere she begins to sing. I don't know the song but the man with her does. He's a bit shorter than she. His skin is the color of Decatur back road puddle water after a soft drizzle. He wears cut-off jeans, bare legs, and a t-shirt, bare arms. He joins her in song. Half way through the first verse they both begin to laugh again. Then they take each others hand, each others bare hand, and fall into each others arms, each others bare arms .... laughing. I'm somewhere between gobsmacked, confused, and disgusted. I've heard about them, but I've never actually seen one for myself. I almost didn't believe they existed. Handsies.

COVID-19 arrived in 2019, and by spring of 2020 it was a pandemic that sent the world into a frenzy. People were in grocery stores hitting other people over the head with wine bottles and stealing their cases of water. Even the multi-grain bread that no one ate went missing from the shelves. You couldn't buy a squirt of hand sanitizer or a square of toilet paper anywhere. There were people dying in China, Italy, Germany, and places we'd never heard of. There were cruise ships stranded at sea, playing "Staying Alive" to empty dance floors, because of outbreaks. Schools were suspending classes one after the other, and asking professors that still had dial-up modems to teach online courses. A state of emergency was declared in most major cities and citizens were advised to stay indoors and practice social distancing. The U.S. government seemed ill-equipped to handle the arrival of this new strain of coronavirus. There was conflicting information coming from the White House, the CDC, WHO and HHS. Some commentators on MSNBC, Fox News and CNN said it was a dangerous and possibly fatal global pandemic, and other commentators, on those same networks, said it was just a bit worse than the flu, and not to overreact. People reacted, the over of it was a judgement call. Erring on the side of caution people stocked up for what felt like the coming apocalypse, or at the very least season two of *The Walking Dead*. They began to bathe in homemade hand sanitizer, some of which smelled like chicken grease, and swim in bargain basement store brand bleach.

People stopped touching, stopped gathering. Stopped. Those
that left home at all would immediately wash their hands under scalding
hot water when they returned. Even then, so as to break the habit of
putting their fingers in their eyes, or mouth, or ears, they began to
practice not touching themselves. Populations the world over weren't
having physical contact with anyone, not even themselves. It led to
rampant depression and a rash of suicides globally. COVID-19 was the
gateway that led to the world we find ourselves in today.

At the same time, in 2020, in small enclaves in the West Side of
Atlanta, there were groups of people who would not comply. They
would not wear the masks. They would not distance themselves from
others. They would not not shake hands with strangers, not hug loved
ones, not feel their own faces. These West End neighborhoods that had
recently gentrified immediately experienced white flight like never seen
before. Even many people of color, feeling like they were surrounded
by Typhoid Marys, left without even packing up their homes or locking
their doors behind them. The few local grocery stores, in what was
already basically a food desert, closed shop and so the people in the
West End began growing their own food. When the coffee shops and
restaurants abandoned the neighborhood and the property value fell
sharply, they bought the buildings for little to nothing and opened their
own. When the clubs went under they started having bonfire
illuminated block parties, all night, at the corner of Lee and Abernathy.
They gathered every Sunday and danced a commemorative second line
up Joseph E. Lowery Blvd, for all who'd passed the week before. No
licensed physician would see them so they became herbalists and

natural healers. They got sick. Some died. Most got well. They reported that cancer and other diseases had fallen to record lows since they'd begun growing their own food and using natural medicines. The suicide rate amongst them was almost non-existent. Their birth rate was much higher than the national average. They rooted in the earth. They danced in the sky. They waded in the water. They embraced each other whole heartedly, and greeted each other with a hug or handshake. Because of this they were called Handsies.

A Handsy medical representative was interviewed via SkyMe once on CNN. I remember watching the video on ViewTube. He warned that if people got too disease free, too clean, too far away from the natural pathogens of the earth, they would have no immunity against anything and be unable to survive even the common cold. This was four months before COVID-23.

COVID-23 was the Rubicon. You either crossed into a life of masks, isolation, and celebrating being together for one week; or you went against everything that every major health organization advised, and breathed deeply the air of the West End. As you might imagine the overwhelming majority pulled on their gloves and settled into their downtown homes and what would become the new normal.

I'd never even heard of anyone that went to the West End. I figured maybe that colony had moved on or died out. I imagined that none of the Handsies could have survived to see COVID-31. And here, dancing, singing, and laughing down the middle of Peachtree Street, two Handsies.

They notice me trying to act like I'm not looking at them. They wave. I look at my phone. The Heli-Car is four minutes away. They don't approach me. They just smile and continue to walk and sing. His hand is in hers. At one point he spins her, dips her, and they kiss. His mouth is on hers, their tongues... She grabs the back of his head and pulls his mouth even further into hers. His hands hold her full weight. Touch her bare skin. They end their kiss, stare in each other's eyes, laugh and continue their song and dance down the street. I look at my phone, two minutes.

I feel flush. In spite of myself I steal glances at them. It takes a second for me to accept the truth of how watching them has affected me. I feel aroused. They look so free. So happy. I can't seem to imagine being so comfortable, not only with another but with myself. Why? I was thirty when COVID-19 arrived. How had I, in just thirteen years, so completely forgotten myself. I look at them openly now. I can't take my eyes off of them as they ease on down the road like Dorothy and the Tin man. Arm in arm, singing and dancing. My Heli-Car lands. I watch until they disappear around a corner. Then I take my seat and in an instant I'm whisked away.

I arrive at Celia's building a few moments later. She has a condo in what used to be the CNN center before they moved. I walk into the lobby, enter her unit number into a key screen by the elevator, and identify myself via retinal scan. She appears on the screen, her mask still on, smiles with her eyes, and buzzes me up. I enter the elevator and go through the building's decontamination protocols as I'm brought to her floor. Unconsciously I discover I'm humming the melody of the song the two Handsies were singing as they danced up the street. I make myself stop.

I look into the retinal scanner beside Celia's door. It makes sure I match with the scan and approved apartment entry in the key pad below. I do. The door swings open and Celia stands there in a robe. She has on her mask, her gloves, and a bath robe, nothing else. We're separated by a transparent flexiwall. All of the modern condos have them. They're for added protection against COVID-31 and just in case someone tricks or falsifies their way into an apartment. Flexiwalls are super thin but incredibly strong moving walls. The owner of the condo can make it so that it's a fixed barrier, or allow it to move freely as the person on the other side walks about. Everyone's microbes are contained on their side of the wall and a disinfecting mist automatically sprays itself on anything of Celia's that I touch. I stand so close to the wall that even with my mask on I can see my breath against it. We're so close, and yet so far.

She points behind me, and gestures for me to sit on the sofa on the far side of the room. I do. She turns and walks to a sofa across from me, on her side of the flexiwall. We must be roughly fifteen yards from each other. She removes her mask, and smiles. In my mind I see the Handsy woman smiling and dancing down Peachtree street. I see her hand pulling her companions mouth more completely into hers. I start to hum a tune I don't know, as I remove my mask.

"Dinner was amazing," Celia says.

"Thank you," I reply, "I cooked it myself." She laughs.

"Three weeks. Can you believe it?"

"I can. I hear that anything you do for three weeks," and we say in unison, "becomes a habit." We both smile.

"I ..." she pauses, turns her head away for a beat, and then continues, "I don't imagine you have a pair of absorbs, and a Virt-Life Suit with you?"

I immediately take her meaning, "Unfortunately, I don't." I see Handsy man's hands against the dancing lady's bare skin as they kiss, and I feel my breath quicken.

"Well I was wondering if you'd, if you'd like to celebrate our anniversary... properly."

I see their fingers intertwined, hers black as pitch, his the brown of Decatur puddle water, "Absolutely," I reply.

Celia gestures to a door just behind me. I stand and walk through it. I hear the disinfecting mist spray on the sofa. Through the door is a bathroom, and hanging on the back of the door is a robe that matches hers, and a unopened box of organisynthetic gloves. They are the Impossible Burger of gloves. Fancy. Expensive. I undress, slip on a pair of the gloves, throw my old ones in her bathroom trash incinerator, and don the robe. I re-enter the room and sit on the couch.

We smile awkward, shy smiles at each other, but she can look at the contour of my robe and tell I'm aroused. She bites her lip and begins telling me the ways she'd kiss me. I match her line for line. I speak of my mouth on her neck, her breasts, her, everywhere. I tell her how I'd kiss her greedily, caress the back of her head, and pull her mouth more fully into mine. We both elevate the intensity and salaciousness of our words as we try harder and harder to excite the other. Her left gloved hand rubs her breasts, beneath her robe and her right disappears into her lap. I reach beneath my robe and take a hold of myself. Her hips begin to grind into the sofa and she begins to softly moan. I rub my entire length, and begin to sweat. We're talking over each other at this point, both pushing the other to ecstasy. Then I see them again. In my mind. The Handsy couple. Laughing. His bare hand in hers. Dancing. Her bare skin against his. Kissing. No mask. No cares. No gloves. I rip the gloves from my hands, and grab myself. I haven't touched myself without a glove on in almost a decade. I'm engorged and throbbing, in my own bare hand. It feels almost foreign. But it feels ... good. I hear a scream from across the room. I look up, and see Celia putting her mask back on, her face contorted in horror.

"What are you doing! What are you doing!?"

I don't know what to say I open my mouth and only manage,

"I...I...I..."

"Are you, touching yourself!? I mean touching yourself touching yourself!? Are you speaking love making to me without a glove! Are you crazy!" She grabs the flexiwall controller and begins to make it shrink around me.

"Grab your clothes and get the fuck out of my place! Get the fuck out!"

The sanitizing mist begins to spray everywhere and everything, including me. I dive into the bathroom and dress as hurriedly as I can. I put on my mask and grab a fresh pair of organisynthetic gloves. I want to say something but I know there is no excuse for what I've done. In some cities speaking love making with an ungloved hand, and not notifying your partner, is a form of sexual assault. When I exit the bathroom the flexiwall is contoured in such a way as to only allow me a path to the front door. Celia is fully dressed, in tears and sobbing into the phone to someone.

"... and then... and then... he touch touched himself!"

I hear the voice on the other end shout, "What!" I don't say a word I just leave. I board the elevator and run through the lobby into the street. My chest is heaving. I feel out of breath. What did I just do!? That was crazy! I feel... I don't know. Different. I can't explain it but it's true I walked into that condo one person and I've emerged, changed in some way. I close my eyes and see the Handsies easing on down the road. A warm night breeze runs across my closed eyelids, and my breathing slows. I look up at the bright moon in the clear sky, something I haven't done in some time.

I pull out my phone to order a Heli-Car. I need to go home, sleep, think, and sleep. I notice I have a message from *hAPPy Dating*. I've been kicked off the platform for inappropriate touching. Fuck. I look around and realize I live about seventeen blocks from Celia's condo. I take off one of my glove and feel the wind against my hand. It's been a rough evening but it's still a nice night. I pull up walking directions to my place, start to hum a song I don't know and walk home.

ACKNOWLEDGEMENTS

First giving thanks to God. My every opportunity and blessing comes from God's love, mercy, and grace.

Thank you to my mother Barbara Goode, my father John E Goode Jr., my sister Tiffany, nephew Joshua, sisters Cheryl, Leisa and Yvette, and my brother Duane.

Tracy Ingraham, Dr. Lia Bascomb, Dr. Fahamu Pecou, Gunther Gordon, Keda Hawthorne, Amir Sulaiman, Spinxx and V Jones, Cola Rum, Ebony Stewart, Dana Gilmore, Christine Platt, Dr. Rhea Combs, Janice Barton, Michael Bettis, Shannon and Ben Kroll, Malik and Kim Salaam, Kym Estis, Amenah Arman, Karen Mason, and Sam Berger.

AIR Serenbe, The Serenbe Institute, my Ebrik family, The Kupcakerie, (ad)Vantage Point, The Atlanta spoken word and storytelling communities, The Moth, Southside Richmond (Oakgrove, Bellemeade, Blackwell), and Atlanta, Ga.

'Aint Blue

"So Nelson are you from Camilla?"

"Oh God no! I'm from Hot-lanta." Nelson laughs loudly as he turns and looks at the couple in the back seat. Nelson throws his head back like a Pez dispenser with every loud guffaw.

Brad and Laura laugh along halfheartedly. They don't get the joke but judging from Nelson's reaction clearly something's funny. Brad and Laura are also from "Hot-lanta," but today they are in Camilla, bouncing around in the backseat of a Bonneville, somewhat happily married and looking to buy a summer home.

Russell doesn't laugh. He just drives. His black hands grip the steering wheel so tightly his knuckles look ashen. The Bonneville is his. Realtors that own property in the area but don't know it very well hire out his services to show potential buyers, and themselves, the lay of the land. Russell was born and raised in Camilla. If you were to cut Russell he just might bleed Camilla red clay.

Nelson, Brad, and Laura continue to talk and laugh as Russell pulls into The Bottom. The Bottom is a quaint collection of houses as old as Camilla itself. All of the houses are home to storied black families that have seen the best and worst that Camilla has to offer. All of the homes except one. That one is for sale, and that's what brings Nelson, Brad, and Laura to The Bottom.

"Oh my God I love these houses!" Laura rolls her window down and stares. Nelson smiles knowing that if the wife loves the house then his work is mostly done.

"Is there an HOA down here?" Brad asks.

"No, why do you ask?" Nelson looks out of the window now too.

"Well I notice that all of the porch ceilings, window and door sills are painted ... Blue?"

"I never noticed that before."

"Yeah it's like a Tiffany Blue," Laura says.

"'Aint Blue," Russell interjects and it's as if everyone in the car realizes for the first time that the car isn't driving itself.

"I think what you mean to say is, it isn't blue," Brad responds. Brad, Nelson, and Laura trade smiles.

"That's 'Aint Blue," Russell says again. "After what happened here in eighteen and sixty eight you better heed it. There are things darker than you think me to be, that roam the rooms of your mind when the sun gets to hiding behind the moon's skirt. Things so committed to the fire that they won't cross water. That's 'Aint Blue and if I was you, I'd mind it."

A month later Nelson and Laura buy the home in The Bottom, and begin renovations. Brad is on the porch, up a ladder in paint splattered overalls when he and Laura hear the pie plate break. They turn to find one of their neighbors, Sylvia Jean, standing with her hands covering her mouth, and a ruined pie alongside two others at her feet. Through her fingers Sylvia says,

"What are you doing?"

"Repainting," they say concomitantly.

"But that ain't 'Aint Blue."

"No it ain't... ain't blue, it's red. And we looked it up, there's no HOA here so..."

"And you're the third person to drop a pie right there."

Sylvia runs off, her hands still blanketing her mouth.

"... And she's the third person to do that too."

As the sun begins to set the couple watches as all of their neighbors hurriedly gather their children, close their doors, and shutter their windows.

"These people really hate the color red," Laura says. They both laugh as they too head into their home and lock the door.

The screams begin at exactly one minute after midnight, echo through The Bottom, and don't stop until eleven minutes after one. No one dares to go see. Everyone knows.

The next morning at first light Russell and all of the residents of The Bottom gather in front of the house with paint brushes and buckets of Haint Blue. When the porch and the last of the trim are repainted the front door swings open. The house is empty. No furniture. No clothes. No Laura. No Brad.

There is only a single piece of what appears to be ripped, red paint-splattered denim sitting in the middle of the long hall way. When Russell reaches for it all of the windows and the backdoor fly open. A gust of wind moves through the house, picking up the piece of fabric and blowing it out of the backdoor and beyond the trees.